WITHOUT HER

Also by Rosalind Brackenbury

FICTION

Becoming George Sand
The Third Swimmer
Paris Still Life
The Lost Love Letters by Henri Fournier

POETRY

Bonnard's Dog
The Circus at the End of the World
Invisible Horses

NONFICTION

Miss Stephen's Apprenticeship
How Virginia Stephen Became Virginia Woolf

WITHOUT HER

A NOVEL

ROSALIND BRACKENBURY

DELPHINIUM BOOKS

WITHOUT HER

Copyright © 2019 by Rosalind Brackenbury

Library of Congress Cataloging-in-Publication Data is
available on request.
ISBN 978-1-883285-79-1

19 20 21 22 23 LSC 10 9 8 7 6 5 4 3 2 1

First Edition

Jacket and interior design by Greg Mortimer

For Simone and Charlie

PART I

1.

A small, thin girl playing chess, one hand against the other, perched on a bench in the cloakroom where girls milled around and the air stank of coke from the boiler: that was my first view of Hannah. She doesn't remember this scene; even argues that she never played two-handed chess, especially in the school cloakroom. But I see it now: her, the hanging cloaks and raincoats, the muddy hockey boots shoved into open shelves, the hard and dirty floor. I smell it, the sweaty polluted air. I waited for her, and I remember the feeling. She made people wait, even then.

I said, "Do you want someone to play against, ever?"

She looked up. Gray eyes behind the National Health issue glasses with the pink plastic frames; later, everyone would peel those frames off and reveal the wire underneath, copying John Lennon. She flicked back two pale braids of hair so that they bounced on her shoulders.

"Well, maybe. But I kind of like playing like this, I never know which side is going to win."

I watched her stoop again to make the kind of decisive last-minute move that people make when they know what they are doing. There. Top that. The black knight, that little dwarf horse, crossed forward and sideways, took the white bishop. Which side was she on?

"But they are both you."

"Hmm, I know." She contemplated her game for a minute. I didn't know all the rules of chess, though I had seen my father play. It seemed like an adult occupation, remote from me, at that time.

A bell rang, as bells did on and off all day in that place: a jangle summoning us all to the next activity, lining up for lunch. We were always lining up, clattering up or down stone staircases, swallowing food we had not chosen, sleeping in dormitories with people we did not like. Was it supposed to be a preparation for a future life? If so, we were all destined to be convicts. I was impressed that this quiet girl did not put her chess set away immediately, but went on pondering what to do with her black queen. Everybody had left the cloak-room, except the two of us. At last she said, "Well, we'd better go." It was the first time there was a "we." And she swept her pieces all scrambled into their box and pushed it out of sight behind a hanging green cloak.

We walked fast towards the stairs with the kind of hob-bling gait we had all adapted for speed, running not being allowed. We went one behind the other up the back staircase with its dark green paint to shoulder level, a black line above it and dirty cream above that, a worn central strip of dark green linoleum underfoot, and came late into the hush of the dining room. Girls stood already at the tables for grace to be said, heads bent. The housemistress, Miss McKinley, had already bowed her head to begin, but she looked up, sharp as a bird, and saw us, and frowned in a way that let us know that we were in trouble, then ducked her bird-head again against her ruffled white blouse and intoned, "For what we are about to receive, may the Lord make us truly thankful." Then chair legs scraped on the bare wood floor and covers were lifted off dishes and the usual Monday disappointment showed in girls' faces because Monday was always cold leftovers and beetroot, though you could always hope for something more, like an extra scoop of mashed potato. Perhaps there would be a pudding, jam roly-poly that we called Matron's Leg, or even pie. Then everyone sat down and water jugs were passed and the prefects began doling out the food. By this time Hannah and I had slipped into our places, but not unobserved as we'd hoped. Being late for anything was a crime, and would be marked up against us; we would be seen to be potential troublemakers, Hannah Farrell and Claudia Prescott, simply because we had been late together; efforts would be made to separate us as soon as possible. We would be told that the other was a bad influence. It had all begun with our being late for lunch, coming in shamefaced but without even an apology.

Later, we stood before the housemistress on a patch of carpet worn away by many miscreants' feet and muttered, "Yes, Miss McKinley, sorry, Miss McKinley." While we tried to escape her piercing stare—birds of prey, I discovered later in life, especially small hawks, were her prototype—and also not to cry. "What were you doing, Hannah?"

"Playing chess, Miss McKinley. I forgot the time."

"Well, Hannah, there is a chess club for that. Everything in its time and place." This Hannah told me afterwards, with a smirk. We often quoted it to each other. "Everything in its time and place." Later we shortened it to T. and P. "T. and P., Claudia, T. and P.," she'd hiss at me from time to time.

It was McKinley's technique to spot and separate potential wrongdoers before they had even begun to do anything really wrong. She let us know this. She had her raptor's eye upon us, almost from the beginning. She also knew who was what she called the Ringleader, and who the hapless Follower. In our case, it seemed to be Hannah who led, leaving me billed as the stooge. But all this attention to rules and protocol, graces and rituals, tellings-off and forced apologies only made it easier and, yes, more necessary, for us to be the friends we became.

2.

That was then. This is now, a lifetime later. On a hot afternoon in May, I'm in a classroom in a college town in Virginia. Different century, different continent. Green leaves at the high window like hands against the glass. Footsteps on the gravel outside, shouts from down below where students lounge on the dried grass, trees cast dense shadows, chestnut and live oak, and the whole semester shrinks to its end. In here, the smell of enclosed rooms, dust, hot bodies, the chill of air conditioning to keep us all awake. I'm teaching my Advanced Film Studies group for the last time this semester. The credits have rolled and the screen is white again. We all go to sit around the table; there's the sound of chairs dragging on the floor and someone's phone buzzes. We've been watching Antonioni's film *L'Avventura*, made in 1959. It's old history; it's life in black and white. For them, it's strangely dressed people doing incomprehensible things. It doesn't even have a proper ending, they grumble. I was expecting this. We've talked about sound, and how the camera follows each person along the narrow paths of the island. We've discussed the use of light and dark, the attention to detail: a cup on a table in the boat's cabin, a lit cigarette. But what they want is story—and they find it lacking.

If Hannah is briefly in my thoughts as I watch this film again with my students—how many times have I watched it in my life? I forget—it's because I first saw it with her, at the Arts Cinema in Cambridge, in 1962. We sat on after everyone else had left, in the dark cinema; and when the lights went up, we were still sitting there. It was because there wasn't an ending. And also because the two women in it had nearly identical names to ours: Anna and Claudia. So yes, she is in my thoughts, not as a small girl in a school cloakroom, but as her student self, black-clad, loose-haired, smoking. When I look at my cell phone minutes later and see that Philip, her husband, has left me a message, I'm not entirely surprised. This kind of synchronicity still surprises people; but I've noticed over the years that it happens relatively often in life.

I turn to my class, and smile at them because, after all, they have been patient, and it's the end of the semester, and it's hot outside and smells of cleaning fluids in here. "Maybe there are no solutions, then, just further questions." As soon as I hear myself, I feel them shifting their behinds on their seats, like people waiting for a plane to board, who are told it has been delayed or, worse, canceled completely. There's a faint groan.

"It isn't me saying that," I tell my class, "It's him. The filmmaker. Antonioni."

They hate this. They hated the film and they hate having to talk about it, especially this afternoon so near the end of the semester, as the summer burns outside and a hundred other more seductive things are waiting to be done. Their minds, like the phones vibrating in their pockets, are just waiting to be freed. They want solutions, of course they do. They are nineteen, twenty, twenty-one, they are young Americans, my so-called Advanced Film Study class, and up till now their knowledge of film has been mostly what has been playing in the multiplexes downtown. No, that's not quite fair; they opted for this, and they have sat through *Breathless* and *Hiroshima Mon Amour* and early Hitchcock—all of which, by the way, have outcomes, solutions, or at least endings. Antonioni and most of the Italian neorealists have them irritated, even scared. The French New Wave is just downright depressing. The young women with their tight scoop-necked T-shirts, their astonishing décolletées—apples in a net—tanned now from all the hours spent lying out on the grass in front of this building pretending to study for their exams; the young men with their tight muscles moving under tattooed skin. I like them and I think they like me. But it's nearly the end of the semester, it's May, it's hot, and they long to be out of here. Of course they do. And I'm telling them—or letting Antonioni tell them—that there aren't any solutions? There is just life, open-ended, inexplicable? How unfair is this? If you want to feel your age, spend time with college students, let them in on what has been one of the formative experiences of your life. See their bafflement; feel your own

They yawn, fidget, eye each other. Michael Paulson in his faded Grateful Dead T-shirt—maybe it belonged to his father—groans, "Then what's the point?"

"I think the point is Claudia's search for who she really is," I say. A little self-conscious that I share this character's name, although I'm nothing like Monica Vitti, never was. I say, "I know it's hard. We are all so geared to finding one, these days. But I think the greatness of this film is that it doesn't pretend to provide one. No easy answers, no happy ending."

Michael runs brown fingers through spiky black hair, rolls his eyes, grins, sighs, stretches jeaned legs and sneakered feet farther under the table. The table is littered with cardboard coffee cups and laptops, tablets, and other devices that I won't let them use in class. Peyton Mackenzie leans back, flicks blonde hair back over her shoulder, smooth, plump in a spaghetti-strap top. "I guess it's that we've gotten used to mysteries always being solved. Isn't that right, Professor?" She's always on my side. She pads beside me down corridors, almost offering to carry my books, except that I don't carry books, just a light laptop of my own in a shoulder carrier. Teachers hardly carry books now, any more than their students do.

The girls get it. The sexism in the film has made them groan and mutter. He's just so arrogant, he can't spend five minutes without a woman, those Italian men, all he can think about is sex, she's right to want to get away. They get it too thoroughly, these twenty-first-century girls. None of them, they say proudly, would put up with this loser groping them for a second. They become a team, they begin to sit up straight, as the boys in the class slump lower in their chairs. The white rectangle of the screen has been rolled up—such an old-fashioned way of watching a movie—and they have come back to the table to discuss it, as we had to discuss films, always, when we were young. As well as the lack of an ending, what has come up is the old division between the sexes, men's invariable lust. We sit in the clammy chill of air conditioning. Alicia Bond lifts her mass of hair from her shoulders and holds it aloft, for coolness, showing her shaved armpits, the pale insides of her arms. Gerry Shaughnessy can't help looking, then begins to play with the ballpoint pen he has, clicking it open and shut. We sit in the knowledge of failure, emptiness, a retreat from any certainty except this one: that men will always be men.

Eric Nilsen says suddenly, on behalf of his gender, "Nobody would get away with it now. They'd dump him." He's another tanned, blond, handsome young American, and he's playing the girls' team now, grinning sideways.

I say gently, "Yes, that is one aspect of the film that dates it. Good thing, eh?" We seem to have run out, run through, come to a stop. I lift my hands, letting them leave if they want to; but some of them stay. There is something I want to tell them: that film is the one art in which we control time, in which two hours can contain everything. Perhaps I have told them this; perhaps I said it at the very beginning. Now is not the moment for it anyway, as they begin to run out, scattered, into their lives, with their youthful sense that they have all the time in the world.

Going down the steps of the department into the dazzle of late afternoon, I peer to retrieve Philip's message. I'm on my way home. I walk towards my car in the college parking lot, under the spread green leaves of the campus chestnuts and magnolias, thousands of miles and an ocean away from my caller, in the damp summer heat of Virginia. I hear his voice. "Claudia, could you ring me back? It's rather important."

Being English, and diffident by nature, he'd have to reduce the urgency, but I hear it in his voice. Philip, my oldest friend's husband, whom I have known for decades, yet still hardly know well.

I park my car outside the house, let myself in, feel the

chill of air conditioning like a caress before it becomes simply clammy, pour myself a big glass of water from the refrigerator. The old refrigerator that ticks and hums. Ice that crashes into the sink. The silence of the house, my rented college house where, in spite of my years here, I have never quite made myself at home. I pour cold wine left from last night and go and sit down on my sagging couch, my feet up on the coffee table, and press in Philip's number. When I call his house number in England, I hear that Philip and Hannah Macauley have left for the summer but can be reached at this number. The code is 33 rather than 44: it must be the house in France. It will be about my plans for the summer, then; he is a bit of a fusspot, as my mother would have said, wants everything planned in advance, probably wants to know exactly on which train or plane I will be arriving. But—"rather important"? And muted, as if he feared to be overheard?

"Claudia." At last, his so-English voice, across the wide Atlantic. I imagine him, balding now, tall and slightly bent, his eagerness still boyish; a very English way of not quite growing up, something appealing about it from this distance. "My dear." Yes, it does sound affected, from my American side of the ocean. "I'm so glad to hear you. It's rather desperate. I don't know what to do, you see. Hannah has disappeared. I don't know where she is."

"Disappeared? What do you mean?"

"She never arrived. I've waited for two days, she was meant to be getting the train on Friday, and she wasn't there. I waited for three trains, I tried calling her, her phone was dead. I simply don't know what to do."

"Phil, I thought you were going down there together. What happened?"

"No, I was to drive down with our stuff, and she was going to follow on the train. She had something she wanted to do in Paris. Then, I just never heard another thing. Do you think you could come? I mean, as soon as you can? I'm finding it very difficult to cope, actually." He coughs, but I've heard the catch in his throat, the stoic man's alarm.

"Well, yes, I was coming next week, after the semester ends here, but I could come sooner, I guess. I'll see if I can change my ticket." We're not doing all that much, finishing up, evaluations and that sort of thing. All the students are pretty much asleep, anyway, they party every night and they can't wait to get away. "You're at the house?"

"Yes. It's worse, in a way. I mean, if I were at home I'd have more of a clue. Should I tell the police, do you think? I think I must."

"I don't know. I mean, you don't want to start an Interpol hunt if she's just shopping in Paris."

"But it's so unlike her," he says. And I say nothing, but remember times—oh, long ago now, but more than a few times—when Hannah simply did not show up, but wandered in hours or even days later, smiling, with no explanation. I wonder that her husband of nearly forty years has not suffered the same thing before. Do we change, essentially? Can we ever predict how another person will behave, even if we've known that person since girlhood and gone with her through every kind of adventure and mishap? In her sixties, is there still the child Hannah, wanting to surprise, even shock people, making them wait so long that they will call the French police, set up a hunt, call old friends in from across the world? I don't know. To the extent that I have changed or not changed, the same will be true for my old friend. Circumstances change. Technology changes. It would be far harder now in these days of almost total surveillance to hide out in the woods than it was in our childhood, or even our wild adolescence. But do we change? Isn't the irritation I am feeling, here, now, in my little clapboard house in a university town in Virginia, the same that I felt then, when she let me down, hid from me, stayed out all night, and came in brilliant and smiling in the morning, announcing, "Claude, I do believe I'm in love!"

I hunt online to change my flight to Paris, to Marseille, to Nice, even to Toulouse. All the airlines are booked. The only available flight within my shrunken budget—I am on half pay, semiretired now—is Atlanta to Miami and then a Swissair flight to Paris via Zurich. I can get a train south from Paris more cheaply than a flight. I want a night in Paris anyway—ah, the plans our minds secretly make for us while we think we are thinking of other things—because I want to see Alexandre. This I can't say to Philip, since his wife has gone AWOL somewhere between Paris and the south and everything therefore has become urgent; in fact, until now I have not consciously admitted it to myself. But he, Alexandre, would be impossibly hurt if I were to spend even a few hours in Paris and not see him. It is not what we do, anyway. Philip will never know. I will say that the flight got in late from Zurich, it made sense to go to a hotel and get the morning train, and anyway, jet lag is always a valid excuse. When you cross the ocean at our age, you are allowed to feel tired and want to go to a hotel. You don't have to say if you are going to it alone.

When I admit this subterranean plan my mind has been making, I recognize, that no, we do not change all that much, essentially. I've been an expert in stolen nights in hotels all my life; I'm only surprising myself slightly at planning one at the age I am now.

I send out an email to all my remaining students; then I write to my head of department and the secretaries, something personal has come up, I have to leave immediately, before the semester officially ends at the end of the week, and anything important can be forwarded to me by email.

My flight to Zurich arrives at seven in the morning and I walk about the airport with that drained, skinned-alive feeling you get from overnight flights, waiting for my connection to Charles de Gaulle. On the transatlantic plane I sat next to a woman who told me she was eighty-three, and going home after visiting her daughter in the US. She thought the US very dirty compared to Switzerland. I said that she was not the only person to think so—that yes, America was a young, brash country, that it was dirty, that our politics were appalling on the whole but that yes, Obama was an elegant young man with good ideas, and I, too, was relieved that nobody had assassinated him. My neighbor was well coiffed, even after a night sitting up in a plane with eye mask on and tray table stowed after picking at a tray of food. I'd thought—Switzerland is the place for you, if you are this fastidious. Or do we take on the attitudes and manners of the places we find ourselves in? No, I said, I do not know Zurich, I'm only changing planes, to go on to Paris. Yes, it was a good, clean airline. Yes, one had to be careful. And then she had patted her silver coiffed hair and said, "I don't know for how much longer I can go on flying to the US to see my daughter. I'm eighty-three already. It is a great strain on the body. And I do not think she will ever come home."

I felt sorry for her, then, and saw her courage, under the fussy exterior. I couldn't imagine being eighty-three, and obliged to fly the Atlantic every year—not yet. We all have our stories, and sometimes they spill out of us in bits and pieces, and we let ourselves, just for that moment, be seen. I suddenly saw an old woman holding herself together, with hairpins and lipstick and good luggage and morale, and admired her for it.

Zurich airport is even more glossy and removed from any real world than most airports are. I pass shops of incredible glamour, with impossibly expensive watches, bracelets, rings in their windows. Everything is rich and shiny, yet discreet. I notice, glancing at it, that my watch has stopped, and no, it isn't operating on US time, it's simply not moving, however hard I try to make it do so. I see that one of the hands has actually become detached. There's no way to mend it in a hurry. There is just time, as I pass one of the expensive shops, to dive in and buy myself a watch, a Swiss watch, not the most expensive but not the cheapest either; it's a luxury, but when will I ever be in Zurich again? I whip out my American Express card and charge it, and go on, pulling my bag along on its wheels, to find my Paris flight. It's a beautiful watch, with a flat round face and Roman numerals. The second hand is a thin gold wand, it shows today's date, and, at the bottom, near six o'clock, it says discreetly, Swiss Made. I am in the land of marked time and precision instruments. It will be a souvenir of an hour spent in Zurich, where I may never be again. I wear it, and go on to board my plane for Paris feeling better equipped for this world than I have for a long time. It occurs to me, as I settle in to my seat for the short flight, that time stopped for me in Zurich, and I made a bargain with it: I'll buy a new watch, that will see me into my next decade. I slip my old one into my bag; it was a present from my father when I was young, and has ticked on well into this new century; until today. My new watch gleams on my left wrist, showing me the correct time for where I am now, regular as a new heart.

By mid-morning I am walking out through Charles de Gaulle, with no one apparently paying any attention to me; even the couple of men at Customs only look up to give me a passing smile. Then I am on to the RER and the true grime of underground Paris, to surface on a dark summer morning, the sun lurking behind clouds and streets where the garbage collectors have not yet been, streets on which people still spit and dogs pee and it all looks much as it ever did. I think of my airplane companion and what she might have said. Dizzy with lack of sleep, I trundle my bag down the street towards my hotel.

Before calling Alexandre, I lie on the bed in the hotel, nearly fall asleep, then get up to have a shower, wash my hair, and change my clothes. There is no need for the rush and hurry of our younger days, when I would have called him from the airport if I could—no cell phones, then—and he would have been waiting impatiently at whatever hotel we had picked for our rendezvous. We would have pulled off our clothes and fallen down on the nearest bed, washed or unwashed, at that time.

We have a history of hotels, he and I. Cheap, even grungy hotels; rue de la Bûcherie, rue Magenta, rue Gît-le-Coeur, rue Saint-Marcel, rue Saint-Lazare, when Paris hotels were not what they are today. All over the city, wherever we could rent for the afternoon; and the rooms, wildly wallpapered, with bidets or tiny bathrooms where we could not both fit in the shower, with sagging overused beds and, once, even someone else's condom left behind. The younger you are, I now think, the less you mind about such things. The urgency of desire, of the flesh, of coming together like this over distance and time, the romance of it all quite covering up the details. I would not dream of going to such a hotel now. The one I have chosen is in the 6ème, behind Odéon, near Saint-Germain-des-Prés, three-star, *touristique,* and the rooms are clean, and now it is not a question of renting by the hour. But, as I say, we have this history behind us, and so whatever hotel we find our-selves in for the meetings of our mature years, it is one in a long line, a link on a chain of memory, a chapter in a history we have shared between us over more than forty years.

I put in my earrings, turn away from the mirror, think briefly of the students I left behind me only yesterday, in the US. Another life. How we invent lives for ourselves, spinning from one to another with such ease, such apparent insouci-ance. My eighty-three-year-old neighbor, resolutely crossing the Atlantic to meet her daughter in some grim American city where nobody understood her. Myself, professor at an American university, waiting in a Paris hotel room to meet my long-term lover, a man in his late sixties with a shaky heart and thinning white hair. I imagine one of the students, puzzled, asking "But what it the point in falling in love with someone if you don't get together in the end?" The marriage plot—beginning, middle, end. Alexandre and I have had no such plot—he was married to someone else, a couple of some-one elses, for so many of these years, and now, well, there is no longer any need for it, it seems. I live in the US, he in Paris. We meet like this, migrating birds flying in to settle for a brief time on a cliff-face. And part, these days, without pain. Or nearly without pain.

He is downstairs in the lobby, waiting. I've come down in the elevator, to avoid him coming up to my room immediately. We practice these politenesses, these little thoughtful adaptations to our age and station. I see his white head from above, hair thinned across his scalp, and it gives me a pang. Once, it was so rich and brown, thick and down to his shoulders. But like this we forgive our own physical changes, in not noticing each other's. The eyes don't change. The parts of the body that are usually covered by clothes remain pale, unmarked, curiously young.

"Ah," he says, coming towards me. And "Ah," I say too; and we kiss on both cheeks, and then he briefly, almost surreptitiously, takes my hand and squeezes it. We are the same height; he isn't a tall man, but compact, with only a slightly perceptible gut. The desk clerk looks away. They must spend a lot of their time looking away, or at their computer screen, these days. I remember, in our early days, the fierce stares of concierges who parked their bosoms on their desks, watching us and everybody else come and go. So many rooms, so many meetings: and then, so many departures. I walk out through the glass door he holds open for me and on to the street, where the sun has come out and traffic flashes and lunchtime crowds hustle and the long green buses follow each other down rue de Rennes.

"*Tu veux manger?* We can have lunch."

In fact, I am very hungry, after not eating anything at the Zurich airport—nothing since bad coffee in a paper cup and what they call a continental breakfast at 33,000 feet. These days, it is all right to admit it. I don't have to pretend, and listen to my stomach rumbling, and try to stop it. We will have a good lunch, although it's early for lunch, in France. Neither of us will be insulted by putting off the removal of clothes, the rush of body to body, the relief of skin. In fact, probably both of us are glad of it. When you are our age, you need time, and food, and to sit on a comfortable chair in a good restaurant and know that everything is coming to you, all in its own good time.

"Nice watch," says Alexandre. "Is it new?"

3.

In the middle of the last century—a date that now looks
like old history—Hannah and I were at boarding school
together for five long years. It felt like a lifetime; when you
are a teenager, you have little capacity for the long-term prisoner's resignation. Our minds and bodies were impatient, our
souls cowed. When I first knew Hannah, she had long fair
hair, usually plaited in two braids, and wore those National
Health glasses. It's a look that nobody has now: the under-
fed myopic English schoolgirl of the 1950s. She was small
for her age so I felt like a beanpole beside her. Our school
was a well-known girls' school in the deep west country of
England, a mile outside the nearest town, far enough someone had thought from the temptations of shops and boys.
Though we were probably both equally unhappy, we never
told each other this. At our school, we never told anybody
anything that had to do with feelings. When we cried, it had
to be under the bedclothes or in the lavatory, or at the far end
of the games field, and even that was never safe. Girls who

cried were scorned and mocked, probably because every-body wanted to cry at some point, and so those who gave in were derided mercilessly. I remember a girl who cried openly when her father left her at the gates and drove away in his Alfa Romeo; her name was Daphne, which we thought a wet name, and she was thought wet, for crying, and in my mind that connected with the car, that made it look as if her father was enjoying himself rather too much to care about her. So nobody wanted either to have too flamboyant a parent, or car, or to be seen to cry. We clenched our fingers around hidden wet handkerchiefs, and bit our lips, and stifled thoughts of home.

The effects of boarding school on my later life have been var-ied and mostly inconvenient. I can't bear having to share a room with anybody else, after years in a dormitory. So, no marriage bed—although I have several times been tempted. Also, since we had to use each other's dirty bathwater, the prefects getting the clean water, in our twice-weekly baths, I am obsessive these days about clean bathrooms. The men in my life, particularly the Americans, have been curiously interested in all the details of boarding-school life that I find most ridiculous. Uniforms, knee socks, strict mistresses. One of them was particularly fascinated when I told him about the knicker inspection. This ritual was to ensure that nobody was wearing anything frilly or insubstantial; we were sup-posed to wear green wool knickers over white cotton "lin-ings," hence the periodic lineup in which we whisked up our skirts to put our underwear on view. I can see the possible erotic connection, yes. But Alexandre, being French, sniffs at all that and simply calls it *"histoires de bonnes femmes"* and

irremediably, ridiculously English. Knickers and uniforms
and rigid routines apart, our school was a nest of incipient
lesbianism, according to him, although I don't think many
of us knew the word. I've told him, it simply isn't possible to
be in an environment like that and not to long for someone
to love. So crushes and pashes were "in" but I don't think
many of them blossomed into full affairs; partly because the
rules around who was allowed into one's cubicle or dormitory were so strict, partly because we were all so ignorant.

Hannah was a little younger than I was, and in a lower
form, as they were called; so we didn't meet often during
school hours. Neither of us was good at games, or involved
in any school activities. Did she ever join a chess club? I don't
think so. We didn't do clubs, or join the choir, or feature
on any team. She wasn't easy to get to know; perhaps that
was why I wanted to know her. She had a self-containment
about her that was rare. It was as if she lived somewhere else,
inside her head, and all the school noise, the rules and punishments, hardly touched her. I noticed that soon she began
to avoid doing anything that would result in her having to
wait outside our housemistress's door after lunch, where the
miscreants, usually including myself, had to line up. Or perhaps she simply didn't get caught. I was always being accused
of something, usually accurately: I lost my possessions, scattering them across the school, I was late for class, missed
prayers, was caught talking, borrowed someone else's cloak
without a thought when I couldn't find my own. I existed in a
state of permanent rebellion, not deliberately, but by default:
I couldn't understand what was being asked of me, or was
simply incapable of doing it.

As in prisons, I imagine, some inmates are perpetually

in trouble; others get by. When I was tired of all the trouble, I reported sick to the matron and earned a few days' solitary confinement in the Sanatorium, where our school doctor was, we thought, rather too fond of examining girls' chests. We called him The Quack and sat shivering as we waited our turn, topless and goose-bumped, for his inspection and the cold touch of his stethoscope. If you could get past him, cough convincingly or complain of stomach pains, you were ushered away to the San. There, you could cry out your homesickness without anyone hearing, because nobody came near you anyway except to bring congealing meals on trays. It was a retreat for a time from the demanding world of school to a place where you could truly feel the depths of your misery.

I don't know if Hannah ever went to the Sanatorium deliberately, as I did; but there was that one time, later in both our careers, when she was effectively made a prisoner there. Neither did she take part in the violent games of hockey and lacrosse that we had to play every afternoon in the winter mud. How had she got out of them, I wondered? Then I discovered that she was always in the library, during the afternoons, and that being in the library, deep in some book, turned out to be an almost acceptable alternative to games. I saw her there one day when I went to get a book for my history essay—I'd never thought about just sitting there for hours—and whispered, "How do you manage it? Are you off games?"

"I just say I have to work," she whispered back. "My parents wrote a note. It was easy."

I knew I couldn't rely on my own parents writing a note, since they were annoyingly keen on fresh air and exercise, but I did get them to say that I needed extra study time if I was to get to university and that perhaps all this hockey and lacrosse was rather excessive. I don't know if they wrote the second part, in spite of my prompting. So Hannah and I sat in the library on those dark winter afternoons of our adolescence, instead of clashing hockey sticks red-kneed in the mud, and read. We had a French literature teacher who told us in a whisper one day about Proust (he was not on the syllabus so she was not supposed to mention him), and we embarked on him secretly, passionately, travelers setting out on a long-haul journey. We also read Hakluyt and Marlowe and Melville and Restoration comedy and surprisingly sexy books about Mary Queen of Scots—allowed because they were histori-cal?—and Dr. Jekyll and Mr. Hyde and all of Conan Doyle. We read hungrily and at random and quite uncritically, just gobbling up the literary world. If anyone ever asked me later how I got my education, I said it was because I got off games at my school, and read instead.

We were also, Hannah and I, the girls with the unusual names. Claudia and Hannah were odd in the nineteen-fifties, when everyone was called Jennifer or Elizabeth or Jane. Yes, as I've said, we have nearly the same names as the women in Antonioni's film *L'Avventura*. But it was a long time later, when we saw the film together at the Cambridge Arts Cinema, that we discovered this and glanced at each other, amazed, in the smoky dark.

4.

I don't talk much about my schooldays to Alexandre. As I have said, he isn't turned on by stories of schoolgirls—all lesbians, as he will say, as dismissively as he still does of feminists—and apart from some vague hygienic worry about our bathing practices—you mean you actually had to get into dirty water? And there was no lock on the door?—he finds nothing there but a slight historical interest. So I don't reminisce, or make up stories about it; it's an unfortunate part of my past to him, as if I had been a nun, or in jail. A past that was typically Anglo-Saxon, *bizarre* in a word, and not worth discussing from a rational French point of view. He is really only interested in the Hannah-Claudia saga when it starts to include him.

I've told him several times that he's an old-fashioned French sexist, and that times have changed and left him behind. But now—that is, at the moment when we are together again in a comfortable bedroom in a hotel in the *sixième*—there is no scoffing or accusing. We've found, once again, the alignment of bodies that we've trusted and returned to over so many years. We have our heads on the same pillow, his hands are spread across my body, I breathe in the reliable scent of him that does not change over time. Other things have changed, of course. He gestures to his penis that no longer can be relied upon. "You have no idea," he tells me, "how upsetting this is for a man. We count on it our whole lives, and then all at once it is over. Or, not over, but not, you know, responsive. Not like before."

I say that I am not like before, either, but we both know that though I'm just as wrinkled and slack in places as he is, I can always be reached sexually. Orgasm, as far as I know, goes on for women for the whole of life, if approached right. I lie back and let him give me what he knows so well to give, and stifle the thought that this is purely selfish, because he has told me often enough that this is pleasure enough for him. I have never known anyone who has made me feel as he does in bed, that I am perfect in every way. Even in my sixties, even lazily lying here letting him do the work, even when I laugh with the renewed pleasure of it, and his penis only shifts a little against his thigh. He doesn't believe in Viagra—bad for the heart, and anyway, do you want to make love with an automaton? My pleasure is his, he says on occasions like this, and I believe him.

"I love it when you laugh," he says. "Why do you always laugh?"

"Because it's always such a lovely surprise."

I don't ask him if other women laugh after orgasm, or cry. He doesn't ask me if other men have made me laugh with pleasure too. We don't include our other lives and lovers, if there are any, and I rather suspect that these days for him, as for me, there are not. (There's a third wife, somewhere in the background, and an ongoing saga of difficult and expensive divorce.) He doesn't ask about my life in the US—that country he views with suspicion, mostly from afar. My time in California, he refers to as "your hippie days." He came to see me a few times in New York, which he considers worth visiting: there are museums, there are landmarks that even the French, with their immense superior store of cultural monuments, can respect.

After we have done what we mostly do these days and have slept for a few minutes, in the middle of the afternoon here in Paris once again, we wake and roll to lie on our backs and I tell him, "Apparently Hannah has disappeared."

"Really? How do you mean?"

"Philip called me at work. It's why I'm here early. I'm supposed to be rushing south to help him find her."

"People don't disappear these days."

"I know, it's hard to believe. But he says she left home in England and came to Paris and never arrived at the house."

"Perhaps she too has someone to see in Paris?"

I haven't thought of this. "Hmm. I doubt it, somehow."

I've always suspected that one summer, long, oh long ago, Hannah and Alexandre may have had an affair. I've never asked him; it would be outside the bounds of our relationship, and, anyway, I doubt that I would like to hear the answer. It could have been during that summer that she was in Paris alone, when I for some forgotten reason had had to go home to England. Had my mother been ill? Did I have to work? These details of life slip from the mind after forty years or more; and what remains only is a series of unreliable memories. Hannah sitting on the side of a bed, her long hair hanging down; something in the air, in yet another shared hotel room, something she would not tell me. A catch in Alexandre's voice—young Alexandre, with his long shaggy brown hair and his same quick upward glance. A silence. An unexplored possibility.

"What do you think has happened?" he asks me now.

"I've no idea. Either she just wants some time away from Philip—you know how he fusses—or, I don't know, perhaps she's ill, or something happened to her." I want to ask him, "You didn't see her, did you?" Surely, they have not been in touch with each other for years.

He says, "She didn't contact me, if that's what you are thinking." Like this, the shortcuts in our talk, the questions that somehow, not asked, answer themselves. It's all right to have this kind of conversation after lovemaking, when the sails of the world go slack and you are becalmed; not before.

"No, I didn't think so, after all this time."

He says, "Who do you think she knows here, now?"

"I don't know. So many of our friends are dead, or have moved away. The Lenoirs, you know, Madeleine and Sylvain? But they spend the summers in the south, anyway. They'd be gone by now. She has a friend at the Sorbonne, teaches English, a woman called Simone. But, most people will be leaving soon, won't they?"

"So, what are you going to do?"

"Well, first of all, try to calm Philip down. He's probably got the French police or even Interpol combing Europe for her now. Then, I don't know."

He says, "The strange thing is that now it is almost like a crime to go missing, even for a few days. We are supposed to keep in touch, always; we can be tracked down, by our mobile phones, our computers, everything we do is watched.

So, to disappear is more of an effort, more of a plan. I would say, it's almost impossible."

"Yes, it seems she didn't take her phone with her. That's a tracking device in itself."

"Yes, exactly, if it was deliberate."

"But," I say, "why?"

"Who knows? At our age, there is less of life left to us. Perhaps she wanted to do something she could not tell Philip about. Claudie, you know her best, think; what would she do? What would you do if you were her?"

"That's just what Philip thinks. I know her best because I've known her longer than anyone, so I should be able to guess at her motives. But I can't. We live such different lives, now. I only see her once a year, if that." All at once, I am exasperated. Why, once again, are we spending our time talking about Hannah? And, why do I mind—since I brought up her name in the first place?

He picks up on this thought. "All right, enough about Hannah. How long are you here? How much time do we have?"

"I have a train south tomorrow morning. Ten-thirty at the Gare de Lyon."

"Ah. That's good. I have something early this evening, but after dinner I can come back, if you like, we could even spend the night together."

Even though I warned him that I'm only here for less than twenty-four hours, he has something, someone, some place to go for dinner?

"All right. Come back here after your important dinner."

"Claudie, it isn't that, believe me, but I said I would have dinner with my son."

"Ah. How is he?" His son, Dominique the ex-drug addict. He hardly ever sees him, I know that.

"Better. But still fragile. You know, I can't let him down at the last minute."

Yes, I do know that. And I have known, over the years, the agony of Alexandre, the guilt, the trying to make amends, the fights with his former wife, whose side Dominique always took, and finally the boy's struggles with drugs, painkillers, cocaine.

I'm doubtful about spending the night with him, even after all this time. Will we sleep? Will he snore, and kick? The sleeping habits of people our age are often disruptive. Will I spend the night wide awake with jet-lag, haunted by memories of boarding school? Enough time has passed, surely, for this not to be an issue. Sleeping with your lover in a comfortable French hotel is after all not very similar to lying awake in a dormitory in an English boarding school. And I can always ask him to go home in the small hours; he doesn't live far away.

"All right." We are already reaching for our clothes, which are all mixed up on the floor and on the nearest chair, and this makes us laugh, because we have done this so many times before. He wriggles into his shirt, I do up my bra. The undressing was so swift, we flung our things away from us like teenagers, and now we have to sift, separate, collect. He picks up his watch that has lain with a handful of euros on the bed table. I strap on my Swiss beauty. When he ties his shoes, he puts one foot after the other on the chair and pulls the knot tight. I have watched him do this so many times; all my life, as it sometimes seems. Does this make up a marriage of sorts, a repetition over the years, an intimacy that has no home and no address, just this sharing of moments, memories, places to which we will never return? We have known each other since we were nineteen, and now we are on the edge of old age. He flattens his white hair with my brush. "Do I look respectable?"

"As respectable as you ever do."

"Don't tease me, Claudie."

"Why not? Haven't I earned the right to tease you? After the life you have lived, you have no right to look respectable. But yes, you look like a dear old *prof. de lycée*, with that jacket and that briefcase you tote around. Nobody would ever dream what you get up to."

If I'm fluent in French still, it's because of him. A true Frenchman of his generation, he's never felt the need to learn other languages. One day, he says, he will learn better English; it's after all the language of the Internet. I don't say, it has been my language too, since we first met.

He likes the vision of himself that I've given him—the wide boy, the man about town. He likes the disguise, the pretense, the getting by. "*Bon*, I must go. Till later then. Nine o'clock?"

I watch him go, as I have watched him so many times. Once, I used to cry as soon as he had left the room, clean from a quick shower, rushing home to his wife and child, or back to work, back into his life. A night together used to seem so impossible. Now, I don't cry. I smile. It is, after all, quite an achievement, what we have done together in secret over the years. When I am not with him—which is most of the time, ninety percent of my life at least—I think about how we live this love affair of ours, and at times could almost believe that I have invented him. But what I live with him is deep, subterranean, a seam of passion and pleasure that exists nowhere else in my life, as I am almost sure it does not in his. We have invented this together, this way of meeting throughout decades, this lovemaking that goes straight to the point. It's not always yearly; there have been times when we have not met for two, even three years; when I lived on the West Coast, the distance meant we met infrequently. In New York, we stayed in a hotel in Washington Square and watched people's dogs in the little park, and ate bagels that he pronounced tasteless, and even visited the Statue of Liberty. But the conversation our bodies have been having eliminates time and place, as it insists on its own reality. Bagels or croissants, the Statue of Liberty (who started out in Paris after all, he says), hotels in New York, pigeons on Parisian windowsills, once even a fleeting few hours at an airport, I forget where, when one of us was passing through. The décor hardly matters, as the passage of time hardly marks us. It has seemed to me like magic, as well as heartbreak; a juggling of what we are allowed of time and space in one lifetime, tossed up into the heady air.

I imagine that many people might think that meeting a man once a year to have sex with him in a hotel room does not constitute a relationship: that we have made nothing, only repeated a compulsion that does not suit our age or status. But lived from the inside, there is our reality, and it's different from this. I can't say what goes on inside Alexandre's head and body, of course; but there is something that has been created over the years: a trust of the body, a being present to each other. There are the gaps between actions, the in-breaths between the out-breaths if you like, the silences in between words, the inaction between actions, the stillness at the center of life, felt in the beating of two aging hearts. This, the silence, the stillness, the belief in coming together, the showing-up, the being there, all this has created a third thing, as a marriage does, or any long connection between individuals. It has made us both less and more than our individual selves. Alexandre and I know each other, in the Biblical sense and beauty of that word.

I never thought for more than a few postcoital hours about marrying him, even when we were both free. He worked in Paris, became a lawyer, wore suits. He married other women. None of the marriages seemed to work for long, although he always started out hoping they would; but in some conventional French way, he believed in marriage. It was respectable, it gave him weight. Love, sex, was something else. And I, living in America, pursuing my dream of film-making—well, I had chosen this life over the settled one that marriage seemed designed to provide, even if it rarely did. I could not imagine myself married to him, living in Paris, being a foreigner who would always be seen as inferior to all the French *cinéastes* who already existed in such numbers. It was simply not a possibility that either of us could entertain.

We don't discuss it much—our relationship, that is. Our emails to each other are usually short; we used to write real letters, or more often cryptic messages on the backs of postcards whose fronts were to convey their coded meaning: a Bonnard bathtub nude, a phallic chimney somewhere, a satisfied-looking cat. The email era eliminated our use of postcards, but echoed their brevity. All we really wanted to know was, are you still there? Increasingly, as you age, you want this question answered—are you here, in this world, on the planet, breathing in and out? I see his e-address in among the lists when I switch on my computer early—emails from France are always written in the American night—skip immediately to his *Claudie, chérie*, his *mon amie*, his *t'embrasse tendrement*, his *je t'aime*—and know that he wrote it to me at the end of his evening, before taking off his clothes and lying down with a sigh, alone or not, I never could guess, on his bed, in his apartment, in the sixth arrondissement, in the city we inhabit together that is part geography, part make-believe; as we are part-history, part-dream.

5.

Hannah is in my mind now, of course, and if I start running through my store of memories of us together as I sit alone in the bar downstairs after Alexandre has left, it's because the raw anxiety has been there since I heard Philip's voice on the telephone. What has she done? Is she lost, in danger, hurt, or simply on another escapade? I sip my Campari and think, where are you, Hannah? What is going on?

We were Claudia and Hannah, Hannah and Claudia, from those early days. The club of two, the snobby intellectuals, the not-good-sports. We wore the label together, where it would have been intolerable to wear it alone. We walked about with our green school cloaks pulled around us as if we had swords under them, we bent our heads in deep conversation as we marched round the games field, stopping to pause at the fence at the very limit of the school grounds and look out at bare trees, raw fields, sodden grass—and then on again, in our heads, in our books, in the desperate fantasy that made up for

the reality we were in. In summer, we lounged on grass, reading, always reading. I tried to get a tan, she lay in the shade.
We pulled our school hats down over our eyes, slouched
when we walked, wore our school uniforms as slant as we
could, socks dragging down over ankles, skirts hitched high.
Hannah and Claudia. Teachers sighed and raised their eyebrows, but since we both got such high marks in class, there
was not much they could say. Except, on occasion, that our
attitude was letting down the school.

The school, I discovered later, was set up to be let down in
due course by history itself. We were already in a sort of time
warp. While outside, our contemporaries were buying 45s
of rock bands and bopping away to Buddy Holly and Elvis,
then the Beatles and the Stones, being teenagers, flirting with
each other, watching *Top of the Pops* on TV and fighting with
their parents, we were in here, just waiting to escape into
that world and afraid that by the time we got there, it might
all have vanished without warning. Our parents seemed to
have abandoned us and were getting on perfectly well without us. My own parents, with my twin younger brothers and
a new baby daughter to look after, seemed to have pushed
me out of the nest to make room for their expanding life.
Hannah's parents, both busy doctors, had, it seemed, little
time for their only daughter because they were and always
had been obsessed by each other and their careers. They had
always had trouble finding babysitters and now the school
was her permanent babysitter, day and night, until Hannah,
programmed to emerge from it nearly adult and independent, could find her own way. Our parents may well have
had other thoughts about all this, and valued the education
that they believed we were getting, but to us when young, the

way they lived their lives, writing to us once a week to give us all the details of happy family life, in my case, or successful careers, in hers, made us bitter. The letters we received were both lifeline and torment: they were written at weekends, at the tail ends of weekends, so that we would get them by Tuesday at the latest. Darling Claudia (or Hannah), I do hope you are well and working hard. We've had a very busy time with the boys' birthdays (or the new clinic) so this will be short. Everyone sends love. We miss you. (Ha, said Hannah, not enough, obviously.) Don't forget Granny's birthday, darling (or Dad's professorship, darling); she (he) would love a card from you. With lots of love (hugs) from Mum (your Ma).

On Sundays, which always felt like the worst day of the week, we had to sit down to write our letters to our parents, after church and lunch. It was the worst day, strangely, because there were no lessons, and lessons at least filled up time. There were services instead: early Communion (you had to file down the street to the Abbey for this on an empty stomach, because God was insulted if you ate anything before His body and blood, like spoiling your appetite for a special lunch), then Matins for those too lazy or irreligious or interested in breakfast to go to what was simply called Early. Here you had the amusement of a possible, very brief flirtation, eyes only, with some boy from the Boys' School who might be lounging outside the Abbey doors, reading his newspaper or pretending to; but Hannah and I, at this time, were scornful about boys in general and these—what she called Upper Class Twits—in particular. There was lunch, which was the high point of Sunday, because it was roast meat and potatoes (the same meat that would show up again on Monday and, more thoroughly disguised, Tuesday), and we could gorge ourselves for once until our waistbands cut into our stomachs. Letter-writing, which followed lunch, was an orgy of suppressed homesickness as we leaned our elbows on tables and doodled ink blots and contorted our minds into producing acceptable sentences that held no hints of our true feelings.

Did they want to hear that I missed them, missed home with a raw pain that this forced letter-writing only exaggerated? I searched my mind for topics, came up with stilted phrases that must have made my parents wonder if it was even me who was writing them. I glanced over at Hannah's, "Dear Ma and Pa," and at her fat mottled fountain pen that squelched in her ink bottle before it curled blue Quink across paler blue Basildon Bond writing paper, and at the rounded deliberation of her letters. Her handwriting gave nothing away. It was just unusually large for an apparently small person, as if to conquer as much space as possible. We finished our letters, "tons of love," "love from," xxx and ooo, and signed our names and handed the unlicked stamped envelopes to the senior whose job it was to collect them and take them to Miss McKinley, whose job it was to read them—did she really, a grown woman, stoop to this?—and make sure that we had neither complained nor tipped into any unhealthy excess of homesickness. Some of the letters from younger girls had blots and stains; she must have known they were tears. Others—ours, Hannah's and mine— simply said nothing but announced, surely, to any conscious parent, that what we were writing was censored. We became excellent at self-censorship, and this, I might say in passing, is a hard thing to unlearn.

"What about being kidnapped by gypsies?"
"What about running away to sea?"

"What about highwaymen, and you're in a carriage, rushing through the night, and they stop you, your money or your life? What would you do?"

"Which would you rather be, a prostitute or a nun?"

"What about running away to another country? What about India? Nobody would ever find us."

We walked round and round the games field with its white goalposts and muddy hockey pitches until the sun set or the cold drove us indoors, that first winter at school, and began to talk about our secret lives.

We began calling each other by code names, aliases, changing the code weekly, so that nobody would ever catch up. We wrapped our gloved hands in our green school cloaks, pulled these cloaks tight around us, saw our breath puff out on the dank air, stared out beyond the fence at the very edge of the field, where we were not allowed to go. We would be spies. The Russians would have us, they would love two intelligent girls who could put on disguises and slide into their dangerous world.

You do what you can, when you are young, to make life livable; you seize on the slightest opportunity and make of it what you must. Children are heroic, and we were still children, our minds ruled by our imaginations, our hearts in our hidden lives.

6.

I call Philip in the morning to reassure him that I am on my way. He will meet me at the station at Avignon, he says. I hear the out-breath of his relief. He believes, against all likelihood, that I will somehow know where she is. I try to sound reassuring, even calm. At least he will not be alone; at least I can provide company. But Hannah? Who has ever known where she was, when she did not want them to? She was still a child when she perfected her sudden disappearances, her almost Houdini-like escapes. I am perhaps the only person alive who knew her that well, and that is why he has asked me, and why I am on my way south to try to find her.

Hannah met Philip while we were still at Cambridge, in our third year. They met in Heffer's, in the history section; more exactly, he was in the history section and she was twirling around in a roll-necked black sweater, her hair coming loose from its bun, waiting for me to buy Karl Popper's *The Open Society and Its Enemies*. We tried to leave but our bikes were entangled with his, outside on the street.

I heard him say to her, "I've seen you outside the Seeley, haven't I? And maybe at the Arts?"

Even then, it was a clumsy pickup by a man unused to such things. I recognized it and fell back, so that they could casually decide together to go for coffee at The Buttery, a conservative sort of café where serious students went and were to be seen wearing their black academic gowns even in the morning.

I heard her say, laughing, "If you've seen me outside the Seeley Library, I must have been waiting for her." Waving towards me. "So, you're not a historian?" "No, English." "Ah." And they were off, for the next fifty or more years.

He used to wear a tweed jacket and cavalry twill trousers until she laughed him out of this outfit; we were in jeans and black sweaters, all the rest of us, our group as we called it. It was the sixties at last, it was the time of revolt against everything our parents had done and told us to do. Our clothes, our hair, our taste in music, the way we smoked and drank and took dope, the way we stayed up late at night drinking instant coffee and listening to modern jazz, showed the world who we were—and showed us ourselves who we might be, too. It was a club just as rigid as any other, looked at from now, but at the time it was freedom, originality, flair. So, Hannah got Philip out of his conventional clothes almost as soon as she'd found him, but he still looked neat in his ironed jeans—who ironed them?—and a slightly shabbier version of the tweed jacket over a black sweater. He would wheel his bike, and she'd walk beside him down King's Parade, or she'd wheel hers and he, gentleman that he already was, let her go ahead.

He was not handsome, being very tall and thin and beaky-nosed, with flyaway hair, and I wondered what she saw in him at first, but he turned out to be so good-natured and simply kind that all of us—our little gang—warmed to him and took him in. Was that what it was, his sheer niceness? A man without malice, a man who had been brought up to be polite, especially to women. An old-fashioned Englishman. He got up in the morning and went to lectures, as we did not. He sent neatly written essays in on time, she reported. He was set to be an intellectual—not the sort we admired, with existentialist or Marxist credentials—but a solid, thoughtful, respected historian. He was bent on getting a first, and did so in Finals, without ever looking ruffled or overworked. What was it Hannah wanted of him? To be treated well, to be loved. She would tease him for being boring, and he simply smiled and took it, and she went about with him arm in arm, smiling too. She had found someone who accepted her just as she was, I think now, and relaxed into that ease, adopting his aura of pleasantness. He seemed unworried by her occasional flightiness; patiently, he waited for her to come back to him, even when, as she did, she let him down, or was seen with somebody else. What happened to all her other suitors, I did not know, but I sometimes glimpsed one of them bicycling hard up the hill towards our college as if in pursuit of something that eluded him; maybe it was his bicycle clips as well as his impatience to find her that had put her off.

They were married in the early seventies, only a few years after we left university—he was a year ahead and had already gone down before us—and I went to her wedding in East Anglia, among buttercups and cruising swallows, in the pale light of that region where the sky cups the flat earth so completely that every human activity looks small. It was in a flint church, in summer, and there was a garden party afterwards, and I saw my hippie friend transformed into a bride among pages and little flower girls from her new husband's family, all clutching bunches of wildflowers artfully arranged. I was in a floaty blue dress and broad-brimmed hat from Biba on Kensington High Street, and high boots.

It was the year in which we went our separate ways: she into married life and I into the far reaches of North America. Each of us had disappointed the other; the shared life we had imagined, having salons, taking London by storm, had evaporated. But in our twenties we were too busy inventing our individual lives to be aware that this mattered, or to think it irreversible. You just moved on, as life took you with it, and nobody was supposed to complain. I couldn't imagine then why she had decided to marry Philip, of all the young men who had crowded around her at Cambridge, with whom she had claimed, serially, to be in love. Was she in love now? I dared not ask, it was not something you could ask someone on her wedding day; it was far too late. Weddings imply a lot: they almost force you to accept a certain reality, that this woman and this man are in love, that he, she, is the "one," that only one person exists in this world for you, for anybody, that it is "meant" to be, even, that it is all God's idea, and suddenly people who haven't mentioned God for decades are intoning and singing hymns and promising Him that they won't let him down, or look at anybody else, in sickness, in health, for richer, for poorer; they are signing their lives away, old friends hardly count anymore, and this is the beginning of their Real Life. All this can go through the mind of an old friend, at a wedding, and it went through mine. I saw her move away from me as surely as if she were setting sail into an unknown sea. Later, I understood that she had felt the same way about me, when I told her I was leaving for America. If this was betrayal, it was also what was expected of us. In that era in England, you either married as soon as you could after graduating, or you got a job in television with the new channel, BBC2, or in publishing. Or you went to America. It was a foreseen part of growing up, becoming a real adult person; a parting of childish ways. We had set our sights on different lives, moved in different directions, I told myself, and that was that. Yet there was something in her guardedness with me when I saw her again, her rather tight little smile, that told me that perhaps marriage and a house in East Anglia did not quite match up to my American adventure and the freedom it brought me.

On the day of her wedding, when I'd flown back all the way from California to be there with her, I surprised her on the stairs as she went up to change into her going-away suit, after the party. She was already unzipping her white satin that had grass stains around its hem. She had lost a contact lens, thought she might have left it in a wineglass. Her hair was falling in wisps out of its fluffed-out bun. I reached to help her, almost automatically, and she stopped me. "Careful with the zip, it catches easily." I eased it slowly down her back and the white wedding dress slithered down, and she stepped out of it there on the landing and caught it up like laundry under one arm. She was wearing a garter belt, as we call it in America, and white stockings, and a push-up bra and lacy knickers—real honeymoon stuff—and I could see that she was embarrassed. We exchanged a glance, but no words. To me it said, don't say anything, don't you dare, you have no right to comment, I'm doing exactly what I want to do. But I could have been wrong.

I have time to think about all this as the TGV speeds south, as I lean back in my seat and watch countryside change, brown cows give way to white cows, grassy fields to hills, suburbs to vineyards, gray roofs to red. I love train travel in Europe, and can't believe that trains hardly exist in the US today, for all their lonely whistles blowing from the past. This is a journey I have made many times, but usually I have a book, or a copy of *Le Monde*, and I read to distract myself. Today, I can't read, though I have the new Patrick Modiano I've been wanting to begin. Sometimes other people's documented lives are fascinating; at other times, they feel like an intrusion. I think about our lives, mine and Hannah's, as intensely as I can, in case there is a clue, a memory, a story that will turn out to be essential; in case, as Philip has suggested, I myself carry the answer to the riddle. I can't risk Modiano's own potent, seedy memories of postwar Paris getting in the way. I watch France rush past me, or that is how it feels. Really, I am being carried through France at an absurd speed, a speed we could never have imagined in the early days of our travels. I remember Hannah and myself, wriggling into couchettes, lying there pretending to sleep, too excited to close our eyes: seeing France pass and narrowly become Italy through a slit at the side of the blind, where it stretched and rattled against a window, and the mysterious sign that said *E pericoloso sporgersi*; the banging door of the toilet up the narrow corridor, and the pervasive stink. The swinging of the train carriages, the track glimpsed like suicide between the coaches that seemed so slightly linked together, the guard sleeping in his little closet. The train of memory, the train of youth.

And then we're there. I get off my fast twenty-first-century train at the futuristic new station in Avignon, the one that's been set down like an airport or a supermarket in the middle of the red-earth countryside of Provence. I miss the old station, where I had to carry my bag through an underground tunnel to come up facing the high medieval walls of the old city; where Hannah used to meet me, and take me straight to a dark bar across the street where we would sit in a corner and sip vermouth and catch up, before driving out to the house. Here, I step out into blunt heat and see a parking lot full of cars flaring light from their windshields a short distance away. No sign of Philip. I stand and shade my eyes, wondering if he's come, or if I should get a taxi. There's a taxi stand down some steps with a number to call, and a little group of hot people with suitcases. But no, of course he's here, I see a tall slightly stooping figure walking towards me, wearing a floppy hat, dark glasses, a droopy linen jacket, jeans, and espadrilles. His red cotton scarf somehow gives him away as English, and his blue eyes when he takes his glasses off that really do widen and lighten at the sight of me. He waves, "Claude! Claudia! Over here!" as if I haven't seen him, and I walk towards him, pushing my wheeled suitcase beside me, my bag slipping down over one shoulder. The place feels mercilessly hot and dry, but the line of poplars by the parking lot and a farther stand of dark cypress, their tips just moving, remind me I am in Provence, where there will soon be shade, and a cool drink.

"Claudia. How are you? You look marvelous. You haven't changed a bit."

"It's only been a year, Phil." Though I suppose we do start to change overnight, these days. "Yes, I'm fine."

"I wondered if you'd be able to get here, with all the strikes they are talking about. Why didn't you fly?"

"Oh, I've had enough of flying, once I've crossed the Atlantic. I like fast trains. I had something to do in Paris, so I stopped over, caught up with a bit of the jet-lag, so I didn't fall asleep on you as soon as I got here."

He's pulling me towards him in an awkward one-armed hug, so I kiss him firmly on both cheeks as if we were French, and see him blush. We walk to where he has parked his car in the rows of others, a BMW with big English plates. We begin driving towards the city of Avignon, that lies to the right of us like a lion in its valley, couchant in the sun behind its ancient walls. The wide Rhône under its stone bridges. The dark ranks of cypresses, the willows and poplars glittering beside the water. On the left bank of the great river as we go towards Villeneuve-les-Avignon, with its jutting tower, I glimpse the restaurant with the faded striped awning where once we celebrated one of their wedding anniversaries—or was it a birthday?—years ago.

The road divides and he sets off towards Pertuis and the Lubéron, where his house is.

"So," I say at last, "Phil, d'you want to tell me what has happened?"

"Nothing has happened since we talked. She simply hasn't contacted me, nobody knows where she is, and the French police appear to be doing nothing to find her."

"How infuriating. I'm so sorry, it must be awful for you."

"Frankly, I'm at my wits' end." He's staring straight ahead, driving carefully, his profile unchanged but a certain angle to his neck that tells me he's trying to keep control, not only of the car.

"Have you told the children?"

"Yes. Piers is coming on Saturday. Melissa's trying to get

away, but she's still at work and needs someone for the children. They are both absolutely mystified, as I am."

Another silence. "But Claude—I know she isn't dead, I feel it, so there's some hope. I believe I would know it if she was dead."

I'm moved by this declaration. He has a humble man's certainty about some things. He feels he knows his wife. But if she is simply elsewhere, as she has been before? Not dead, but willfully absent?

"Well, that's good. Philip—has she been odd in any way recently? I mean, is she mentally okay?"

"I think mentally she's fine. She hasn't been very well physically, that's partly why I wanted to come down here for a good part of the summer, so she could relax." He glances sideways at me. We're at the age now when things can go suddenly wrong; when the body, or the mind, can crack open and let life out. I see this new nervousness, which is making everything harder for him. His hands grip the wheel more firmly.

"I only asked because you hear sometimes of people wandering off, you know, forgetting things, not knowing where they are." Not for a moment do I think that my astute friend would be in such a state, but I wanted to cover all possibilities. "D'you mind talking about it while you're driving? We could wait till we get there if you like."

"No, no, I want to use all the time we have. This is fine."

"So, do you know what was wrong with her physically?" I think, I have to start here.

"I don't, really. She's been run down, complained of aches and pains, cramps in the night, that sort of thing. She's been seeing a doctor in London, our local hospital leaves a lot to be desired, with all the cutbacks. But you know Hannah. She didn't want to talk about it, so I didn't ask. She seemed better, recently, more like her old self."

Her old self. How many old selves we have now. My own include the rapt young woman hanging out on houseboats in Sausalito, the itinerant would-be filmmaker in Central America, a dozen others, as well as the girl who left London with two suitcases to follow a dream six thousand miles away. How many are there of Hannah's old selves? I've been remembering how we got a night train down to Marseille to catch a cargo boat to Turkey, the summer of our second long vacation from college. All the way down the Mediterranean for twenty pounds, steerage. The Turkish musicians who played as we ate our dinner, and the slipping deck under our feet as we learned wild dances with young Turkish men. That old self? Or the old self of her wedding day, demure under a white veil, but swigging champagne with a devil-may-care look in her eye. Or the self with the quick glance, looking up through her hair one evening as I asked her— yes, I did—if she'd ever slept with Alexandre, and she'd said, "Claude, please. Trust me."

Trust me, she must have said to Philip, trust me to be a good wife, a mother, a companion, trust me to stay with you, trust me to be respectable. Trust me to arrive where and when I said I would, and not let you down. To me, her oldest friend, she had only said it once, that evening when I suspected her, and apart from that one time we had based our friendship on such trust, over years, over decades. She could trust me, but could I trust her? Could anybody, over a lifetime of questions left unanswered—did you sleep with him, where were you, where are you now?—trust another human being this much? Like Philip, I feel betrayed by her disappearance. Could she not have told me, I have a rendezvous, I had to get away for a bit, you know, you understand. I feel demoted, somehow, by her not having told me anything. And heaven only knows what Phil must be feeling—insulted as well as worried, angry as well as perplexed? Leaving someone, a husband, with no explanation must feel like such an insult to the person left: you are not important enough for me to tell you what I'm doing. In a way, an accident or even a kidnapping would feel less degrading: it would not be his fault. I wonder now if she has some plan, or project, that will let him know that life with him, this marriage, this car, this house in France, this use of what is left of her life, is not and cannot be enough?

Plane trees flicker past us; we come down into the flood plain, turn at the T-junction, and go through the shuttered village where the few remaining shops are closed up for lunch, no one sits out on the street, and probably the church is locked. To reach the house, there's a narrow unpaved road along the canal, with a bridge over it and bamboo growing thickly along one side, so that Philip's big car hardly passes. It's years now since they bought this house, at a time when it was easy for English people to buy houses in France and do them up, or have local contractors do it for them. Their house, on the outskirts of the village, built against one of the foothills of the Vaucluse, is an Englishman's idea of what living in France means: living free of having to work at anything in particular, or be near a school, or even have a supermarket nearby. It's a luxury house—not big, not full of expensive furniture, but a luxury in that most of the things that ordinary people need to live are not present. You have to have a car to live here, and the Internet of course, and someone to look after the place when you are away, and a gardener for the big garden, a pool-person for the pool, probably a woman to come in and clean. You have to have made your money somewhere else. You have to not care about local politics, which are mostly right-wing and nationalist these days, and you should be able to vote elsewhere. You have, in short, to be a rich, mobile foreigner with another place in your own country to retreat to, even if you also have a French bank account and credit card. But it's a beautiful stone four-square house with a rose garden and honeysuckle and a courtyard with a paved terrace and a swimming pool and a mountain behind it, and a view of the further mountains of the Lubéron. They have made it very comfortable, considering that it was once a ruined farmhouse, and I'm always happy to step inside it and be told to make myself at home.

The electronic gates open to admit the car, which crunches across the gravel. The garden is planted with oleanders, roses, lavender, and the table and chairs on the terrace are scattered with small leaves blown in the wind. It is where they have given parties; where we have sat out on so many evenings, drinking aperitifs. Today, it has an abandoned look: nobody has had time or inclination to sit out here.

"Your usual room?" says Philip, opening the doors, and I pull my suitcase up the winding shallow stairs—"No, let me, I can do it"—to my room on the first floor with its view of the hill behind us. He follows, anxious. "I did ask Marie-Laure to make the bed, I hope she has." The bed is smoothly made with clean white sheets and topped by a green and white duvet. The white curtains flutter a little in the breeze from the open window. The broad tiles under my feet are polished. The chest of drawers is oak, its top covered by a lace runner. A vase of peonies stands on the dressing table, their blunt heads not yet opening; they must have been picked this morning. Marie-Laure, I think. I put down my suitcase, and feel Philip hovering behind me. "Everything all right? Come down for a drink, and then we'll have lunch. You haven't had lunch, have you? I'm starving."

I smile at his almost absurd Englishness, the schoolboy enthusiasm and exaggeration, the way he longs to make me comfortable, make it all completely right. "I'll be down in a minute!" And when I've washed and combed my hair, I go back down the wide oak staircase into the open-plan room they have made of what was a farm kitchen. How did Hannah end up here, I wonder once again. Or has she decided not to end up here, not to come back at all, but to take up her life somewhere completely different?

I meet Marie-Laure on my way down, as she is taking off her apron and finding her car keys, to go home for lunch. She's younger than I am, but has a grown family: her son works in a bar in Avignon, her daughter lives in Nîmes with a husband and children; she often shows us photos. Today, she looks worried, and raises her eyebrows at me, jerks her head slightly in Philip's direction.

We kiss on both cheeks. "How are you? Good to see you."

"Well, I'm fine, madame, but this is all very worrying, don't you agree? That poor man, he is beside himself. What can have happened?"

"I hope we're going to find out."

"It's wonderful that you could come. It will make such a difference. Men. They are lost without us. Now, I'll be back tomorrow, but if you need anything, call me." She slips into her light jacket, jingles her keys. Her new little red Peugeot sits outside in the drive, next to Phil's car. She waggles her fingers at me as she leaves.

Philip has poured himself a pastis and is getting food out of the refrigerator for our late lunch. I sit down on the white sofa with the Moroccan rug thrown across it. "Yes, pastis, that would be fine." We are, after all, in the south, and I'm thirsty. I fill my glass to the top and the water clouds.

He puts out the plates from the pottery in Aubagne—I went with Hannah to buy them, years ago, when we loaded the car with green and yellow Provençal plates and enormous pots. We sit at the glass-topped table and face outward towards the garden, the oleander and roses, sunflowers and clumps of lavender, and young olive trees with their gray-green leaves. The light is the familiar yellow light of Provence, and I find it hard to summon any anxiety as I relax into its warmth.

But what will we do? Eat lunch, talk about Hannah, wait for her to appear? It's as if she might come downstairs, smiling, at any minute. I realize that Philip has no idea, that he has reached the end of his imagination, because he has never for a minute imagined that she might leave him—probably, she has never given him cause—so what is happening now is the unimaginable, it is outside reality.

"I don't really want to talk to the police again," he says. "They ask all the wrong questions and somehow everything"— he smiles apologetically at me—"gets lost in translation. She was the one who could always make people understand."

He has relied on her, for so many things. For his life, for it all working as it does, for the fact of his children, for the framework she has given them all. What nobody would ever have expected of restless Hannah: to become a faithful wife, effective mother, good housekeeper, keeper of the status quo.

"I'm so glad you're here, Claudia. It makes all the difference. I'm afraid I've been feeling terribly alone with it all, these last few days, and I'm sorry if that sounds very feeble. The truth is, I don't know how to live without her."

I reach across and pat his knee, and he taps my hand briefly and swallows the rest of his pastis. "I mustn't get maudlin. But with you, at least, I can tell the truth."

Part of my job here, I see, is to listen to him while he talks about Hannah, about his feelings, their life together, how she can't possibly be dead or in harm's way: to hear him out while he convinces himself. The other part is presumably to think of something we can do, some way to find her. That I have no clue how to do. But a drink and lunch is a good start, as I'm hungry again, having eaten nothing on the train. Marie-Laure has made soup, he tells me; we only have to heat it up. Like orphaned children, we are being mothered by a woman who comes in and cleans, makes soup, and then goes out of sight; one of the invisible helpers who keep life on track.

Spooning up the soup he's heated in a big copper-bottomed saucepan that must have cost at least a couple of hundred euros, he says, "You know her so well, Claudia. I'm sure you'll be able to find out where she is, what she's doing. I can't tell you how grateful I am that you're here."

"I'm glad to be here," I say. The soup is delicious, home-grown tomatoes, I guess, with basil from the herb garden outside. Nothing I have tasted in the last year has had this freshness and flavor; it's like seeing a black-and-white film suddenly turn to color. "Now, tell me how life has been since

I last saw you, how Hannah was, what you did together, and about this illness, what do you think it was?"

It's the last sentence I speak over lunch, apart from asking the occasional question; he has been waiting for my arrival to pour it all out. I hear his misery, his confusion, his embarrassment at feeling this way, but he does not sound angry with Hannah. He slurps his soup sideways out of the spoon, drinks often from both water and wineglasses, tells again the story he must have told to the police, to his children, but to me he tells it unadorned by the fierce self-control he must have been imposing on it till now. "She wasn't on the train. I went to meet her. She simply wasn't there, and she wasn't on the next one either, and her cell phone was switched off, and what was I to do? I simply came back here, waited for a few hours, tried her phone again, and then called the police. I don't know, Claudia; I have no idea. I am at my wits' end. Thank God you are here."

I sit catty-corner to him and notice how familiar he is— that profile, somehow Roman—and yet how changed by his present tension. We have known each other, not well, but for all this time, because of Hannah. I don't think I've ever been alone with him for more than a few minutes in all the years.

"Well, I don't know what I can do, but maybe talking it over may help. I'm sure she'll come back, Phil. I know, it must feel awful. But I'm here to listen, and do anything I can."

I think, maybe it just makes a difference that I am another human being, to sit here, to hear him. Maybe that is all. For I don't have an answer, either; I have no idea. We sit as if at some terminal, beyond which we can't go. But we go on eating, drinking, crumbling bread between our fingers, as if this, life in its smallest details, is what must go on.

7.

Hannah and I used to spend weeks of the school holidays in each other's houses. The strangeness of other families fascinated me. The way they lived, what they ate; the smells of their houses, their bathrooms, especially their bedrooms. It was like visiting another, alien tribe. Her mother wore ankle socks over her nylons; they sometimes had wine at dinner; her father used to leap up halfway through a meal because the gadget he wore at his waist had let him know that some child was dying. Often, he was not at breakfast because he had been up all night with a child patient. He seemed to be entirely devoted to other children, the ones in the hospital we never saw; but he was kind, if vague, and used to ruffle my hair and tell me I was a genius, on no evidence at all that I could see; and he'd kiss his daughter and wife absent-mindedly and go gangling and urgent, his shirt outside his trousers, tie loose, out through the door.

At my parents' house, Hannah was made welcome as if she were a refugee.

"Are you a lonely child, really?" my brother Calum asked

her when she first arrived. My mother, laughing, covering up, told him that the phrase was "an only child" and that it was nothing to be worried about. The boys, Calum and Chris, were careful and thoughtful around her, though, as if that first adjective "lonely" was really the right one. They could not imagine having nobody else, no other child to play with—partly being twins, I suppose, but also because everything they knew was to do with being one of a crowd. We, in our family, were a crowd, a clan, a gang, even if most of the time I wasn't at home and they were four years younger: we existed plurally in a way that Hannah's absent family did not. The presence of the latest baby, my year-old sister Joanna, even hinted that there might be more to come. Babies could appear when you were not paying attention, taking your parents' time and devotion and letting you know that you were to get on with your own life now.

I went to stay with her and her family, that first summer we knew each other, on the east coast, at Aldeburgh in Suffolk. There is something about that time, that holiday—but what? Hannah's parents, like mine, slept in twin beds. Yet in Aldeburgh, at the house on the sea front, there was only one bed for them, a saggy double. I once passed the door in the morning and saw Hannah's mother's white breast emerge from her slippery-looking nightgown as she reached for a cup of tea that Hannah's father handed her. I looked, and went on fast and silently downstairs. There were more aspects to people's lives than you ever knew. There was the surface, what you saw every day, and then there was this secret geography of bodies; this ballet of flesh behind closed doors. I needed to know how other people really lived, beneath their surfaces: what adults did when they were alone. I sniffed up their secrets like a trained dog.

Hannah's parents spent a lot of time at the Yacht Club, where they had friends who sailed and kept a boat. For some reason, Hannah and I were never invited out on these trips. I think now, they involved drinking, and maybe flirting; laughing a lot with other couples, anyway, and coming home late to stand propped against the kitchen counters, talking over late cups of tea or cocoa, their faces flushed. But we were happy on our own, Hannah and I, striding together through the town, marching to the seawall, sitting there to gape at the vastness of water and hear the roar of the shingle dragged back down the beach. We liked our solitude, and were censorious to each other about adult activities we considered stupid.

They gave us money to buy fish-and-chips suppers, and, sometimes, for the cinema that was rigged up for the summer behind the Moot Hall, where we watched Buster Keaton and Chaplin and *Seven Brides for Seven Brothers*. The sun went down late over choppy water, and nobody was left on the beach except ourselves.

I took photographs with the box Brownie I had been given for my birthday; but they have been left somewhere behind me, those gray-and-white images with their thick white borders and crinkled edges, the two of us sitting on a slant wall in a photo taken by someone else, our feet in sandals, our legs bony and scarred, or Hannah alone, a strand of escaped hair blowing across her face, against the background curl of the sea. I wanted, even then, to preserve these times, to make something of them that would say more than words can, even without the fluidity of film. Even then I knew that you could preserve an image, make it reach out into the future; I took my undeveloped film to the chemist's shop in a passion of anticipation, to see what I had made. I knew that already there was a gap between the photograph and the original image; in this gap, an ache opened that I did not know how to fill.

She was just twelve, I nearly thirteen. The sea was beside us always and there were the long slow sunsets over the town and the marshes, the Moot Hall, and the alleyways where nets were stretched. We took our warm paper packets from the fish shop and carried them to the seawall, where the tide moved all the pebbles up the beach. Every evening, when her parents had gone out, the same expedition. Our feet slipping on cobbles, the smell of hot newspaper soaked in grease and vinegar; we made our way to the seawall and sat, dangling our legs, to bite up the scalding chips and break off pieces of battered fish in our fingers, as the sky darkened slowly over the North Sea and the lights came on one by one, and the lighthouse beam turned.

We went in to that cold sea daily, hobbling over pebbles, the east wind rushing in over the land; afterwards we had hot baths, to wash the salt off, and I sat with my knees up against my chest, so that nobody could see I had breasts. She was flat-chested, her nipples flat as coins, like a boy's, and she was afraid they would never grow. In the afternoons, we went to hit tennis balls against a wall, whacking them with old wooden rackets, for something to do. The sea and the sky were huge. I'd never seen so much sky. Just one summer, and then others, but it's that first time I remember, when we hung out with our hair in rattails and our brown legs dangling, on the seawall, tasting freedom. We were outside normal life— outside the rigidity of school, the ordinary routines of home. We were at an edge, a margin, we were in some liminal space together that felt wild and free and unpredictable. There was no agenda for us, and we had none ourselves. We were guile-less, because here there was no need for guile.

My parents thought we had been neglected. I loved being neglected, I loved the fish and chips and the late evenings and the skies we watched slowly change and darken, the red stripe of sunset late over the marshes. I loved the space, the silences, the sound of the sea, and being up late in the evening. We didn't talk much. There was only school, and we didn't want to talk about that, and there was everything left behind in the land to the west of us, everything in this free place, this margin between childhood and adolescence, when we didn't know who we'd become, only I was Claudia and she was Hannah, and we were sealed, sure, proud, and certain, little girls still before the chaos of puberty, and there were only my secret small breasts under my striped T-shirt to remind us that we would ever be anything else; so I hid them, I pretended. We sang, and marched up and down, and told jokes, and hit tennis balls against a wall. When it rained, we got out her father's chessboard and she tried to teach me to play, but the moves confused me, her long silences as she con-templated a move were too long, and we resorted more often to two-handed Scrabble and Monopoly. We curled in the big old stained bathtub together, she at the tap end because I was the guest, and her mother looked in our ears to see that we had washed away the sand, and scrubbed our backs red. We slept in a high-up room in the rented house on the seafront, and the sound of the sea was in everything we did, even when we were asleep.

There's a point before adolescence tips you over, fuddles your brain, and distracts your body; a point of balance, between childhood and the opening adult world. I think in little girls it is particularly clear—but we rush past it, all of us, in our eagerness to become who we will be next. Here. Perhaps it is here, the clue I have been waiting for; where the wild open sea stretches all the way east before us and we turn our backs to the land.

There was the night of the maroons, sometime in July, when the sun still sets so late on the east coast that it is only really dark for a few hours. The emergency siren wailed across the town to bring everyone out of their houses. We woke, hearing it, and already Hannah's parents were calling upstairs to fetch us down.

"What? What's happening?" We were bleary with sleep, but quickly excited.

"It's the maroons. Everybody's going to help with the boat!"

A ship was sinking out at sea, and the lifeboat was to be launched. People were running down the street, even leaving their house doors open so that yellow light spilled here and there on to the pavement. Down past the Moot Hall we ran and saw it emerging from its shed like a great whale slithering towards the water, the people of the town all heaving and shoving to push it down faster over the shingle, so that it could strike out into the waves. It was midnight, and a starless windy night: the sky still held its pallor, but black water slapping up against the stones and against the sides of the boat as it was launched, and the sound of it was grinding stones and a kind of groan and then a sudden rush, and the spray that hit the bow. We all wanted to have a hand in it, and people crowded up to help. Hannah and I in our pajamas with raincoats over them, and sneakers pushed on with the laces still untied. We'd all run out together in our nightclothes, and everyone else was strangely dressed too, in wellington boots and jackets over nightdresses, and hastily thrown-on rain gear. It began to rain, and the rain slanted down in the light from the boathouse, and we saw the stern light of the lifeboat as it left shore and struck out towards the horizon. In just a few minutes it was out of sight. No lights out at sea, but still over the land the remains of that long summer twilight, pale over the marshes, and the sounds of the maroons, that siren wail in our ears still, that ghost-sound that had woken the whole town.

People stood on the shore, straining to see the boat's passage, or a dark shape that could be a ship out there, but nothing was visible. There was nothing to do, but go home to the open houses to bed, or wait out on the seawall watching for a return. We stayed out, I remember, because it was too soon to leave, although some people did, wanting to get back to children and warm beds. We sat on the seawall, Hannah and I, and her parents smoked, and then her mother said, "Well, it will be a while. Perhaps we had better go back in." But I could hear that nobody wanted to, so we stayed.

Her father said, "Maybe I can be of some help. They may need a doctor. I'll wait and see." We waited with him, proud of ourselves as if elected to be of use too. There was the continual grind and suck of the sea on stones, and then a whisper, a ripple that told us the tide had turned. I don't know how much time later—an hour, more—it was that the boat came back in, the men shouting into darkness, lights at the bow, and the foreign sailors were brought ashore, one of them dead, someone said, a young man. People were saying that it was a Norwegian ship, so the young man was Norwegian.

"Hannah, Claudia, come on! Come back with me, now. There's nothing more we can do." Hannah's mother called us away from the scene and walked ahead of us, her arms folded. Her father was down by the boat where the ambulance men were running down the shore with stretchers. Maybe he was examining the young man, or helping others out of the boat. I wanted to see for myself, and I think Hannah did too. We moved close to him, pushing through the crowd, and they let us, because we were with her father. The foreign sailors in their dark wet clothes stood apart from the crowd. They looked shocked, as they rubbed their arms and hunched into themselves. People reached to hand them blankets, flasks. Someone was saying that the ship had gone down. Nobody knew if there had been others left on board. The boy being lifted out of the boat and laid on a stretcher looked young, not much older than us, and he couldn't have been in the sea for long, only he looked completely soaked through and very pale under the lights and his features were blunt, somehow, like those of the dead kitten I once saw our cat give birth to, quiet and left to one side, still wrapped in its caul while all the others had been torn open and licked to life; and then I saw that he had a cut on his head, and blood had come from it, so something must have hit him before or after he fell into the water. Hannah's father was holding a wad of cotton to the cut, as if to keep the blood inside, and the ambulance men were lifting him and the last we saw of him was a small dark wet shape on the stretcher that was being lifted into the back of the ambulance like something being put carefully away on a shelf, and all the while I saw that his arm and hand dangled down, the way they never do when you are conscious, or even when you are asleep.

I thought when someone was dead you could tell: the body was heavy, different; and there was that boy's hand, dangling as if disconnected to anything alive. Hannah's father turned on us when the stretcher was gone and looked almost angry. I'd never seen him look fierce like that. "I thought you two girls had been told to go back to the house. Go on now, and I'll be back soon."

We had no excuse. We just wanted to see what was happening up close, because we wanted to be part of it all, I suppose, we wanted to know. We walked back towards the house, not talking, all along beside the seawall till we saw the light in the kitchen and Hannah's mother waiting up to scold us. Only, she didn't, but just said, "Go to bed now." In our room facing the sea we dropped our outer clothes on the floor and got straight into our beds, because there was nothing more we could ask, or say. And that night and the days and evenings to follow, we stood alone together at the edge of the long shingle beach, away from the smallness of the town, deafened by the roar of the sea and its withdrawing grind over pebbles; the gulls scream over the shore and the marshes, their swarming and squawking around the fishermen's huts. We never talked about the boy whose body we had seen taken away in the ambulance. In the local paper, it said that he was nineteen, from Oslo, and must have fallen, or jumped, overboard. All the other sailors apart from the five rescued by the lifeboat men, had gone down with the ship.

We looked outward together at the endless gray movement of the waves, imagining other shipwrecks. Anything was possible. The wind, we were told, came straight here from Siberia, nothing in its way. Even in summer, you could feel its chill. The east coast of England, a bulge, an excrescence, where land used not to be, and a wildness to it still, a lift of the light and air as if solid objects might fly away. The old town lay buried beneath shingle. I discovered later that it was among the crumbling Saxon churches with their watchtowers, inland farther than you would think a great ship could enter, that the invading Vikings—the early Norwegians—had first made their way upriver, in from the North Sea.

How many summers were there? How many times did I go with her and her parents to this place at the very edge of England? More than once, anyway. I remember coming back there, a little older, probably the following summer, and taking up our old habits, but somehow they were not quite the same. The wild freedom of the first time has stayed with me. The freedom, and the danger, the strangeness of that night of the maroons when we first saw someone dead.

8.

We knew each other through all those invisible years, when people think you are simply a blank slate, a page for your education to write upon. When you have been children together, you have a past that no others can share; it has to be a secret, in order for you to survive. Often, we suffered in silence. But I saw her, and she saw me, across the enormity of this silence, and there was something admitted between us that said, not now, but later; not this reality, but another; we will wait it out. We have glimpsed it, we were on that beach, we know it's there.

It was necessary, we decided when we were back at school, to run away. We talked about it, worked out how it could be done, made plans. Why had nobody ever tried, as far as we knew—or was there such disgrace, such punishment, that nobody ever heard again of girls who had tried it. Perhaps they had been expelled, and their names expunged from history. We didn't know. And, where could we run to? I had an aunt in the New Forest, only about a hundred miles from our school. We could disguise ourselves, hitch lifts. I thought she might take us in.

"I'll tell McKinley my parents are coming down, and they've asked you out too," Hannah muttered to me as we crossed the courtyard to go into the school building, our green cloaks pulled around our shoulders, our heads bent together. You could never tell when someone could overhear you: a prefect passing, apparently unaware, a couple of girls who would inform on you just to curry favor.

"Right. This Saturday? Or is it too soon?"

"This Saturday. Be ready."

We passed each other notes in a code we had worked out, based on substituting some letters for numbers, so that it looked as though we might be passing answers to an algebra problem. We were in the Big Prep Room, where girls sat in rows, doing their preparation work, waiting for the shrill bell to ring that signaled a rush out of the building and back to our houses for the cold meal of Spam, sardines, or Marmite on toast called supper. It was in the spring term of our second year.

She told our housemistress, saying that it was hard for both her parents to get away together, so it was a last-minute decision, an opportunity not to be missed. Our names were written in the exit book. We dressed in our scratchy tweed suits, pretended to wait for the car to come up the drive. When we were sure that nobody was looking, we walked fast down the drive, not looking back. Our berets on our heads, our hands in gloves, our socks pulled up tight, we must have looked less like escapees than a prim pair of young ladies heading for church. We had hidden a bag behind a bush at the bottom of the drive with our nonuniform clothes in it, and enough food stolen from the larder the night before for a picnic en route. We picked up the bag and walked fast into town, to the railway station, where we bought single tickets with no comment from the ticket seller. We waited on the platform for the train, on which we would change our clothes and our hairstyles, and join the crowds of ordinary commuters on the train that would end up, three hours later, in London. We hardly dared speak to each other as we were doing all this, except in whispered asides, got the money, good, platform three, only a few minutes. The platform clock ticked on as slowly as ever the clock did in the Big Prep Room. We sat on a bench, trying to look inconspicuous. We handed over change at the newspaper stall to buy packets of crisps and chocolate, and film magazines to read on the train. No girls from our school were ever allowed to travel unaccompanied on a train. Just before the board went up, announcing the train, we saw feet in brown lace-up shoes, legs in brown lisle stockings, a tweed school skirt come in to view. We couldn't hide, except behind the magazines we'd bought. We waited to hear the voice of a school prefect—the only girls allowed to come in to town, and even they had to come in pairs, so there must be two of them. Our hearts hammered, as we told each other afterwards, we expected every minute a voice to say "Prescott and Farrell? What are you doing here?" and for hands to seize us and drag us away. Amazingly, as we kept our heads bent and our copies of *Picturegoer* and *Photoplay* in front of our faces, we heard nothing, and the feet in the brown shoes moved away. The whistle of the train sounded. What were the prefects doing here, if not hunting us down? The train was stopping, very slowly, up against the platform. Doors were opening. We were nearly free.

"Just what do you two think you are doing? Thought you were getting on that train, did you? Well, you'd better think again. Come with me, both of you."

It was Janet Richards, eighteen and captain of cricket as well as head girl, a tall beefy blonde who seemed to us far bigger than any adult woman we knew. She was like a Nazi in a film. She and her friend Penelope Wright marched us back to school and straight into our housemistress's study. There was nothing we could say. The punishments were various: being shouted at for half an hour for wasting our time and our parents' money, telling lies, being in fact lower than the low; they included being made to stand in the corridor with books on our heads before breakfast; having to run around the hockey field three times in the fog; not being allowed any dessert for three weeks; and most serious of all, being threatened with expulsion. Our parents would hear of it—and did. We were not allowed to speak at meals, nor to walk together to church on Sundays. No one was to talk to us. I can't remember what else they thought up that came short of beating us; but the general sense of being outcasts was hard enough. Perhaps some girls admired us for trying; but trying to escape and failing never carries much glory. We suffered in imposed silence. And then Hannah wanted to try again. "We were too obvious, Claude, anybody could have seen us walking downtown when my parents were supposed to be picking us up, we were sitting ducks, maybe even the stationmaster called the school. Next time, we'll go after dark."

I objected: I didn't want to risk being expelled, mainly because my own parents would have been so horrified. More than that, I had been made simply afraid. Being told day after day that you are a wicked, ungrateful, lazy, lying failure has an effect. Or, it did on me: I felt weakened, as if I could stand very little more of the general opprobrium.

Hannah felt it as a challenge. She was caught up in the idea of escape, at whatever cost. I see it now as her practicing the art of fugue.

"But what if they catch you again? There'll be huge trouble. You'll probably get expelled."

"Come on, we can't give up now." She looked at me, her head on one side, pulled a face. "Oh well, if you can't, you can't. Really, Claude, you're sure? Then you'll have to cover for me, till I'm really and truly gone. Promise? You'll just say you haven't seen me?"

"All right." I wondered what I would do, if questioned; how I would act my part.

"You could pretend we've fallen out with each other."

I thought, they would never believe me. "I'll think of something. Don't worry, you'll get a head start."

She would go out at night, before the main door was closed, and she would change immediately into ordinary clothes, put on makeup and pretend to be one of the town girls going out on a date. I saw her off, with a whispered "Good luck," wearing her school raincoat, heels—we were allowed to wear them on Saturdays—her hair inside her beret, a slash of lipstick across her mouth.

"Call me Sharon," she laughed. "And if you never see me again in this hole, look me up in Bournemouth. My dad's cousin lives there. By the sea, Claude!" And she was gone, into the darkness of the drive, flanked by laurel bushes, out of sight.

When they brought her back, she was shut up in solitary confinement in the Sanatorium for a week, and I couldn't see her or find out what had happened. Her parents were called, and she was threatened with expulsion, but her father was a fairly well-known pediatrician who wrote letters to the *Times* and had given money to the Chapel Roof Fund, so she was given another chance. When I finally saw her, she was pale and looked exhausted. "Claude, thank God you're here still. I suppose we'll just have to wait it out, now. It's impossible to get out of this place—worse than Colditz, if you ask me."

So I remember, as I go through my memories in Philip's house, Hannah's early addiction to the art of escape. I search for something that may possibly be of use, but may equally be of no importance at all. What about the time when Hannah decided she was going to learn Russian? It was the year we saw Dino de Laurentiis's *War and Peace*.

My own film passion had begun early, when I went to a children's party and saw my first-ever cowboy film, sitting in the dark watching Hopalong Cassidy, who was William Boyd on a white horse. I sat on, wanting him to return, long after the film had ended with its fizz of exclamation points, stars, and numbers, and all the other children were in the kitchen eating ice cream. I thought—so this is what you can do? You can be a man on a white horse, rushing through canyons? You can be someone completely different, live another life? At school, we had a film once every term and you had to sit on an ordinary school chair and watch the starbursts and numbers flashing upon the wobbly screen and then flashes like lightning, and spots, and grainy gray nothing, and then, miraculous, a human face. Just as we were getting enthralled, the film tended to tear, or stop for no apparent reason, and the projector wound down, and we all groaned in chorus.

When we were fourteen or so, her mother took us in the

Christmas holidays to see *War and Peace*. That film, Techni-color, Cinemascope, glorious stars, aching music, the death in battle of the one you loved most (or wanted to be), the crowds, the ballrooms, Natasha in her gray scarf searching for Andrey in the ruins of Moscow, Pierre lost on the battlefield. Complete suspension of disbelief. If we could have had freeze-frame and replay in those days, we would have sat rapt, for hours, going back and back to those scenes, till we knew them by heart. I would have stayed with one scene until I knew its every detail. As it was, there was the one unrepeatable (until years later) experience: Hannah and her mother and I, in a London cin-ema—yes, we had come up for the day—drawn into Russia, or its Hollywood likeness, uncritical, heartbroken, moved to tears. There was an interval, in which we stumbled out into the cruel daylight of real life, Leicester Square glimpsed outside, the taxis and buses and passersby, none of which I wanted to let in to the rarefied place in which I now lived. We ate sand-wiches, drank Coke that came in cold glass bottles with straws, went back in to the holy darkness, immersed ourselves again. Afterwards, Hannah and I were speechless. I never wanted to talk again—and we noticed here our common dislike for any-one who began talking about a film after it was ended; the only correct response was an awed silence. We followed her mother, got ourselves somehow back to King's Cross, may have had tea somewhere—it was the matinee—but I don't remember. I remember Hannah's look across at me as we came out of the red plush of the cinema into dingy afternoon London, and what it said: we are different, we are Russian now, this has changed life forever.

When you are young, you can't say what you have liked or disliked about a film. It simply swallows you whole, it becomes your life. Nobody could have asked me at that time what I thought about *War and Peace*. It had simply become a sacred object.

It was not until I was older, and saw Bergman's *Wild Strawberries* at the Arts in Cambridge, that I first thought, somebody made this film: it is connected with a person's life.

Hannah and I lived *War and Peace* for at least a whole school term. In dancing class, we conjured up the ballroom scene, in which Andrey asks Natasha to dance, at her first ball. We clicked heels, bowed over each other's hands. We reenacted the balcony scene in the school cloakrooms, where you could perch on lockers and gaze up at the hanging gym clothes on hooks that were masking a Moscow night sky, and take turns to be Natasha on her balcony and Andrey standing smiling in the shadows, hearing her rapture. We played the death scene, over and over, Hannah lying on the narrow gym benches, expiring, "I saw a door . . ." as handsome Prince Andrey closes his eyes forever and distraught Natasha bends over him. We did the field at Austerlitz, and Pierre stumbling among the war dead; but at fourteen, fifteen, we preferred the love stories, the ballrooms, the Moscow nights. Much later, when I saw the long Russian version with its magnificent wolf hunt and its grimmer battle scenes, I knew that it was a far better film, and that the Hollywood one we had so loved was—well, Hollywood—but I could still not forget the poignancy of Henry Fonda wandering on the field of battle, and Hepburn herself searching for her love among the wounded.

That was when Hannah announced that she was going to learn Russian. Her parents had written a letter, and they were going to have to fit the whole timetable around her

Russian lessons now. And that winter, long before everyone else began wearing fur hats because of Julie Christie in *Dr. Zhivago*, she sported a fine black one that sat upon her fair hair like a prize, and made me envious all over again, of how she not only had ideas, but acted on them. She was as Russian as she could be, in her own eyes; and so she was in mine. She had invented an elsewhere for herself, where nobody could follow.

Was it here, the continuation of her need to escape? To have an alternative life? I can't believe that she has gone to live undercover in Moscow, like Edward Snowden. Yet anything is possible.

9.

Philip and I move about in our solitary ways in this house that feels so empty without her; I hear him in the bathroom, his footsteps in the corridor. I've slept for eight hours straight when I come downstairs again to find him at the breakfast table. It's as if he is waiting for her to come down, and for a moment I almost expect her, sleepy, in a dressing-gown, barefoot on the stairs. I wonder: if somebody trusts you absolutely, is there something they are unwilling to look at, to consider? I can never quite trust Hannah the way he seems to, because I know her, I know better. But I love her still, with her occasional flightiness, her bouts of secrecy, her refusal to name names.

He sits opposite me at the table, unrolls his table napkin, and begins to butter a croissant, just as if she were not missing somewhere in Europe, with the police looking for her, and all the attendant possible danger this entails. He takes a big mouthful of coffee and says, "Marie-Laure brought the croissants. She always looks after us so well, I don't know what we'd do without her."

I nod. It's almost as if his losing Marie-Laure and her soup-making, croissant-buying abilities would be just as serious as having lost his wife.

"Phil," I say, "we should talk about Hannah, shouldn't we? I mean, time might be vital. How many days since she went missing?"

Does he, I wonder, assume that if he keeps the outer structure going—unfolding a napkin, drinking coffee, going through the ordinary motions of life—that this will bring her back to him? Apparently, it always has. He's holding the stable door open, a stable full of dry hay and bran, so that the errant horse can return of her own free will.

"Let's see, I arrived on Tuesday, it must be, what, three days. Since she was due to arrive. She wasn't on the train to Avignon. It seems she was on the Eurostar, though."

"Do you remember her doing anything like this before?" With you, I mean, not with me. She has left me in the lurch, and come back to me with a smile and no apology—how many times?"

He goes on eating, as if all this were simply normal. "No, she hasn't just disappeared before. I've always known where she was, even if she only left me a note. More coffee, Claudia? Try this apricot jam."

I can hardly bear it, the peacefulness, the calm. I put down my bowl. "No, no thanks. Phil—I don't know, but shouldn't we be doing something?" Yet I'm also thinking, if Hannah wants to go missing, then she won't want to be found.

Later today, his grown children are to arrive. We will not have the opportunity to talk about Hannah on our own. Piers and Melissa, her twins, must be in their forties by now: I haven't seen them since they were kids, or at least since they left home to go to college and on into their apparently successful lives. He's waiting, I see, for them to know what to do: to tell him, Dad, we must act. Until then we will hang about the house, eating meals that Marie-Laure has mostly prepared, although I say I'm quite willing to do some cooking. I will swim laps in the turquoise pool that sits in its flowery frame under the mountain. I'll lie out with a hat and sun cream on, making up for the muggy heat of Virginia summers that makes you want to stay indoors in air-conditioned cool. I'll behave as if Hannah hasn't disappeared, but is about to join me, slopping out on to the terrace in her flip-flops and swimsuit, setting down a drink, a book, coming to join me with a sigh of pleasure in the cool water blued to perfection by the paint on the bottom of the pool. I'll try, anyway. He too must be trying not to allow in the scenes that lurk so easily in our minds, from all the photographs and news items we have seen: murdered women, women gone missing, a bag, a shoe found, the dread implications accepted at last.

He wipes his mouth with a napkin and says to me, "You're right. Think, Claude. Please. Anything you can remember about her, anything she may have said, the smallest clue. Is there anything? I know you two write to each other."

Apart from a jokey exchange of Christmas cards, mine lazily online, and an email or two about summer plans, I haven't been in touch with Hannah this year. I think back to a year ago, here, in this same house that seems so eerily quiet and uninhabited without her. I came for a few days only. I was going to Croatia, for a conference. Or was that when I went to

Rome for the Cinecittà festival? Anyway, I was only in Europe for a short time. And yes, I stopped in Paris to see Alexandre. The summers have resembled each other, over the last few years: the times I've visited them in their house, the meals, the swims, the books, the talks, the growing anxiety—still then a small cloud on the horizon—about Europe, and refugees, and climate change, and distant war. Last time, what was different about last time? I remember going into Avignon with Hannah, sitting in a café—it was, must have been, after the theater festival there, as the streets were fairly empty. We faced the great red walls of the Palace of the Popes. We were going to see a film, that was it. The one about the two women in Switzerland, with Juliette Binoche. Philip had not wanted to come—no, you two go, I want to see the match, it's the quarterfinals, anyway that's more of a women's film, isn't it? I remember not saying what I wanted to, irritated once again at this division into films for women, films for men, it always seems so infantile, as if we aren't all involved together in this huge event, called Life. But yes, Juliette Binoche and Kristin Stewart, and clouds coming down a valley. Hannah and I in a café beforehand, drinking Campari, watching the sun paint those famous walls. If it was the quarterfinals of the World Cup, it must have been before the festival. June? And what did we talk about? Hannah was thinking about getting an apartment in Avignon, I remember now. The house, all the way out there in the country, we're too isolated, we have to use the car to go anywhere, what will happen when we get too old? It's too big for a holiday house, and it costs a fortune to keep it going when we're not there. I remember that I nodded and agreed with her—I've recently found the house slightly imprisoning, with its automatic gates and alarms, its remoteness from other people and their lives.

"*But I thought you and Phil loved the countryside?*"

"*Well, yes, we used to, but now we hardly go out into it. He has to put up taller and taller fences to keep out the wild boars, or they'd come in and eat everything, trample the garden to bits. Anyway, I'm thinking that if we had a flat, I could just come down sometimes on my own.*"

She said that, and now I wonder if I should tell Philip; or is it an open topic between them, have they talked it over, even made plans?

"Did she ever talk to you about getting an apartment in Avignon?"

"No? Whatever for? This house is quite enough for us to deal with."

"It was just something she said, last time I was here. One evening when we went to a movie. She thought it would be easier for you both as you got older."

Philip flinches, or it looks like that to me. "After all the work we've put into this house? Anyway, we aren't in our dotage, exactly."

"I know." I want to be calming, agreeable. I see how easily, now, he is upset. I see too, there have been cracks, there have been disagreements, and things not said.

"What else did she say?" He's on to it now like a detective; as if I have all the clues.

"Nothing, really. What about this illness you mentioned? You said she had been unwell?"

"Yes, just this last winter. She was seeing her doctor. You know how she hates talking about that sort of thing. Very private. Very discreet. She probably didn't want to upset me. But I wish she'd told me, I really do."

"What sort of doctor did she see? Gynecologist, neurologist? Cardiologist? Osteopath? What?" I'm thinking, how peculiar their marriage is, really: these people live together for a lifetime and don't talk to each other when they have been to the doctor?

"Oh, I think just our GP. We don't go to specialists all the time, the way you do in the States."

"You said she went to London, Phil."

"Oh yes. The one time, she did. Or maybe, once or twice."

"Do you have any idea what it was?"

"Not really. Aches and pains. Used to keep her awake sometimes at night."

I imagine Hannah wrapped in a shawl like a Russian heroine, awake and staring into the night. And Philip, asleep in the bed she has just left. It's unbelievable. I wonder if all marriages are like this, with dark areas like on the satellite map of the world seen from space, intense clusters of electric light in just a few places, linked by invisible power lines.

"Phil, before the twins get here, I think it's really important that you tell me what you know about this mystery illness."

He stares across at me, distress written across his face making him plainer than ever; but honest, caring, truthful to a fault. "There were some pills in the bathroom cupboard. Painkillers. Also stuff for epileptics, I think. Neo-something. I suppose that was what she was taking." He sees and accepts my amazement at the dark spaces I have glimpsed in his marriage, in his long years with Hannah.

"She seemed better, with the spring. I thought it might be seasonal. You know, we had a hard winter."

"And you never asked her, Phil? Why she was taking that drug? Do you think she would have talked to Melissa? Maybe a daughter would be an easier person to tell?"

"Knowing Hannah," he says, as if I don't, "I don't think she would have told anyone."

"But this might be a major clue. She could have gone off somewhere to—I don't know. Be alone? Get over something?"

"Without telling me?"

"Apparently, yes."

I'm thinking—do we know the same person? And what can come of this talk? He's showing me a strange mixture of calm and desperation; I can see from his grip on his spoon how tense he is. But he has decided—yes, decided—that she will come back to him.

"Claude, there isn't somebody in France, is there? I mean, someone she might have gone to see. You know, and not tell me about?"

"I don't think so. I can't think of anybody." I watch him get up to make coffee in their incredibly high-tech espresso machine.

He comes back with two tiny cups. "She's been to Paris a couple of times in the past to meet writers we publish. I just wondered if she might have needed to—well, see someone without telling me."

"There was somebody she knew at the Sorbonne? Apart from her, her name was Simone someone—I don't know."

I think, of course, Alexandre. But no, I've just seen him; both his initial surprise at news of her disappearance and his lack of interest in her whereabouts were evidently real. I put the thought away.

PART II

10.

Hannah and I met Alexandre on a train. We were going to Italy, on our first trip away from our parents, she and I—our first foray into Europe. She was eighteen, I nineteen. We had finished our first year at university, it was the long vacation, we were facing outward at last into the world we had dreamed of through the years of our incarceration. This first summer of our freedom we had three months stretching ahead of us that would lead, we knew, into the rest of life: France, Italy, the future.

He got on in Paris, after our train had made its long loop round from the Gare Saint-Lazare to the Gare de Lyon. As the train pulled out, as we faced south, really going into Europe now, no fear of being turned back, he leaned in the corridor, smoking a cigarette, a boy in a black leather jacket with shaggy brown hair. We had a way of sizing up boys in those days, with a lifted eyebrow, a moue of interrogation, copied from some sixties' movie star. We exchanged a glance behind his back, as we slid past to go back to our compartment. It was evening, and Paris was settling into long summer dusk as the train moved out between the shadowy buildings, the pools of yellow light.

"We're off, then," Hannah said, bouncing back on to her seat, crossing her legs in their tiny skirt. "Life, Claude. Life is a big adventure."

We said things like this to each other, then. Statements about Life, Love, Loss. One of her favorites was, "Here is a girl who has lived, loved, lost, and lived to love again." She had it pinned up over her bed in college; if it sounded tragic and solemn, I privately thought that Hannah's loves were never long-lasting enough to deserve such an epitaph—but then, whose were?

We smoked, and swigged from a bottle of water. The train lurched and rattled, swaying along the track of our future, which, unknown to us then, contained this shaggy young man we had just passed in the corridor. A man in uniform came in and began to pull down the blinds quite violently, but as soon as he had gone, we pulled them up a foot; we were not going to miss a single view that this journey offered. Later, he came round, scowling, to turn the seats into couchettes, and we and the four others in the compartment began shuffling and hitching ourselves and our belongings around, to fit us to the narrow shelves on which we would spend the night.

"Let's find the bar," Hannah said. "It's far too early to go to sleep."

A big Frenchman in shirtsleeves who seemed unlikely to fit into a couchette, headed out in front of us, smelling of Gauloises. We followed him along the swaying corridor, in the direction of where a bar might be. There in the corridor, staring moodily out into the growing dark of eastern France, was Alexandre. Perhaps he was being a movie star too: Alain Delon turning a pure profile; Belmondo running his thumb along his upper lip.

I said in my schoolgirl French to him, "Where is the bar?" It was the first sentence I ever spoke in what was to be our life-long friendship. He sometimes reminds me of that.

He says he had always known that English girls were both lesbians and alcoholics, and I say, you were wrong about one thing, at least.

He jerked his thumb down the corridor. "But it will be full of *mauvais types*. Why don't you join me, I have a not-bad bottle of wine and some *saucisson*, a sandwich if you like."

He fetched his bottle and we passed it back and forth, filling our mouths with red wine as if we were gargling. Then he passed the sandwich, a whole baguette in which we all left teeth-marks. It did have some very good peppery sausage in it. Then he passed his cigarettes. We all stood in a row, peering out, in the train corridor, while behind us large people seemed to be getting into various stages of undress to pass the night with strangers both above and below them. Couchettes were six to a compartment, with the sexes unsegregated, so there was some pretty loud and intrusive snoring, as well as the smell of feet and cigarettes. We hung out in the corridor with our new friend as long as our legs would hold us up, and we all laughed increasingly loudly until the guard came and told us to shut up and go to our compartments. Since there was a group of French soldiers, en route for Algeria, just up the corridor doing exactly what we were doing, only louder, this seemed unfair. People want to sleep, the guard said. It's late. Then Alexandre said, "*Oui, faut dormir . . . ,*" so we all cranked our doors open—he was in a compartment two doors down—and slunk in past the snoring sleepers, tripping over our feet and various parcels and bags in the dark, to find our ladders. Hannah and I had the top bunks, and climbing drunkenly up the ladders made us giggle and snort, and I put a foot on the prone body, or perhaps face, of the person below me and heard an angry protest, *ça alors*, before I tumbled face down on my bunk. The train clattered and roared through darkness, only a flash behind the drawn blinds showing where a station passed; then it slowed in a series of bumps, with an unbelievably long-drawn screech of brakes, and we all banged into the wall beside us and a collective rumble of alarm spread through the train, as if we were caged animals woken to some trauma in our jungle past. What had happened? Were we stopping in a station? We heard shouts in the corridor. The man below me sat up, banged his head on the bottom of my bunk, swore, *putain de merde*. I looked down on a bald crown surrounded by ruffled hair. A woman was clutching her breast as if she was having a heart attack. The big man on the bottom bunk sat up in his undershirt, hairy shoulders and broad furred back. "*Ils ont arreté le train.*" They have stopped the train.

Footsteps in the corridor. Shouts. We must all have been remembering films about the last war, people being searched on trains, being thrown off, bodies hitting the dark invisible earth beside the tracks. It felt extraordinarily exciting. Something had interrupted our smooth onward progress through the night: something had happened.

The guard put his head round the door, his cap a little askew. Perhaps he had been asleep too in his closet at the end of the carriage. "*Messieurs-dames*, no need to worry, there has been a disturbance, someone has pulled the cord, we will be moving again soon. Someone has to be put off at the next station. No cause for alarm."

Hannah whispered, "What did he say?"

"Someone pulled the communication cord, I think."

The emergency communication cord, locked in its box behind glass, with its announcement of a huge fine for anyone who interfered with it—who would have dared to pull it, and why? We all crouched on our bunks, in our various stages of semi-undress: children woken in the night, our journey suddenly become dangerous, unpredictable, a train that had plunged into the unknown, and been stopped. The long nightmare scream of brakes would stay with me, although I had been half asleep. The roof of my mouth was furred and sour with wine and cigarettes. I looked at Hannah. Had we taken on more than we could manage? No, of course not. Life, as she had said, as we both believed, was an adventure. And the definition of adventure is that it is sometimes uncomfortable.

I slid my arms into my shirt and slithered down off my bunk, swinging down the ladder. "I'm going to see."

"Claude, don't."

"Just to see, we have to know, don't we?"

In the corridor, there was nobody. I looked up and down the train that had been stopped and silenced in the middle of nowhere, in the middle of France. Then there was Alexandre, the boy with the bottle and the sandwich his mother had made; beside me in his T-shirt and jeans, his hair tousled, eyes bleary but amused. "Some dick pulled the communication cord." He used the word *connard*.

"Do you know why?"

"No idea. There's a big fine if it was just for fun." *S'amuser.
Une grosse amende.* My French was coming on. I noticed his
wide lips, with a kind of frill at their edge. He pursed them
around another cigarette and inhaled and blew out, a perfect
O. *Tu veux?* I took one, not because I wanted to smoke, just
to be with him, part of his little cloud.

Someone, we learned—he learned—had pulled the cord
because a fight had broken out, one man had attacked another
with a knife in the next carriage and a third person had broken
the glass and pulled the cord that stopped the train. We would
have to stop at the next station in order to get one man to the
hospital and the other into the hands of the police. By this time
the corridor was full of people leaning, questioning, lighting
up cigarettes, shouting, asking questions. An elderly woman,
her hair in a gray plait down her back, was in tears. Hannah
was beside me, asking, pushing closer to Alexandre in order to
find out. But it was too late. I had got there first, to stand beside
him, to hear the news, to take his cigarette and have him light
it for me, bending close, to get my first whiff of his body smell,
mark of his maleness, the scent that was to be his all his life.

We all went back to our bunks eventually, and there was
a mass settling of bodies to sleep again, or to lie awake tense in
the darkness. At the next station, which may have been Lyon,
the train stopped and there was another brouhaha outside, and
people were hustled off, I heard the voices, the carriage door,
the brief invasion of the outside as an engine was rattled into
life, and then the train door slammed again, in the next carriage from ours, and darkness overtook us again, and sleep.

Dawn cracked the narrow line at the bottom of the blind, and
when I pushed it up, there was Italy, and the light we had

dreamed of. There was the future, the world; and we were going into it. I leaned across and poked Hannah. Look! She pushed her blind up an inch, then two. Light filled the compartment, spilled down on the lumps of the sleeping bodies of our night-companions, who stirred and grumbled. It was early. Outside, sleeping locked houses, far mountains, fields still hazy with the night's dew. The sun spread long fingers slowly across the land, and cypresses raised their paintbrush tips and we stared, silenced by the beauty.

"Italy," said Hannah at last.

We'd tunneled through the Alps in our sleep. We'd be in Florence by midday, dragging our suitcases full of Marks and Spencer's clothes and the stomach medicines our mothers had made us bring, to find the bus to the youth hostel on the hill just below Fiesole. We'd be really there.

And Alexandre? We'd exchanged nothing but wine, a sandwich, cigarettes, and a question on an indrawn breath. Who are you? When will we meet again? Alexandre, who was also getting off in Florence but who was meeting up with an Italian girlfriend who had been in his class at the École des Beaux-Arts.

"Ciao," he said, and left us behind.

We next saw him gazing at Botticelli in the Uffizi, his arm around a girl, who was gazing at him. "Hannah, Claudia, this is Lucia." It all sounded very properly Italian. Lucia, languidly disentangling, was a slim girl with dense black hair and eyebrows that very nearly met in the middle, and a seductive downward look. She wore a straight brown shift to the knee, like a linen sack really but incredibly chic and correct, and she moved like Monica Vitti stepping her way through Italian real-

ist debris. We'd both seen all the films Antonioni had made so
far, Hannah and I, so we recognized the blueprint. We stood
there gaping and irritated at once, two English girls with bad
complexions, in our rumpled cotton dresses and cardigans
and our un-chic sandals, all wrong. We'd lost Alexandre to
a better model of girl, and there was nothing we could do
about it. At the youth hostel we ate spaghetti with no meat
in the sauce every night because it was cheaper, and danced
with other foreign boys under the moon, and went at eleven
to our segregated beds. The moon stared in at us through a
bare window and we lay awake, whispering, not daring to
talk out loud, or dreamed our separate dreams.

In Florence, we plodded around the Uffizi, took photographs of the David in the square, drank cappuccino in cafés,
learned how to eat spaghetti, and lost weight with all our
conscientious touristy striding. Alexandre—well, there he
was again, right at the end of our stay, and he'd obviously not
been doing anything as banal as staying in a youth hostel. He
looked sleek, in a pink button-down cotton shirt and black
jeans, his jacket slung across one shoulder. He looked Italian.
He waved across the tracks to us. "Come to Paris!"

"What? Can't hear you!"

"I said, come to Paris! I'll be there in a few days. I'll give
you my address!"

Then he was suddenly there beside us, having run up the
stairs and across the bridge that separated the two platforms,
and arrived at our sides. We all kissed, two each, bumping
cheekbones in our haste. He scribbled on a bent postcard he'd
pulled from his pocket, the Botticelli ladies with the shell.

"Come in a few days! I'll be there. That's my phone
number, call me."

And Lucia? "Oh, she was an old friend, nothing serious, over now, good to meet up again, but you know."

We didn't know. We had no idea how French boys and Italian girls conducted their affairs, no. So, Lucia was over; he shrugged. "I have an aunt in Rome. Why don't you come to Rome? Ah, *zut*, there is my train . . ." and he bounded away and three steps at a time up the stairs and back across the bridge, and down the other side, and we couldn't see him as he leapt into the Rome train and then, presumably, was gone. I had his postcard in my hand, and shoved it into my shoulder bag. "What a poser," said Hannah. I remember my surprise.

We did call Alexandre's number when we were back in Paris, at the end of our summer. He lived at that time in an apartment in the Marais, then a grimy district of dark stone and narrow alleyways, not the fashionable tourist neighborhood it is today.

"Claudie, Anna! Come in. Yes, put your things there. My flat-mate is away, you can have his room, one bed only, you don't mind? How glad I am to see you, you can't imagine, Paris is so dull at this time of the year, I had to come back as I have work to do, also no money left, and you, how are you, how was your summer? Tell me everything. No, first, there is the lavabo, here your room, leave everything. Now."

He made us thick dark coffee in a Mokka on a small gas ring and we sat on the floor in his room and sipped, our legs tucked up under us. He had the posters on the wall that everyone had then—Che Guevara, Marilyn, James Dean. The room was full of dusty rugs and unwashed clothes and smelled of patchouli, coffee, and smoke, under the prevailing musk of himself and his clothes. We were instantly in love with it all—with his Paris, with the noises of it and the smells of it and the whole ambiance—a word we relished—of this next stage of our lives. Hannah had undone her plait for the last time in Italy and these days let her fair hair fall across her newly brown shoulders. We were both thinner, more mobile; we had broken out of the mold that we had grown up in. My hair was a wild black mop and I stretched my tanned legs out, admiring my brown toes in their dusty sandals. Everything that had been boring and inelegant, because far too English, seemed to have been burned away from us after our time in Italy; we were new, we were becoming who we wanted to be, and we had that startled confidence I now see in young women—in my students, sometimes—who are at last realizing their own power. It happens to them much earlier, now, of course. Hannah and I had been in the chrysalis of our school's uniform and rules for far too long.

It wasn't then that I suspected her; it was later. But some ambiguity was set up then, there, in Alexandre's grubby apartment, as we three sat, smoked, talked, swigged rough red wine, inventing our lives. Officially, she said, he was mine. I'd earmarked him, hadn't I, that time in the train? Anyway, she wasn't interested, he wasn't her type. Far too self-centered, who did he think he was, French men were all the same. And he never washed his hair, you could tell. Was she overreacting, in order to give him to me, a reject, a cut-price secondhand sort of gift; was she pretending, criticizing him in order to hide the fact from me that she was secretly intrigued? Girls' friendships become women's, and a third thing intervenes: the lure of a man. It was here, during this summer of our first trip away from England, that I noticed—tried not to notice, but noticed—her possible duplicity.

We fell into the flat-mate's bed, she and I, late at night or in the small hours, and Alexandre stretched out on the messy divan in his own room. We'd been out to bars in the *quartier*, and nightclubs in cellars down by the Seine where jazz poured out and sweat poured down and we kissed anonymous boys up against damp walls till our lips were sore, and Alexandre smooched with girls behind their curtains of hair and sometimes disappeared with them—but never us, and never him. It was as if we had a pact to behave like brother and sisters, that summer. Perhaps it felt safer. Perhaps the hint of the implications of any of us ever embracing warned us in advance, in our genes, our cells, the unconscious wary places of the body. But I knew that I sniffed him up in secret, that I loved his skin and his movements and the rank smell, even, of his discarded T-shirts, and the way he smoked and threw the cigarette ends away from him, the way he tossed back his head, hair flying, to laugh. It was a secret I kept almost from myself; certainly I kept it, I thought, from Hannah.

But she mocked me: you fancy him, Claude, you fancy him something rotten, come on, admit it. And I would not. Why, because of the safety of our threesome, that end of August in an emptied Paris, in our shared lair on rue du Temple, in our nighttime excursions, lights falling into water, trees black along the Seine, jazz clubs sweaty and dank and blaring, bodies packed together, everything about it I wanted to keep. Stasis, if you like: safety, balance, an equilibrium none of us wanted to disturb.

Then there was a night in early September when I woke alone. I turned in the rumpled bed to find a surprising space beside me: no warm presence of Hannah, no hair spread across the pillow, no human breath. We kept our careful distance from each other in the bed, but there was no mistaking her absence. And the cooled stretch of the rather grubby sheet, which meant she had been gone some time, she hadn't just got up to pee. I got up and peered round the door into the rest of the flat. A light was on in Alexandre's room, I saw it under the door.

I thought I heard voices. A low laugh. I walked forward on bare feet, curling my toes down after my heels on the dusty floor. I was in my knickers and bra; we never slept naked. And yes, voices, Hannah and Alexandre, and then a light switched off, and then silence. She came out past me, walking close and unaware as if sleepwalking, and went into our room and got into bed. I followed. In the morning, Claude you must have dreamed it, I only got up for a pee, really, what did you think we were doing? And then, leaving me there, one day she was abruptly gone.

11.

That time in Paris, in Alexandre's apartment on rue du Temple, she did leave me a note. I didn't find it for a full twenty-four hours, but there it was tucked into the frame of the cracked mirror in what had been our shared room. How had I not seen it? I was not looking for it, that was how. I'd accepted her departure without a word as if it were normal—because it was the kind of thing she did? I unfolded it.

Chère amie, forgive me! He's all yours now. See you in Cambridge. xox H.

All mine? Alexandre, did she mean? And why had she chosen simply to go, leaving the two of us alone? She must have got up early, dressed without waking me, even after she'd stayed up late with Alexandre, crept out and down the stairs to the street, she must have walked across early-morning Paris to Gare Saint-Lazare, or taken the Métro or maybe even hailed a taxi, and simply got on the waiting train. I tried to imagine her journey, how it was, how it felt; as if I wanted to be her, not my confused self, left as if holding the baby. The baby who was Alexandre.

I stayed another week, and went home on the boat train,

following in her tracks as I supposed. In the meantime, Alexandre and I talked.

"*Elle est bizarre, ta copine*. Your friend is weird. Why did she go?"

"I don't know. She does that sometimes, just gets up and goes. At parties, if she's not enjoying herself. Anything she finds boring."

"She found it boring, here?"

"No, I don't think it was that." *He's all yours now*. But how could he be? In removing herself, she had destroyed our safe triangle, and it would be even less easy to get close to Alexandre. We were both of us, already, pulling away from each other as if in fear.

"What did her note say?"

"Nothing much. She said she'll see me in Cambridge. Term starts in another couple of weeks."

"But you will stay, Claudie? Please stay."

"Okay, if you're sure."

"Of course I am sure. Now. Shall we have coffee here or go to the café, have a treat? Then, I don't know, we could walk. If you like. If you don't want to be alone."

He was as unsure as I was. No, of course I did not want to be alone. What I wanted was to throw myself into his arms; but I didn't, not yet. It would be too much to handle, I felt, to start anything with him; also, I didn't want to do it just because Hannah had in her airy way given me permission. He handed me an untipped Gauloise from the squashed blue pack in his jeans-jacket pocket and we smoked, and looked at each other, and looked away. That was what we did then—put things off, changed the subject, moved on with the flare of a match, the crackle of tobacco, the sudden creation of a cloud of smoke. Everyone did, not just us. It was the way things were—in films, in books, in life.

After a while I dared to ask him, "What were you talking about last night?"

We'd got ourselves down the street and into the café on the corner, and were sitting over our tiny cups of black coffee. I preferred *café au lait*, really, but black seemed more sophisticated. We smoked. I drew in the dust with the toe of my sandal—we were sitting outside, our backs to a wall, so I didn't have to look at him.

"Oh, life. You know. What it's all about."

I didn't know. I wanted to know. "Did she say anything specific, about, I mean, wanting to go home?"

"She didn't want to go home. She wanted to go to bed with me. I said no, that would not be, in my view, chic: not with you there in the next room."

"Oh." I was silenced. Hannah had suggested going to bed with him, and he had said no? The world, the street reeled about me. A big garbage truck went past, very close, and the men emptying bins, clanging down lids, only feet away from us, so we couldn't say anything that could be heard.

After they had gone, Alexandre said, "I had thought of it, of course, with the two of you staying with me, but not then, not like that, I mean, just because we were awake and talking and you were asleep."

"Oh," I said again. "But you'd thought about it."

"Of course. It's normal, no?" The way he said it, *c'est normale*, made me want to laugh.

I remembered a conversation Hannah and I had, that first year we were at Cambridge, about sex and friendship. It was the beginning of the summer term. We'd been lying in long grass, at the edge of one of the Girton lawns, under a tree. We had our textbooks with us—mine Stubbs's *Charters*, hers *Gawain and the Green Knight*—but it had been too hot to read, and our minds were elsewhere. Which do you think most important, sex or friendship? Her question to me. I said, oh, I should think sex, it's such a driving force, don't you think, it overrules everything else, it carries you away. And she said, oh, friendship. Because when you are old it is what is left. At the time, I was a virgin and so I presumed was she. All we knew about sex was from reading, and films. But when I did lose my virginity, later that summer, it was such an anticlimactic act that I wondered what D. H. Lawrence and all the others were talking about. I was on a bed with a boy I quite liked, who had suddenly, after a party in Emmanuel, taken me to his room and become very urgent about making love to me—passionately, as he put it, I want to make passionate love to you—and I'd thought, well, here goes, this is the moment then, and I can't wait to tell Hannah in the morning. It was nothing like what I'd imagined, as I'd touched myself to orgasm under the boarding-school sheets. It hurt, and I bled, and he got apologetic, and then we had to scramble to get me out of his college because if we were discovered, we could both be sent down, and he didn't know about me, but it would kill his parents.

It's normal, said Alexandre in his practical French way, of course I'd thought about it. And yet, when he had the opportunity, lovely brown Hannah with her long fair hair and her body fined and strengthened by all that walking about Italy, he'd turned it down.

And then she'd left, and given him to me.

* * *

It was a few years later, when he'd moved to the *sixième*, a *chambre de bonne* on the rue du Dragon, just round the corner from the church of Saint-Germain-des-Prés. He had given up the arts, and decided to become a lawyer, to everyone's surprise. He was studying law at the Sorbonne. We were in our early twenties, a time when several of my college friends had already married and were pregnant; we all believed then that you could do this and still lead a bohemian life.

I went to Paris to find him, in the end, having tried sex a couple more times with young men with floppy hair in London, and an American hippie who had showed up from California and called me his old lady. I bought a plane ticket this time, arrived at Orly, got on a bus. It's all a very long time ago, but what strikes me now is how we draw the patterns in our life when we are young, and there they remain, to be ignored or acted upon—there is still that choice—but never quite to go away. I am still buying plane tickets to Paris, getting on buses and trains, going to see Alexandre. It seems to have been the most stable, as well as the most secret, aspect of my life.

We hardly left his "maid's room," except to forage for food in the then fairly cheap neighborhood of Saint-Germain, where now there are expensive shoe shops and designer boutiques. We pleased each other enormously. We fitted. We knew what to do. Our bodies greeted each other with a kind of sober recognition. We were almost embarrassed by our pleasure in each other. Sex as a memory is as elusive as a dream you don't write down because you think you will never forget it. But something of it, our early fire, our young shyness, lives on. The body has its own memory, its own agenda, quite apart from any common sense. Perhaps the only way to have lifelong sexual pleasure with a man, as I do with Alexandre, is to see him only once a year: it's always the first time and, now, always the last.

12.

Hannah's twins arrive in a large rented car driven by
Piers, who has picked up his sister from the airport
in Marignane. I hear the automatic gates grind open and
the wheels crunch across gravel, and Phil's voice, and their
voices, raised; I look down from my window onto a cluster of
heads and see: a family. This is what Hannah, my Hannah,
has made. A husband and two adult children, their names
as posh English as you can get, who are now about to make
plans to find her, flush her out, and bring her back. I dread
the conversations we will have, the stridency of the young
knowing they are right. I wish that Hannah may have run
off with a lover, hitchhiked across Europe, taken a plane to
Patagonia, emigrated to Australia—I wish for her, seeing
her family down there, only escape. Melissa is taking her
father's arm and apparently shouting at him, though I can't
hear what. Piers is getting suitcases out of the back. This is
the scene that Hannah has made, in being absent. This is her
fault. Her legacy.

I go down to greet them, and am surprised when Melissa, who was only about seventeen the last time I saw her, comes to hug me hard and thank me for being here. Am I a stand-in for her mother? She is close to tears. This is what it is to have a daughter—someone who minds this fiercely that you are not there. Piers, who has Hannah's straight fine hair, now growing around a bald patch like his father's, is a tall, round-faced rosy man, wearing a denim shirt and dark trousers. Melissa has the same hair, but hers is up in a bun, rather severe, and she is wearing white linen pants and a blue top. With their blue eyes, their fairness, they are as English as could be, as English as Hannah and I tried hard not to appear when we were young.

Melissa says, "Claudia, how wonderful of you to come and keep Daddy company. Oh, it's been ages, hasn't it? Too bad we had to wait for such a sad time, to meet."

I say, "Lovely to see you. Yes, I'm glad to be here." What else can I say? Piers is handing a bottle wrapped in white paper to his father. "I thought we should all have something good to drink. Can't hurt, anyway." I spy a gold clamped top. Champagne, when their mother has gone missing? It was always—is—Hannah's favorite drink.

Melissa says it, "Should we be drinking champagne, when she's—well, we don't know where she is? Isn't it rather heartless?" She holds out her glass, all the same, and we clink glasses, all four of us—am I standing in for Hannah, here?— and we drink, to her safe return.

"Mum, wherever you are, come back to us," Melissa says.

"Come back to us," Philip intones. We all stand there in the immaculate salon with the huge black screen of the TV emphasizing absence, and the sky outside, blue with a scattering of birds in the wind, a long way away. Do they think that a champagne toast will miraculously bring her back? I don't know. I don't know these people. But I know, or used to know, Hannah.

As if reading my thought, Melissa turns to me, plumper in the face than her mother ever was, and with her straight hair more emphatically blonde. "Claudia, you've known her longer than any of us, nearly all your lives, haven't you? What do you think, where do you think she might have gone?"

I hold my champagne flute like someone at a wedding and look at Hannah's daughter, who was a baby, then a schoolgirl, and who is now a woman in early middle age. She's emptied out by the absence of her mother; she wants reassurance. Her father and brother won't, can't provide what she wants. So I try. A little carefully, I say, "You know, she used to do this sometimes when we were young—just vanish, without much or any of an explanation. She always came back. I think she may have had, all her life, a need to be absent."

Melissa says, "But she isn't young now." She sounds indignant: the old have no right to such foibles. "And you say she came back. But what if she's in danger? What if she's lost? What if she's lost her memory, doesn't know where she is?"

I say, "I don't think it happens as suddenly as that, losing one's memory. When did you last see her?"

"Oh, at Easter, I think. I took the kids over for the day. Yeah, she seemed okay. A little vague, maybe. She was getting a little vague."

How scrupulous, how careful, this vetting of aging parents by their offspring. I'm glad that nobody is examining me like this for signs of senility.

"Vague, how?"

"Well, she seemed to have forgotten that we'd said

we'd come for lunch. There wasn't any. So we had to go out to the pub."

Ah, so Hannah has given up providing for these greedy creatures, has she? "Perhaps she didn't feel like cooking. Or thought the pub would be a nice change."

Melissa looks severe. Mothers aren't allowed to not feel like cooking, even now. "We had the kids with us. They more or less had to live off crisps for lunch. She had forgotten that we were coming."

Like Hannah, she has a way of looking at you while she's speaking and then staring out into middle distance, as if something else has caught her attention.

"Mel," says Piers now, "it isn't a crime. And it isn't a sign of having lost her marbles. Come on. She was perfectly fine when we last talked, and it was only a few weeks ago."

Philip says, "She hasn't lost her marbles. She isn't getting senile. She was just supposed to get the train south last Wednesday, and she didn't arrive. Come on, finish up your drinks, we should eat." The champagne has lost its easy appeal. We are a distracted little group as we sit down at the table, perfectly laid, with tablecloth and napkins, and Marie-Laure's soup, a *soupe au pistou* today, to be followed by beetroot salad and a fish terrine.

All at once, I don't want to be here. I don't want to be a surrogate part of this family that has lost its director, its raison d'être. I feel sorry for them, but I don't belong with them. I want to be with Hannah, wherever she is now. No, I want to be with Hannah in the past, before any of them, when we were alone together, before we had to grow up. Before we met Alexandre, even; in the innocence and wildness of our youth.

* * *

I think of the note she left me, all those decades ago: *Chère amie, forgive me* . . . Surely Philip deserves similar consideration. Is there a note somewhere that he has not found? What would be an obvious place, their house in East Anglia, her study, her desk, his desk—it's a house of desks—propped in the bathroom, written on a mirror, left behind a pot of flowers? No, notes are not part of this twenty-first century. A message, on his computer, on his phone, in a memory stick, perhaps? Was he too panicked to look?

People go missing all over the world, and here in Europe, surprisingly, and whatever Alexandre says, tens of thousands of people, adults, manage to go missing every year. At a time when increasingly the whole continent is worrying about people appearing, out of the sea, out of unsafe boats, swimming ashore from other countries, desperately seeking sanctuary, nobody except perhaps the police is concentrating on people who disappear. The vast migrations from countries wrecked by war and hunger and violence of all sorts are beginning to enter Europe; appearing, not disappearing, is this year's concern. Of the disappearances, the nameless numbers swallowed up by the Mediterranean, we hardly dare speak. Disappearance means tragedy; appearance in a new place, survival. Shouldn't we all feel relieved at the ones who do reappear?

One woman vanishing is not a big story. Perhaps nobody is even looking for Hannah. Perhaps nobody except her immediate family cares. I saw a photograph recently of an elderly woman sitting weeping on a rock on a shore in Greece, having been persuaded by her children to take the uncertain journey from Syria towards a new life in Europe. Was she simply wishing that she had stayed at home? The old do not migrate easily. Habits grow and settle throughout lifetimes.

What could it be like to be old and leave everything, one's house destroyed, one's family on the run? She was someone's mother, someone's grandmother, she was once loved, and safe. Now, she was lost and far from home.

Life will go on without Hannah. As if she had gone down beneath a wave, beneath a wrecked boat. It is what life does. It is in the nature of things, and people. It is our heartlessness.

In the salon, Philip is talking to the police on the telephone. Or rather, the police seem to be talking to him.

I hear him stumbling over a couple of phrases in his awkward schoolboy French. There are long silences, and he paces up and down. I look down on the balding top of his head, and come down the stairs. He gives me a look of annoyance, pulls a face, holds the telephone away from his ear. "*Oui. Merci. OK. Merci. À bientôt. Oui.*"

"They don't seem to get that it's urgent. I don't know what they are doing. Nothing, it seems, except stare at their screens and ask for things to be signed in triplicate."

"Perhaps they have too much to do."

"They say lots of people disappear. That's hardly the point, though, is it? Is that what they say in murder investigations, lots of people get killed?"

"If I can help?" I don't say, my French is better than yours, and I'm not in such a state.

"They just keep saying they are doing their best. And that they are *desolé, monsieur*. I ask you. D'you think we'd do better in England?"

"Well, you might try in England. But if she got on the Eurostar, she's more likely to be here."

"Not that I trust them to be any more efficient, but at least they might make more of an effort." He huffs and puts the phone back, the landline that they keep here in case of emergencies. "They keep on about how many people are already missing in France. French people. People who have a right to be here. You'd think we weren't part of Europe, the way they go on."

I think of the stories of men who go out to buy a pack of cigarettes and never come home. That happens often, at least in the stories. My husband said he was just going to the corner shop for cigarettes, and that was that. We never saw him again. But women? Do we do that? Do women like us, like Hannah, with comfortable homes, jobs, friends and in her case, children and grandchildren, just get up and go? And where would we go to? A hotel, an ashram, the center for some cult, to another country to start again in our sixties? Do we ever just want to go missing from our lives? Hannah, were you lacking some vital ingredient of life—sexual, spiritual, intellectual, something that you simply had to have before you die? Have you a secret lover, waiting for you in India, in Australia, in Japan? Have you joined some religious order? Are you locked up somewhere, captive, and we don't know? Have you lost your reason, are you unable to find your way home?

The swallows swoop around the house and the sky changes color outside. We will sit down to another meal together, all of us with our unanswerable questions. Philip with his misery, Melissa with her anger, Piers with his disdain; I, with my lifetime knowledge of their missing spouse and mother, unable to offer a theory, a reason, even a clue. I've been here twenty-four hours, and in this time we have received no new information about Hannah at all.

Philip says, "Maybe I should just get in the car and go and look for her."

I can hear that he wants to be contradicted, that he wants us to stop him.

Piers says, "Dad, that would just mean that we lose you too."

Melissa says, "Didn't the police say anything?"

Philip drums his fingers on the table, pushes his plate aside with its pâté and salad half-eaten. He looks harassed, as if the questions annoy him. "I've told you what they said."

"What about the house in England? Is anybody there? Might she have called, left a message?" My suggestion, as I hope to calm them all.

Piers wants life to turn out right; to be explicable. He hates to be baffled. We can't maintain this, I see: we are breaking up.

"I listen to the messages every day. Twice a day. Nothing."

"Daddy, we can't just sit here and wait." It's Melissa again, angry at her mother—for the missed lunch, the unfed grandchildren, or does it go much further back? She wants a solution too, and she wants her father to find it. To be active, reassuring, once again a parent.

Piers says, "What else can we do? We can't rush around looking for her. We can put something out on the Internet, on Facebook, ask her to contact us, or anybody who sees her, to get in touch. That might work. Social media, really effective."

"Facebook," says Philip with scorn. "Only children look at that, surely."

"Now, it's only their parents," says Piers, "Kids find it old-hat. They're all into Twitter and all the rest. Instagram. But anyway, what does it matter what age the person is, if they have had a sighting of Hannah, or any contact with her? Someone, somewhere, is bound to have seen her."

"I suppose it's worth a try."

Lunch is abandoned, apart from Melissa and me. We sit on at the table as if in protest. Philip goes off with his son, to plug in computers and start the search for Hannah in the endless looping maze that is the Web. It gives them something to do, that isn't just waiting. I hear Piers ask, "Dad. Do you have her email password?" Presumably not.

I say to Melissa, "Your parents seem to live very separate lives." She looks alarmed, and I wish I had not said it. Here, she is a daughter, vulnerable, momentarily pushed back into the uncertainties of life. She needs to see her parents a certain way, and no longer can.

We look at the debris of lunch, the stained plates and half-full glasses. Should we clear this away?

"D'you want to walk outside a bit?" She wants to confide, or at least talk. I stack a few plates and carry them to the kitchen counter, leaving the table with its wine-stained glasses and bread crumbs. We go out between the heavy sliding glass doors on to the terrace, flagged with local stone, and down the garden to where Philip has planted fruit trees and olive trees, all of them now surrounded by iron spikes like trees in parks, to keep them safe from the wild boars from the mountain. The grass is dry underfoot, as he has not yet turned on the sprinklers, and the gardener has not been up from the village for days. We pause to feel the velvety but still hard flesh of apricots. The shadow of the mountain falls upon us. The water in the pool behind us is for the moment dark, with falling spirals of light.

Melissa says, "We don't know what she was like, before

she had us." She sounds plaintive, her voice floating up into the air between us.

"No, that's always true of parents. What do you want to know?"

"Well, she's always been our mother. She's always been there."

"But you knew that one day she wouldn't be."

"I knew she'd die, sometime, of course. I didn't know she would just go off—and not tell us where she was going." She is close to angry tears, I can tell. We pause at the end of the grassy orchard, beside a small olive tree that already has a few hard green fruits.

"No, of course not." I make my voice gentle, although at forty, surely she knows that her mother is a separate person, that she cannot in the end be explained or accounted for? "None of us did. It's a shock."

"It's fucking irresponsible, is what I think. She hasn't thought about what it's doing to Dad, it's absolute torture for him."

"Melissa, I think she probably *has* thought about him. You don't live with someone for forty years without thinking about them."

"How do you know? You've never been married, have you?"

Touché. "No. I'm guessing. It's all I can do. I think she may have just gone somewhere for a little while, for a change. I don't know, but I feel almost certain she will come back. She always has." I reach to touch her shoulder, but she isn't having it; my hand drops.

"That was when you were both young—fucking ages ago. It was another century. You all had these crazy notions of being bohemians, hippies, dropping out, all that. We can't afford that now. That's why I think she's being irresponsible."

That anger again, and a sob in her voice, the voice of a small child.

"Have you never wanted just to go away?" I don't look at her as I ask. I look at the solid shape of the mountain behind us, where the wild boars roam, where a knotty pine tree sticks out at an angle from the rock face. The mountain that Philip has fenced off, in order to grow his garden without animals breaking in.

"Well, of course, everyone has these fantasies. But we just don't get up and do it. It's so self-indulgent."

"Melissa, I think you just have to try to imagine a bit more what's it's like to be her. She's not your age, after all. Perhaps there is something in life that has waited for her, that she just has to do alone."

"But nobody would have stopped her. Dad's always been very tolerant."

Yes, she's always been her father's girl. Families are per-haps always divided up this way: you are his, or you are hers, and Hannah as a mother was perhaps too much competition for a daughter; who knows. I think, I have avoided all this, the complexity of family. Tolerant, she says. Yes, but who wants to be tolerated? I think, there's something at the root of this that dominates this young woman's life, and we aren't going to reach it in an afternoon. I don't answer. I watch the struggles in her face.

She pulls a gray-green leaf off the olive tree. "She has so much—Daddy, us, the house in Suffolk, this place, why would she just leave it all?"

"To go off with the raggle-taggle gypsies-oh? Just because

of all that, maybe. Who knows? Remember the song—what care I for my new-wedded lord, and my sheets turned down so bravely-oh?"

"Well, yes, but she's hardly new-wedded, is she?"

"Just so. Maybe that's it. She's been doing the same thing for a very long time, as a mother, as a grandmother, as a wife, as a member of society, as someone who has to answer when her name is called. Maybe she just wanted a break? Whatever it is, she hasn't done this to hurt you, or Piers, or Philip. Mel, perhaps you could go and spend some time with your dad, I'm sure he'd like that. I'm going to walk a bit. I need to move. Okay?"

13.

There's nowhere obvious to walk, except along the canal that runs between the house and the road, a track beside it that reaches the next village. I set off, after struggling with the electronic code for the gate, down the white path, stands of bamboo on one side, the canal fast-running on the other. I always wondered how anyone with small children could have bought this house, and dreaded to see a small body one day, carried along on the fast brown current. But here they both are, Hannah's and Philip's children, alive and well into competent adulthood. It is only now that the house has all these complicated locks and alarms and the gates have to be opened by remote control, and the shutters are impossible to open from the outside. Once, there was an old key under a flowerpot. Now there are these electronic combinations. People come through here, Philip says, gypsies, all sorts, and there have been burglaries. Relieved to have time alone, I set off in hat and sandals to walk in the stinging heat.

I've had the thought, of course I have, that she may have

killed herself; and I have not shared it with Philip, who presumably has had it too. I walk beside the fast-flowing water and think of Hannah's body showing up somewhere, an image of herself that bears no resemblance to her in life, yet is also irrefutably recognizable. Of ourselves, Philip and I, having to identify her. If this is the outcome, I don't want it; anything is preferable. There's the unpaved white road that turns off to the village, and a plank bridge crossing the canal. I stand for a moment on it looking down. There's a crack, through which I can see the slither of the water. The children did not drown here, and neither, I tell myself, has she.

A kilometer or so down the road, I come into the village, and see a café open, with dark green doors and shutters, one table outside with an umbrella with "Ricard" written on it. It's tempting to order a pastis, but I ask for coffee and a glass of water. The owner brings it out to me. Shade slices the table, as the umbrella tips. There's a row of cypresses opposite. I'm struck by the ripple of shadow, and film it with my phone camera for a minute. In all the years I have been coming here, I've never sat down at this café; it is something that Philip and Hannah would never do. Why not drink at home, and be comfortable? The metal chair cuts at the backs of my legs, and I sip water and look out towards the trees. I film the trees, their dark slim presences. Their tips bend like the ends of cats' tails when they are annoyed. There must be a breeze at that level, even if there isn't down here. I think of Van Gogh, Cézanne, those obsessed painters of this light and landscape, of how they made it their own. I feel as if I have escaped, and that in my escape, however brief, I have the chance to think, to remember, to let my mind clear, perhaps to understand: Hannah's fugue, the world without her, the way she has left us floundering in her wake. Those painters, they didn't care what effect they had on people. (What did Theo van Gogh think about his brother's departure from all norms?) They had their vision. Perhaps Hannah has hers, and it has driven her from us, to make her own way, to do what she has to do. Perhaps there is a completeness to her actions that none of us can see. For the first time I think, what has she made of us, by vanishing; what does her absence show?

An old man walks very slowly down the road towards me, heading for the café. I ask him, monsieur, may I film you? He gives me his smile of assent, sits down at the next table, lays out his tobacco pouch and papers, and I film him as he tells me that he has lived in this village all his life, apart from the war. "Yes, things have changed. You see foreigners all the time. But that's life, isn't it, change?"

He is missing a couple of teeth and his accent is thickly Provençal. He's the first person I have spoken to in days who is not obsessed about what has become of Hannah.

"Yes. May I go on?"

"Ah, well, if you like. It doesn't happen to me every day."

"What else would you say about your life, monsieur?"

"It has been rich. That's true. Not always happy, but rich. Not rich in money, you understand. Other things." He gestures around him. "I am happy in where I live."

"Are you married? Do you have children?"

"I was married. Forty years. We had five children. My wife died. But she's never far away from me, now. It's why I stay here, where she can find me, you understand?"

"Thank you for telling me."

"And you, madame?"

"I am not married. I am a filmmaker." I use the word *cinéaste*.

"Ah, yes. Hollywood?"

"Not exactly, no."

"And you are here—why? In this place? I never saw you before."

"I'm staying with friends." I wave towards the mountain.

"Ah, the English people. It was my brother-in-law's farm, that house."

"Really?"

"Really. Long time ago. He sold it, couldn't keep it up. Ah, the English, they love to do up houses, don't they?"

The waiter has brought him a pastis, without asking. He pours water, enough to turn it milky white.

"I should get back. But thank you, monsieur, it was a pleasure."

"Leblanc. Louis Leblanc."

"Claudia Prescott." We shake hands, his hand warm and rough.

I thank him and watch him begin to make a hand-rolled cigarette. Then I lay my coins in the saucer, pick up my hat, and turn to walk under ancient plane trees, back to the plank bridge that crosses the canal, and I feel his mild gaze following me as I go. People come and go here. Others stay, for their own reasons, to continue conversations with their missing spouses, knowing it's possible, or choosing to believe it so.

I walk slowly back towards the house. There's the scent of wild fennel, its dry stalky plants, seeds bursting, heated by the afternoon sun. The shape of the mountain shifts and comes closer. The swift-flowing canal water surges regularly in a way that river water never does, as if propelled. Now I'm walking in the same direction, but it's faster than I am. I walk the straight white line of the path beside it, the movement of walking a solace in itself.

Coming in through the iron side gate, which I'd left unlatched, I hear a shout from the swimming-pool—"Claudia, come and join us!"—and see Melissa in a smooth black one-piece, her hair up high on her head in a ponytail, walk towards the pool and then dive, cutting the water, disappearing, appearing again, yards away, her paintbrush of hair soaked and dripping. Piers is already swimming laps; a white arm raised, then the other, slicing through the blue. Behind them the mountain is sharp and steep, all its planes flattened in shadow, as the sun moves round. One day I will film the changes of light on the mountain: that steady presence in our lives that yet seems to advance and retreat.

I drop my bag, throw off my clothes, dive in my underwear and swim a couple of laps, and surface breathless between them, shaking water from my eyes. There is no need to say anything; we allow ourselves just to enjoy it. I duck my head again and swim underwater, back to the far end. The chains of light snake across the bottom of the pool. A blue world, peopled only by white legs, thrashing feet. If we could only go on doing this: simply exist in the underwater glow, splashing our way around each other, made equal in the pleasure of cooled limbs and active bodies. The light of early evening changes the air around us, so that when we come out it seems thicker, denser, warmer than the water, closer to blood heat. We stand toweling our heads and bodies, freed for the moment. An owl calls from the mountain, there's the silence-numbing chorus of crickets in the grass. None of us wants to go back in to the house; none of us wants to confront the conundrum of Hannah. We are rueful, ironic, regretful that the moment of freedom must pass.

"See you in a minute!" Melissa calls out to us as she runs lightly upstairs, leaving wet footprints on the tiled floor. She's springy, her head wrapped in a towel, drops still flying off her, running up two steps at a time.

"Time for a glass of something!" Piers calls after her. "Tell Dad!" They are both freed for the moment from anxiety, and I can like them better, as I go to my room to shower and change. Life rescues you sometimes with the slightest things: a plunge into water, a walk through countryside, a good night's sleep; a small hope to greet you as you close up shutters for the night.

Philip has driven back into town during the afternoon to speak to the police again, and sign more documents that prove to his relationship to Hannah. "God, French red tape, you'd think that with all that, they would be more efficient at actually finding someone."

I think, but don't say—You think the English police would have been any better? To soothe him, I say, "They are probably doing everything they can, don't you think?"

Piers says, "You should have told us. One of us could have come too."

"No, no, I was fine. Better alone."

"So?"

"They seem to think people have a right to disappear, unless they are minors or have been kidnapped. I don't know."

"So you didn't get any new info?"

"He said he's done everything he can for now. They are

checking with the hospitals, here, in Marseille and in Paris."
Philip sighs. He's exhausted by this; by driving in the heat, by
trying to explain himself in French, by his own rising panic.
He looks pale, worn. "They'll check the frontiers too. She'd
have had to use her passport if she left the country. If she
hasn't, she must be still in France, they said."

Piers says, "Dad, you really have to let us help you. You
shouldn't have gone off on your own like that."

"Well, I didn't want to bother you."

"It's what we're here for. To be bothered. Now don't go
off without telling us again, will you?"

I sense Philip's annoyance, at not being allowed to "go
off" and look for his wife on his own, as if he were incompe-
tent. "I think I should go back to England," he says. "There
might be a clue among her things, on her computer. I'm not
doing any good hanging about here."

"But, if she got off in Paris? If she's in France, as you
said? Shouldn't that be where we start?" I see Piers and
Melissa glance at each other, then at me. We know each other
a little better than we did only hours ago.

"Dad, you don't have to rush back anywhere," Melissa says.

"But who does she know in Paris, these days? Where
could we start?"

"If the police sound calm," Piers says, "it's probably
because they don't think it's very worrying. They think she
will come home." He wants, I can hear it, to believe this;
that normality will reassert itself, because he wants it to. His
mother has always come home before, she has always been
there. (Wives come back, mothers come back.) Perhaps this is
just a brief aberration, a blip, a hiccup in the smooth progres-
sions of life that he has always been led to believe in. Melissa

nods. They don't want another evening of anxiety, having to deal with their distraught father; they want to be allowed to enjoy the pool, the drinks outside, Marie-Laure's cooking, the beauty of the sky under which we sit, its pallor punctuated by swallows flying after gnats. The house that Philip has made for Hannah, who is not here; for their family, this continuity, parents and children, summer vacations, the right to their untrammeled lives.

I say, "Maybe we should just take a day or two here to calm down, Phil. At least let's wait to hear if they find out anything from the hospitals. You rushing off to England won't solve anything; and if the police do find something, they'll need to find you here. Meanwhile, I can ask a couple of old friends in Paris if they have any news, okay?"

After a lifetime of having escaped the bonds of family, I seem to have taken on the role of mother; the one who soothes, explains, makes rational suggestions. The role that Hannah can't stand anymore, or perhaps never could stand—I don't know. The words sound strange to me, as if I'm acting, reading from a script. They sound effortful, even to me. But they seem to work.

I come downstairs an hour or so later, after a shower, to find Melissa marinating lamb chops while Piers has started up the gas-fired barbecue. The grill is heating up, and we'll eat outside. This is now, this is the present. It is where I am and where Hannah is not, it is the reality of this summer of all the many summers in our lives. Once again she is eluding me, as she eludes her family. I have to accept it—as I had to when she let me down, didn't show up, missed dinner, wasn't in her room at college, when she was officially "in love" with that boy in the Sailing Club who had a car—"a car, Claude, and he took me out to a real dinner, three courses and wine, imagine"—and so missed a film date with me; only now I am older, and have until today forgotten just how it felt. Accept what you cannot change: it is one of the mantras of today, borrowed from twelve-step groups. Can anybody really do it? I wonder. Are we not all under the illusion that we can change things and even people, if only we try hard enough? Hannah is demanding this near-impossibility of us: perhaps to find out, once and for all, if we can accept her, just as she is? Absent, irresponsible, uncaring, not thinking about us at all?

The story I am telling myself about Hannah is full of gaps and holes: of course it is. There are the gaps of memory, the times between our meetings, times when our lives went their separate ways, details she will have remembered and I have forgotten. Between two people, always the third thing, the story; neither will ever have the whole picture. All I can extrapolate from is what I already know. There will not be any new evidence. In this house, there are four people who each have a different view of her, as husband, daughter, son—and friend. Her children are the angriest. Aren't our parents the people we know least well, even though from babyhood on we watch them intently from day to day, like spies, sensing their moods, noticing their habits, because we need them in order to live? We can't know who they were before we were born; we don't know who they become when they leave us, tiptoe out of the bedroom, sigh with relief as they drive away for an evening out.

Melissa is angry with Hannah for not being the mother she wanted, the grandmother she ought to be. Piers feels the remoter irritation of the son who wants to be in control, to know always where his mother is. Yet they both managed to throw off their old feelings with their clothes and swim with me; we all came close in those few moments to living quite happily without Hannah. Philip, who has loved her and tried, I really believe, to let her be who she is, must be feeling a sense of bitter failure: she has not been able to trust him enough to tell him, to let him know. All of them are volatile, easily moved from one extreme of feeling to another. I have to tread carefully with all three of them, not impose my own portrait of Hannah that after all is decades out of date. I have to wait, for them to ask, to want to know: the only thing I can provide them with is my patience, and a certain hope, based in my knowledge that she has always—until now— come back.

"Claudia," says Melissa, ruling in the kitchen, "will you do the salad?"

"Sure." I get busy with oil and vinegar, in a huge olive-wood bowl. I think, she wants me with her, now. I turn the salad carefully, leaf after leaf. Piers is outside, keeping an eye on the barbecue. Men like barbecues, I remember, because there is always something to control: fire, meat, the original things. They will even put on aprons for the ritual. Philip is out there too, opening a bottle of wine rather too energetically, as if he wants to look busy too.

"About Hannah," Melissa goes on. Not "Mum" this time, but Hannah. "I was thinking about what you said, that she might have wanted some time off. Do you think there is possibly someone else in her life? A man, I mean. Could she be having an affair? I know she had boyfriends when she was younger, before they were married, she told me, but Dad doesn't like talking about it, surprise, surprise. It would be one reason she couldn't tell him."

"I honestly don't know," I say. "It's possible. If she ever had a lover since she was married, she didn't tell me."

Melissa says, "I think she may have done. I saw her open a letter once, and blush, and hide it away in her desk. I asked what it was, and she was quite snappy, said it was private. I was only about fifteen or sixteen, and I never asked again."

"I think she would have made some excuse, wouldn't she? I mean, not just vanished without a word. Mostly, if people are having affairs, they make up too many excuses."

She says, "You do that beautifully. The salad, I mean."

"Hmm, thanks. What about you, Melissa, are you happy, what's going on for you?" I hardly know her, this younger woman, this married mother of Hannah's grandchildren.

"Well, my life is fine. My husband, my kids, my job. But you know, Mum's been a hard act to follow." She glances up at me, checking my attention. "So good at everything, so complete. And hard to know. She's so private. I've had a hard time not being like her, yet being like her too. She never really let me in, somehow. Piers was closer, when we were young. I know, twins are a lot of work, but it always felt as if she was exasperated at having two of us to deal with. She looked after us, she did what she had to; but I always felt it. As if she couldn't wait for it to end—our childhood, her obligation to us, I don't mean life—and for something else to happen. Do you know what I mean?" She's getting lunchtime's plates out of the dishwasher, she straightens to glance at me again: are you really on my side, do you really want to know, do you understand?

Yes, I know. I too have seen that Hannah. That sudden cold look: well, what do you want now, haven't I given you enough? I try to imagine the effect this would have on a child. My own mother, similarly faced unexpectedly with twins, always said cheerfully that it was two for the price of one. I think of Margaret Thatcher, of whom people said, trust her to get it all over with in one go. But neither of them was Hannah.

"And what about your father?" He's still out there with his bottle, sniffing the cork. The glass between us makes us safe in here, to talk for at least another five minutes before Piers, aproned, summons us out to eat his flaming chunks of meat.

"Daddy was always sweet. He always had time for us, as if he realized that she didn't. Couldn't, maybe."

I remember being angry with Hannah, and not telling her so, because as soon as I expressed it, she would have already been charming, lighthearted, she would have moved on. Nothing sounds more petulant than going back to the scene of yesterday's crime.

Oh, Claude, isn't life exciting? Guess what? I can hear her now, coming in late at night, waking me up, alight with the evening she has spent with some boy, the cold touch of outdoors and autumn upon her, her coat still on but flying open. After climbing in to college through that girl Fiona's window? After hours of kissing and maybe more in a parked car, out there in the dark of a lay-by on the Huntingdon Road? And I, sleepy, annoyed, wanting to say, where were you, you could have said, I waited for ages. Not saying it. Doing what she wanted me to do, instead, saying, wonderful, yes, terrific; agreeing with her, having to, life is exciting, yes! Life, as we had designated it, was an adventure or it was nothing. And for the great adventure to unfold as it should, nothing must get in its way. No, I would not have wanted to be Hannah's daughter. I would have loved her hopelessly, as perhaps Melissa did, and longed to be her equal.

Melissa and I carry trays outside and set them down. Grilled lamb, with rosemary and thyme from the garden, smells good in the slight chill of a June evening. Philip, his bottle wrapped in a napkin as if he were a waiter, pours our wine. Under the willow and between the bushes of lavender and oleander, a few dark butterflies flit and settle. There's a thin moon, its sliver just visible in the sky. Everything is as it should be, except that Hannah is not here. We are peaceful at last, the four of us, going about our preparations, sitting down to eat. We have not forgotten her, or forgiven her, but life does have its own onward momentum, adventure or not. A family meal, without the main member—it's as if she's only just walked out for a minute, maybe to fetch a sweater to knot around her neck against the slight chill; it's also as if she is never coming back.

At what point do you know that someone isn't coming back? Do you need a body, a certificate, a final note? I don't know. This mystery that Hannah has dealt us is making us all ponder the unknowns of life. Will she return quite suddenly—a taxi at the gate, a flurry of her getting out with perhaps a small bag, perhaps not, a rush to greet us, a question, what's all the fuss about, of course I'm here, did you really think I would not be? We have tried, with all our plans and arrangements and assumptions, our smart phones and social media and tools of surveillance of each other, to pin down what can't, in the end, be pinned down. The desires of an unpredictable and finally unknowable human heart.

We clear away the plates and stack the dishwasher, we put food away in the refrigerator, bread in the bin, napkins in the cupboard

"A *digestif*?" asks Piers, holding up a bottle of Armagnac.

"Mm. Why not." Another ritual in an evening of rituals. We don't want to let go of each other yet. Melissa goes outside to smoke a cigarette, scolded by her father. *But, Dad, I only smoke two a day.* As if she has to placate him still. I see the thin line of her smoke rising in the still air. Bats flap across the garden. Philip goes to water his vegetables, the ones that have been awaiting him here, tomatoes, zucchini, lettuces, all tiny and just about existing in the cracked earth of this summer. Piers and I sit in deck chairs and he hands me the small glass of Armagnac and leans forward to see me better in the growing dusk. It's his turn now.

"Dad mentioned that she hadn't been well. Did you know? Do you know if it was anything serious? I can't believe he didn't ask her, but you know him. Or, I do. Anything wrong with her and he panics, he can't stand it. So the result is, we never get to hear. It's very worrying. I don't know how it will be when they are really old."

So, he is thinking of his parents when really old—not just on the way to being old, as they and I are now. A good sign, I think. He thinks that everything will go back to normal, after this crisis, whatever it is, has been sorted out.

"To some extent, you have to let them do things their way, even if it feels worrying." I'm beginning to feel like the resident therapist. "People aren't rational, often, about stuff like that."

The Armagnac goes down, burning my throat, warming my stomach. Flies dance under the fruit trees at twilight. The bats zigzag, one, two, and away. The mountain is huge and tawny at our backs and the sun won't disappear completely for half an hour, but all the colors are changing, the sky turns greenish, the earth black. The wild boars are snuffling up there in the bushes, among the broom and stunted pine trees, preparing their raids.

Philip comes and stands uncertainly before us.

"Dad, a drop of this good stuff?" Piers asks.

"No, I've had enough. I'm tired, I'm going to bed. It's been a long day."

He leaves us, shoulders hunched and long thin legs, going into his house. We see the light snap on in the upstairs room that he has shared for so long with Hannah, with the en-suite bathroom he's so proud of, the freestanding bathtub, the glass handbasin, the last addition he has made to this house to please her. I noticed earlier that he has left his car abandoned in the middle of the gravel drive, as if he simply could not bear to drive it for a minute more; this, more than anything, tells me how upset he is.

"I feel sorry for him," says Piers, "He's lost. Claudia, talk to him. Reassure him. You are the only person who really can."

"All right, if I can find something to cheer him up, I will. I don't want to give him false hope, though, and really, I haven't a clue what she is up to. Or where she is, or anything." Sensing his easily renewed despondency, I add, "But of course, we did a lot together, and I do know a side of her he probably doesn't. Okay, Piers, I'll do my best."

Covering for Hannah, bringing her anxious family some hope, is turning out to be more challenging than I'd imagined. Damn you, Hannah, I think, going up the stairs to my room under the eaves—come back, come back now. The game's over. It's tiring. Come out of hiding. It's gone on long enough.

I dream of her in the small hours. I'm waiting outside a

locked house, I've tried various keys and none of them fit the lock, or I can't turn them. Then I hear a window open and look up. Alexandre is there and throws me down a bunch of keys. I have had the wrong keys all along. Is Hannah with him, in an upper room? I'm not sure. I fit the new key to the lock and the door opens, and I wake up.

I'm thirsty, and reach for the glass of water beside the bed. For a moment, I don't know where I am; the shape of the room in the half-dark is unfamiliar, my body has been removed from one continent to another, my mind hasn't caught up. Then I remember; as if pieces come together in my brain. This house. This time. The shutter is half open and creaks on its hinge, and the sky outside is already paler than night. It's nearly midsummer, in France. I'm in Philip's house. Hannah is not here. I get up and lean out of the window, as far as one can on these windowsills, where there are bars to stop people climbing in. I see the outlines of trees, blots against the pale gray of the sky. I can hear the fast passage of the canal, as it passes the house and goes on—where?—to join the canalized Durance. I hear the rustle of some animal in the bushes, perhaps the fox that comes to raid the garbage bins if you don't fasten the lid down. Night here is different, wilder than the daytime. I lie back on my bed, spread out on the white sheet, after plumping up the pillows. The room glimmers with predawn light. I can't sleep. I sleep again.

I get up again hours later and cross the cool tiled floor to the bathroom, sun poking at the shutters, a hose running somewhere outside, perhaps filling the pool. Everybody must be up and about except me. I open the shutters and look out, and see Marie-Laure's small red car parked on the gravel. Someone has put Philip's car in the garage and closed the doors. Things are being moved around, without me; this is normal—why should it matter? At night, are memories rearranged, resorted as dreams juggle with them, use them, let them fall differently, into new patterns?

You were closer to her than anybody, Claudia; don't you have the key to the mystery? What are you holding back?

14.

Telegrams arrived: urgent and succinct, the first we'd ever had. During the same week, we were both summoned to Cambridge for interviews. We met at King's Cross and went up on the train with a girl called Mary, who wore a hat and later became Education Secretary in a Labour government. We were not in school uniform, but in another sort of uniform that our mothers had thought up for us, based on what they wore themselves: tweed suits, nice blouses, nylons, sensible shoes. We looked like middle-aged social workers. Mary had added the hat, as if she were going to a wedding. We all wore gloves. It was already the sixties, but nobody could have guessed that if they had seen us setting out, embryonic suburban matrons with Pan-Stik makeup and a dab of our mothers' Chanel for luck.

When we arrived, there was a thick fog. We found the bus to Girton, the college that had summoned us both, based on our exam papers in which we had quoted lavishly from all the authors we had been reading, from Machiavelli to

Montaigne (me) and Langland to Eliot (her). The college was gothically spired and pointed like something out of a horror film, hidden behind trees and fog. It was miles from the town. We gave each other the glance: if we hate it, we won't even try. We went in through the high red-brick arched doorway and saw students shuffling or sliding past in the corridors in various versions of the Girton slouch—the polished floors meant that there was no point lifting your feet, apparently, so everyone walked as if on ice. They wore black, these girls, they had long hair and pale faces, their gowns flapped from their shoulders like blackbirds' wings, they wore furry bedroom slippers and carried armfuls of books. The tiled corridors smelled of floor polish and gravy. It was altogether far too much like school. Hannah and I gave each other the look, eyebrows raised, mouths pursed. We thought it looked French, or at least sophisticated. What now?

In her interview, she told me later, she had talked about Yeats and Irish liberation and Maud Gonne, and the woman who questioned her had given her a glass of sherry, on account of the cold and the fog. She came out with pink cheeks, laughing. My history don was a kind woman in mothy wool and tweeds, who, after asking me briefly about the implications of the Peace of Westphalia, showed me photographs of her large family—I didn't know that history dons had families—and we ended up talking about film. I would love it here, she said, as the Arts Cinema was showing all the new films from France and Italy, at least three a week, though of course there was more to Cambridge life than the cinema; and had I seen the new Polanski? She got me to admit that my real desire was to be a film director—the first adult who had even asked, the first person who had ever let me know that it was possible for a woman—and told me about a friend of hers in Paris who was making films; a woman, yes, of course.

In the hall, as we met to eat cold meat and lettuce with salad cream under the high ceilings and portraits of stern and regal women, we glanced at each other a little differently, allowing our new excitement to show. This was not boarding school. The dons were not dried-up sticks. We had already been given something, a mirror in which to glimpse our future selves. Mary, in her hat, joined us. Had the wedding hat brought luck? She admitted it was her mother's idea that she should dress up, but that now she wanted to get rid of it. After lunch we found a row of bins at the back of the kitchens and buried Mary's hat deep in garbage. All three of us now wanted only one thing: to be allowed to come here, to spend three years in this place that seemed to want for us only what we desired most ourselves. When we met the Mistress, as she was called, we were greeted as competent adults who might only want a little guidance or practical help from time to time as we settled in. She was vague, with prematurely silver hair; we'd heard that she was a pure mathematician, and she made jokes about it, "I wouldn't know, I'm only a pure mathematician." Years later, reading an interview with her after she received a Nobel prize, I discovered that her method for choosing new students was based on putting a bunch of variously interesting girls together, as you might arrange a random bunch of flowers. Our essays, our voluminous name-dropping, had got us there, but it was apparently our eccentricity—the very thing that had given us the most trouble in life so far—that had allowed us to stay.

At Cambridge, there was no real need for escape; we were both so thoroughly enchanted by the life it gave us, with its relative freedom after boarding school, no need to go to lectures, no need to get up in the morning or go to bed at night; and of course, young men everywhere. You could spend most of the day at the cinema—and I did, for a whole year, until my tutor called me in to complain about my sketchy essays.

The only regular rule-breaking we had to indulge in was climbing in at night. Students were supposed to be back in college by ten-thirty in the evening, and men were supposed to be out. You heard the tramp of male feet down tiled corridors at ten-fifteen and then the great doors shut, and Girton girls were supposed to be in their rooms, if not in their virginal beds. A few girls had ground-floor rooms with no bars on them. The Scottish girl on our wing, called Fiona, had just such a room; it was her window that we, among others, used for getting in to college after hours. We'd stow our bikes in the undergrowth and creep across the grass, through the flowerbed beside the rosebush, to Fiona's window. We'd tap, and she'd open. We would heave ourselves over the sill, drop into her space, land on the rug and pick ourselves up, mutter thanks and goodnight, and be off to our own rooms. I doubt that she got much sleep, with all the traffic coming through, but she was a good-natured person and rarely complained. Och, nae bother. When the men visiting college—boys, really, but we called them men—had to get out late too, they went through Fiona's window, to sprint across the expanse of lawn to where their bicycles were hidden, and pedal away down the road to town.

I remember our first year and all the comings and goings, and Hannah, in love with a boy in Magdalene, coming in at two to wake me up, sit on my bed, and declaim, "Claude, I'm in love!" for the first of many times in her life. Being in love justified everything, even betraying a friend or waking her up in the small hours; certainly it justified handing in essays late, not going to lectures because you had to sleep in, not showing up in "hall" for mealtimes because you were cooking up baked beans on a gas-ring in some boy's room or living off beer and peanuts at the pub on Magdalene Street. It justified lying about where you had been, and with whom, turning down one date to go with another, newer love, simply not showing up at all; it justified everything. It was the great achievement of life: love, true love, experienced to the heights and depths. Everything we read and saw in films echoed this belief: it was as if we were being initiated into a new cult, acolytes with a purity of vision and a remorseless drive to achieve it.

Looking back, I doubt that any of the young men involved felt similarly, glorifying their sex-drive with such romantic feelings. Maybe some did—we were all reading the same books, after all. How many of us actually indulged in real penetrative sex, our holy grail after reading Lawrence, I don't know. Contraception was still hard to get, abortion was still illegal, the stories of girls who "had to" go to London for it, to back-street abortionists, terrified us, and may well have terrified the boys who "had to" pay for it, or get married as the only other option. We kissed, long and passionately, sometimes for hours. We necked, or smooched, or petted, or felt each other up. I remember hard lumps in trousers and groans from boys whose hands roamed over our black-sweatered breasts, and only sometimes, amazing us with their daring and ingenuity, felt their way inside our bras. I remember a great deal of frustration on both sides, but a great deal of goodwill too— we were all more or less in the same boat, desperate, ignorant, scared, burning with lust and calling it true love. At the Arts Cinema, where the films changed twice weekly, we lived on a diet of passionate sex, with Fellini's, Antonioni's, and Godard's latest films. In everything we read and saw, this was the crux of the matter; it was what life was all about.

Then, after Cambridge, there was our year in London: was it here that I lost her? Freedom, independence, swinging London, the King's Road, all the new music and parties every night: that was what the late sixties were famous for, the version that is so easy to adopt: and yes, we were there, at the heart of it all, Hannah and I. But what were we doing? I was taking the Tube each day to teach in a school in Ealing. She was doing a secretarial course, the one thing she had sworn she would never do, because she wanted to work in publishing and that was then, for women, the only way in. We shared a two-room flat above a shop that sold paperback books and magazines but never seemed to be open; it may have been a front for something, or not—we never discovered. It was on the wrong end of the King's Road, in Fulham rather than fashionable Chelsea, and it was cheap. There was brown linoleum on most of the floors, as there was in the shop downstairs, and the bath was in the kitchen, with a lid to it that could double as a worktop or, coffin-like, hide the person in the bathtub if someone visited unexpectedly. From the back window you could see Battersea power station with smoke drifting up from its chimneys; from the front, the traffic that churned past towards Portsmouth and the west. There was a little park opposite, with a few benches, and shabby trees only tall enough to give a little shade in summer, and tangles of elder, old-man's beard, and sticky-willy that grew up against the fence.

We were there for the year that followed our graduation

from college. I had just met Bud the wandering American and heard about cool California, where independent film-making was taking off and the films of revolution and protest were being made. One young man—Bud—told me, come to California, the other—Alexandre, in Paris—wrote urgent postcards to say, in fierce black art-school handwriting, that the revolution was happening, and why was I not there? The beach was there under the paving stones, the future was ours, the old orders, whichever continent you looked at, it seemed, were going to crumble. Meanwhile I was trying to teach history to a bunch of teenagers who only wanted to talk about the Beatles.

It's like having had several lives running concurrently. I was in love—I'm sure I was—with the young man studying law in Paris; I was also slouching up the King's Road with my hand in the back pocket of the ragged jeans of the tall, tanned, bearded American who taught me to say cool, far out, and call people "man" whatever gender they were. I was trying to teach English history to girls in blue uniforms who were interested in nothing except John, Paul, George, and Ringo; and I was dreaming of being a film director, of making the ultimate avant-garde movie. I had signed a lease here in London with Hannah, and I was making plans to go to America with Bud, and make films. I stood each morning on the platform of Fulham Broadway tube station waiting for my train, and imagined Los Angeles, the Hollywood hills. My mind, like a tethered kite, was tugging me elsewhere. In my spare time I got the Tube across London to Hampstead to go to the Everyman and see films: Kurosawa, Satyajit Ray, Resnais, Eisenstein, Bergman, sometimes going straight from one to another. I watched Cassavetes's *Shadows* at least five times. I'd stumble out late at night and get the Northern line home, exhausted but on fire with what I had seen. Hannah herself was doing her tedious daytime shorthand and typing course and at night going to parties in Chelsea to meet people in publishing, and presumably dating Philip, as we didn't call it then. We'd arrived in London to make films (me) and to publish books (her) and here we were, the most brilliant girls of our generation, living in penury and spending our days doing work that bored us. We had trained ourselves, during the long years of school, and even the hectic flurry of Cambridge, to wait for the prize, to work for it if we had to. This, sixties London, was supposed to have been that prize. And it eluded us still.

On a Saturday morning I stood at the kitchen window watching the columns of smoke rising from the power station and mixing with a pattern of cloud and plane trails in the summer sky. She sat at the kitchen table. We had found a shop nearby that sold croissants, and these, with coffee, were our Saturday treat. We lit up Gauloises after the croissants; we were still pretending to be Parisian intellectuals.

I said I had something to tell her. I don't even remember how I said this; but she sat upright suddenly and said, "You're not!"

"Not what?"

"Pregnant."

"No, of course not."

"You're not getting married."

"No. I've got a chance of a job in LA. Los Angeles. With someone Bud knows. It's in film, Hannah, it's an amazing opportunity."

She put down her coffee mug, threw back her hair,

reached for a cigarette, and lit it with a little gold lighter I hadn't seen before. She didn't speak for what seemed like a long time. Then, "Oh, Claude." There it was again, the disappointment; I had failed her.

"But what about this? London? Our life?"

I said, and I'm ashamed of it now, "Well, we knew it wouldn't go on forever, didn't we?" As if the plans of women are always to be this easily interrupted by the slightest proposition from a man.

"We've only been here a year. Less than a year."

"I didn't expect this, Han. I hadn't planned it."

"But some stupid American only has to breathe a suggestion about a possible job in film in your ear, and you rush off, just like that? It can't be a real job. You haven't any experience, after all. He's just a lost soul, anyone can see that, all this beatnik stuff is just put on, I can't think how you can fall for it. He just wants to get you into bed. Or are you there already?"

"It could have been you, and you'd take a chance like this, I know you would. I know it's the right thing."

She gave me a level stare, and blew a smoke ring. "I know what I want, and it's here, in London. I'm not going anywhere. I've got an interview at Macmillan, in publicity. Anyway, I thought you were thinking of making experimental films, where everything had to be discussed and democratic before anyone did anything. Or is that over now?"

"You never said! About Macmillan."

"I know, I was going to tell you."

"When?"

"When I've got the job. The interview's on Monday."

"That's wonderful! Great news. I'm sure you'll get it, they'll love you."

She did not congratulate me in return until a few days later, when she brought home a bottle of cheap Italian fizzy wine and we drank it, still too warm, out of tumblers, toasting each other in the bathroom-cum-kitchen while pasta boiled over on the stove.

"Well, here's to California, anyway."

I thought she had forgiven me, that she understood. But that was the year, it's clear to me now, that she agreed to marry Philip, who was setting up his own small press in East Anglia, and leave the great job in publicity to someone else. I was in America by then, waiting tables in San Francisco, not making films after all.

"Oh, Hannah, it's been great, you know it has. But we were bound to move on, weren't we?"

"Of course!" She lit a cigarette, waved her wineglass around. "No stopping us. We're the future! *Plutôt la vie!* Isn't that what they've been writing on the walls in France?"

She was trying to be cool about it, and at that awkward moment I loved her for it. It was only later that I knew how much it had cost her.

Are you really going to live in America?

You know they are all morons, don't you?

But Claudia, what about Alexandre? You won't be able to flit across the ocean to see him . . .

If you think you can trust Bud, you need your head examined.

I've heard that there aren't any women filmmakers over there, anyway.

All these remarks came out during the next couple of months, and were met by me with sulky silence. Her effort at being existentialist hadn't lasted. She was miserable and angry, and I knew it. Yet for once—and it did feel like the first time I had confronted her with wanting something different—I did not give in.

I remember her coming in late, when we first moved into the flat, our first really independent home. I remember her flinging back her hair and dumping bags of food on the table and pulling out a wine bottle. I remember her exuberance, her delight. I remember taking a series photographs of her that first summer with the old Leica I had at that time: Hannah with her hair in a towel after washing it, Hannah leaning against the grimy windowsill, the chimney pots of south London behind her.

Where I am now, in her house, I have to get up quickly, take a shower, and towel myself hard so that the tears that are already beginning to spill can be sluiced away and dried, so that I can go down and face her anxious family.

15.

I left her for a mirage. That is at least what it looked like shortly afterwards, when I had made the kind of leap into the void that you can only do when you are young and have no idea what you are taking on. The dream job turned out not to have existed—she was right about that—and Bud's friend's movie was not going to be made. Bud himself had disappeared back to Ibiza, which was the place to be at, with a woman called Miriam, and I found myself lost and adrift in Los Angeles, that most transient and inhospitable of cities. It was a few months before I realized that nobody in the movie business was going to employ a young English woman, ignorant of most things except European films and seventeenth-century history, except for activities to do with sex. Then, I hitched a truck ride north to San Francisco, where I got a job waiting tables in a café down by the waterfront that served oysters and crab and whatever had come in on the latest boat.

I remember looking out across the gray water where the

seals swam, pushing up their heads from time to time like old whiskered men coming up for air. I cracked open crab claws and oyster shells and my hands were raw and red and I was waiting for a green card and being paid under the table. I recognized this as the immigrant experience; there were many of us, European, Australian, Chinese, Mexican, skirting round the edges of legality at this place flung up against the endlessly shifting walls of the Pacific. I was far, very far from home; and yet, as I wrote to Hannah, it seemed easy in a way, you just did the same thing every day, and strolled home uphill to a tiny apartment shared with a Korean coworker, and got up again and went to work.

I missed Hannah, and I missed Alexandre. I missed my family. On bad days, or if a customer was short-tempered or rude, I missed England and our flat in London and my friends there, in a blur of tears. But I had cast my lot, made my move: I was here, and would do whatever it took to stay, as immigrants all around me did and could, however they were feeling.

Making films seemed very remote at this time, but it was still there, the dream that enabled me to get up every day and go to my job. I wanted movement, not the stasis of photography. I wanted to be behind the camera, not write scripts. I saw my material all around me. A girl in a long stained apron—myself—shucking oysters. Hanging up her apron to carry them to a table. The great cargo ships straining at their moorings as the wind came in across the water, all the way from Asia. The grayness and the salt, the way paint peeled, the tarry ropes that tugged at bollards, the high swooping movements of gulls. Seals' heads in the bay, like swimming dogs. The look of things in movement; the weight of meaning in places, in objects, in people as they moved around. The gait of one person, hobbling across concrete: an old man, a fisherman's cap pushed back on his head. The way buildings disappeared and reemerged, through fog. I was training myself to look, without really knowing it; while my hands worked, my eyes noticed and my brain stored what it needed.

I borrowed money, bought a secondhand camera. It was a year, two years before I decided to apply for film school. I arrived at UCLA on the unlikely strength of an interview—it was my "eye" they liked, apparently—and some grainy film of the San Francisco waterfront and my café there. Once again, as at my Cambridge interview, it was not what I thought I knew, but something apparently invisible to me, that had worked. My "eye." The way I saw things. Something so intangible, so personal, as instinctive as the way I walk, or speak; or maybe they had also liked my English accent, my Cambridge degree.

It helped that there was a radical arts collective at UCLA at that time, and that black, revolutionary, third-world, and Cuban films were being taken seriously, that the mainstream—Hollywood—was more or less an object of scorn. Dorothy Arzner was teaching there, having retired from Hollywood. Francis Coppola was a student of hers, about to graduate. George Lucas was at USC, across town. But there were so few women. Women were evidently not expected to be film directors; even Arzner had stopped directing. Women were not generally expected to be anything but coffee-makers or willing "old ladies" to their men. I told some of my contemporaries what I wanted, and discovered not only that it was impossible but that I had the wrong idea, for a start, of what making a film was. Francis, who was working on editing, let me in to the sound room, showed me what he was doing, and eventually took me in hand. Film was a language. Filmmaking was cooperative; forget the idea of the solitary genius behind the camera. Film was unpredictable yet exact; it was organized yet instinctive; it involved everybody, it was a team effort. It was more like being in a beehive, I discovered, than involved in the kind of individual effort I'd imagined. You filled in where you could be useful. You learned to edit, you learned about sound, and how it was added on afterwards; it was about endless learning; you shut up and listened, and there were no shortcuts. You made coffee. You sat up all night listening to men talk, not out of the usual deference, but because of what they already knew and what they were boldly discovering as they went along.

I wanted to be Antonioni, or Fellini, and then I wanted to be Truffaut. Of course I did, and so did everybody else. We'd all had the dream of being the genius *auteur.* At least in Europe, I protested, there were always Agnès Varda—who was even there for a while in Los Angeles with her filmmaker husband—and Marguerite Duras; great women directors— but one was married to Jacques Demy and the other already a respected novelist.

In California at that time it hardly seemed to matter; so much was in flux, including filmmaking. I gradually discovered the work of Maya Deren, Ida Lupino, Arzner, and at the margin, Barbara Hammer and Julie Dash. Women were more often allowed to be editors—the people who joined things together, like knitting, like tapestry. There were Dede Allen, whom I met, who later edited *Lawrence of Arabia*, and Annie Coates. I learned that if you simply did what had to be done next—if you became a useful person, that was, even made the coffee—you would be included. If any of us succeeded, we might include the others in our success. That being considered a wild-eyed narcissist, as some of the people at UCLA seemed to be, would have you dropped from the little gang that formed between five or six of us. We had all grown up on European films, but unlike me, the others were not surprised at the state—nonexistent—of independent filmmaking in America at that time. The thing was to reinvent film; to learn its language; to innovate; to start from exactly where we were.

I pushed up my hair into a beret like Jeanne Moreau in *Jules et Jim,* and they called me Claude, Claudius, or kid. "Hey, Claudius, where are you, take a look at this, what do you think?" I threw myself into it—the long nights' discussions, the pot-smoking—I was cautious with other drugs—the intoxicating assumption that the whole of society was about to change. There was a boy called Spoon whom I shacked up with for a while. We worked together on a film about someone asleep, a topic about to be taken up by Andy Warhol. We made films using collage, and dolls, and postcards, we scrimped on food to pay for film, we stayed up all night talking. We planned what we would do when we graduated. We learned about editing, and about mixing, those unsung, nearly invisible jobs without which no film can exist. We learned about sound and how it could be faked, reinvented, made to sound "realistic." As a child, I'd listened to radio every night, as we all did: *The Goon Show, ITMA, Uncle Mac,* various adventure serials that had me sitting beside the old wireless in the kitchen, shushing my brothers, the three of us a captive audience. I knew that the clatter of horses' hooves was made by coconut shells clapped together. I knew how to

listen for the sinister sound of the wind, the patter of rain.
A footstep on a wet street. A dog's bark, letting me know
the hero was about to be discovered in hiding. The wash of
waves as the Count of Monte Cristo was taken to his island
prison. I'd never thought of it as an education in sound, but
of course it was. At school, we'd listened to pop songs on our
transistor radios, Radio Luxembourg under the bedclothes: I
knew the words of songs by heart from all the hit parades of
the late fifties.

I wrote to Hannah, "Who'd have thought, I'm finding out so much, I miss you, write to me, tell me who sang
"Memories Are Made of This"? What year was that? Do you
remember?"

We were the last generation in England to grow up with
radio as our main entertainment; in our house, we only got a
television in time for the Coronation. It was somehow disap-
pointing: too small a screen, and not grand like the cinema. I
wanted to watch film in the dark, unobserved, with nobody
to talk to me or notice me in the paradoxical total privacy of
a cinema.

She was getting married, Hannah wrote back. "Claude,
please come. I'm giving you loads of time, and I know you're
in a different world, but I can't get married without you."

That year, I flew back across the continent I had crossed,
switching time zones, bug-eyed with fatigue, to be there. Flying east is always worst: your body is moving against the sun.
But I saw her married, I was there.

That year, after graduating again, I went back to San
Francisco, encouraged by the fact of the Zoetrope studio, Francis having established it there in 1969, and hung out on houseboats in Sausalito with my new friends. I bought a better used

camera and began to shoot my own first short feature, the story set on the San Francisco waterfront in the café where I'd worked. The script was, à la Cassavetes, improvised by the actors, who were my fellow waiters and dishwashers and oyster shuckers. Even the boss wanted to be in it. It cost me a borrowed thirty thousand dollars—my kind father sent me pounds and I translated them into dollars, promising to pay him back. Spoon organized a crew for me and we found a studio where we could mix it. The Zoetrope team invited me to their family homes, where simply listening to the talk was an education. The kindness of strangers, who became not-strangers—my American friends, who also happened to be great filmmakers, pioneers in the field. The waterfront film eventually got foreign distribution, through a boyfriend of a friend and someone he knew in Stockholm, and was shown at a film festival in Uppsala. It even got a review in Swedish. I thought in my excitement that this was the beginning of my glittering career; it was only a dazzled beginner's luck. I discovered that you need more money than you are ever going to have, and though I had some now, it didn't last. I went back to waiting tables, this time in Haight-Ashbury, down the street from the old cinema where in the afternoons you could sit on sagging sofas, drink tea, and watch foreign and experimental movies. I would go there after work and immerse myself, as I had at the Hampstead Everyman and the Arts in Cambridge, in the place where I felt most at home.

I did write to her, I know I did. I thought of her often; I wanted to include her. She answered; I still have some of her letters with the flimsy blue airmail paper, its edges stuck down to be torn open, and her large handwriting crossing the page to tell me not very much. We were in different worlds, she was right. I had moved west with the thoughtlessness and careless energy that must have fueled the early pioneers. I was a Californian now. Hungry, sometimes homeless, but never friendless, never depressed for long. She was married, living in the country, publishing local history books; then she was pregnant, then she had twins. It became harder to tell her about my life; I imagine that it was the same for her. I had behaved the way that men do—and get away with—putting my career first. Had she forgiven me? She never mentioned it; her "I miss you" was easily answered by "I miss you too." I did not tell her in my letters about what was difficult; I'd left for a dream, and it had to succeed, whatever it felt like at the time.

I decided that if I couldn't shoot 35 mm, I could still shoot 16, if I couldn't shoot 16, then I could shoot video. If I couldn't do that, I could shoot Super 8. I would not give up. It wasn't a mirage, but was mostly far harder than I'd imagined. When young, we don't imagine obstacles to our ambition, I think now—we have to learn to expect them. I don't regret any of it. Not the hardship, not the homesickness, not the feeling like an idiot because I knew so little. What I learned in those years was essentially that I could look after myself, learn to do anything in film that a man could do, and that if I was quiet and helpful and ready to learn, I would in turn be helped. I let go of my life in England—and Hannah—because I had to, to survive, to flourish where my gypsy path had taken me.

I worked in a cooperative we set up, for a while; on the strength of my waterfront film, I finally got a few grants and was able to live, eat, and work on a short feature and later, half-a-dozen documentaries, as well as a couple of fairly well-paid docudramas, then a miniseries for TV and several short experimental films. My mentors went on to Hollywood— Coppola got *The Godfather*, then *Apocalypse Now*; Walter Murch worked on most of the really great films of that era, always behind the scenes; George Lucas made *Star Wars*. I went to New Mexico for a year and stayed in Taos, interviewing and filming people who knew Mabel Dodge Luhan. I moved to New York, stayed in my friend Joanie's apartment in SoHo while she was in South America, and made a short documentary film with the help of the NYU film school on the poet Wallace Stevens, who reminded me that a poem is itself alone, not representative of anything—as is a film. It was shown at a few festivals in the US and got me the Guggenheim, third try. I went to Honduras and lived on a barrier island there, filming a community that lived in stilt houses in water, their children going everywhere by boat, tiny kids steering with ancient outboard engines into the waves.

Money was short again; I'd used up my small inheritance from my father. I was too old to go back to waiting tables, too nomadic in my habits to contemplate any sort of regular job. I thought of going back to Europe—but where, and to whom? Alexandre was getting married again and wanted to give the new relationship a chance. My parents were dead, first my father, then my mother; I'd flown home for their funerals but not stayed; when you have left home at twelve, it is easy to leave again. My siblings were busy; even my baby sister was working in IT in London. Hannah was growing roses, opening village fetes. A book—someone's—was doing well. The twins were walking. She and Philip had bought a house in France.

My country was no longer mine, except to visit; I had

become American. I moved at last—fifteen years ago now—out of New York, where I was back from the increasingly murderous streets of Tegucigalpa, sharing Joanie's rent-controlled apartment and giving occasional talks at NYU, where they liked my Wallace Stevens film. At last I applied for a job that came up to teach film studies in the English department in Virginia. I can only suppose it was my English accent and my small résumé of unusual movies that made them take me. Perhaps there was simply nobody else. It was then that I began visiting Hannah every summer, in France; we connected again. What had I missed? I'd never know. You can't, as a Jewish friend of mine once quoted to me, "dance at two weddings at once."

What else? I discovered to my surprise—I told Hannah this—that I loved teaching, simply for the "ah, I see" look on students' faces when they understood something for the first time; it was not unlike the look of people coming out of a cinema, a little dazed, inspired by what they saw.

My last film, called simply *Susana*—which did show at Sundance—was a story about a young immigrant student at college, learning about science. Very little happened in it. But the beauty of that young Mexican woman's face as she saw her world transformed by knowledge was something that film audiences did not forget.

I wanted Hannah to see that film; when I came to stay in the house in France one time, I brought a copy with me and we watched it together, having managed at last to get it transposed to a French DVD.

"This is what I do," I was telling her. "This is what it was all for."

I still dream of the next film, the way fishermen perhaps dream of the next fish: the gleam of its body as it comes up through water into sunlight, thrashing, whole and alive. It's there just waiting to be caught; as in a dream, I am often back there on the San Francisco waterfront, hopeful, naïve, ridiculously young, open to what comes next. One day perhaps—but I have never said this aloud—I will fling my line again to hook it, haul it up to the light of day.

16.

We have decided to do nothing over the weekend but be together and try to be normal. The twins will have to leave on Monday, and by then we will have made a plan. Deciding to make a plan seems for a moment almost as good as making one. We spend the weekend swimming, eating, and drinking, with occasional tears from Melissa and increasing gloom from Philip. Piers occupies himself by changing plugs on equipment, testing outlets, fixing a toaster, oiling the mower, making things work. It seems that after the initial shock of someone disappearing, you almost get used to it; you cannot stay in shock forever, the body and its habits take over, the days resume a subdued but recognizable normality; you begin to forget. You long, guiltily, for normality, progress, the illusions of ordinary life. You begin to re-create them.

Piers then begins to spend hours online, doing searches on the Web, contacting friends who might know, websites for details of missing people, support groups for those who miss them. He gets lists from his father of everyone who knows

Hannah. Her doctor. Her massage therapist. Her dentist. Their investment advisor, their bank manager, the garage that last serviced her car. Nobody, none of her friends, none of her acquaintances, has any idea where Hannah may be.

"The woman who gives her massages says she did know she was going away. She assumed she was coming here, to join me."

"What about the bank? Had she taken money out?" Piers asks.

"They won't tell me. She has her own account. All these passwords, you can't even talk to a human being these days."

"I just get the feeling that I'm spreading bad news and getting no answers. Dad, does she have any friends you don't know?"

"Well, if she does, I don't know them, do I?" He's hovering above Piers, looking at the screen, but he's wearing gardening gloves, obviously wants to go back outside to—what?—prune, dig, rake up grass, be occupied?

Piers says, "I can't believe you don't know any of her passwords."

Well, as I said, I may have a note of some of them at home. I think she uses her birthday."

"You're not supposed to do that. It's too easy."

"But at least you can remember it."

"Well, let's give it a go. April 12, right?"

They are both irritated by their failure to come up with a single clue. Men like to solve things, they like to make clear progress. Melissa and I seem to have fallen by default into the female role of just keeping things going, making coffee, getting the next meal. I'm trying not to go on feeling angry with Hannah, that she is putting us all through this: trying to keep in mind that she may be in danger, lonely or sick, and deserving of our best efforts, trying not to entertain the irrational idea that forty or more years ago, I abandoned her to follow a path of my own choosing. It's a mental juggling act that is only partly soothed by getting my hands in the sink, washing up coffee cups (Claude, we have a dishwasher, leave them!). I go outside to look for something else to do, under the blue arc of today's sky, in the still-cool-enough air of the morning.

Then it's Monday, and the twins are leaving together this afternoon in Piers's rented Peugeot to go to the airport at Marignane and then home.

I stand outside by the pool, just breathing the air and looking up at the mountain, close and pale in the morning light, its shadowy presence illuminated, its foliage simply a tangle of broom, small pine trees, and rosemary. It's a benign presence by this light: warm rock and herbs, pine trees with cones and twisted roots, a summit that glistens white. I tuck my phone in my shirt pocket and come back to begin raking cut grass from the blue pool's edges where Philip, after sweating at the cleaned mower, has left it. Is the gardener on vacation, then? Does Philip simply want something active to do? I can't stand being in the house any longer, listening to the murmur of anxious voices, the quiet mutter of English irritation and concern. Surely Americans would be yelling by now. I rake the grass into bunches that are green and damp as wet hair. My phone buzzes. I'm alone out here as I press the green button and hear Alexandre, that clipped French telephone voice he has, as if life is rushing past him at such a rate that he really doesn't have time to talk.

"Alex, *bonjour*." I drop the rake. The pool shimmers in a slight breeze; swallows dive across it. The cypresses at the end of the orchard flex their tips in the air current.

"What's up?" Relief—it's you! But why, and why now?
"You can talk?"

A cloud passes over the sun, just a small one, enough to make a shadow pass across the water, across me.

"Yes."

"She has called me," says Alexandre. "Hannah has called me. She got my number at work. Are you alone?"

"Yes, at the moment. Tell me."

"She does not want her family to know. She is in Switzerland, in a hotel. She is going home to England. She wants to meet you, here in Paris. Can you come?"

"But why doesn't she want Philip to know? He's going nuts here." In fact, he seemed remarkably calm this morning, when I came down: driving the mower up and down, turning at the end of the lawn and coming back, leaving long pale stripes in the grass, almost as if he has forgotten what's been going on; as if he can forget, for ten minutes, then for half an hour, that his wife is missing. It was only when Piers began questioning him about who Hannah knew, asking for their emails, that he became flustered. It must have felt like having taken a painkiller that has worn off too soon.

"Because what she wants to do, she thinks he will stop her," Alexandre mutters into the phone. "She thinks her children will stop her. Claude, it's all very *bizarre*." In his voice I hear his need not to be coping with it alone, the strangeness: to pass it on to me as my business, not his. We do know each other well.

"Do you know what's going on? Why she's in Switzerland?" I can hear the hee-haw scream of Parisian sirens in the background, the hum of traffic. His voice comes and goes, fainter.

"No, she didn't tell me."

"I can't hear you!"

"There, is that better?" I can see him on a street corner, turning away from the traffic noise, one shoulder hunched, trying to find a clear way through in this chaotic semblance of conversation. "I said, she didn't want to tell me."

The cut-grass smell, the heat of the sun, the close presence of the mountain, all seem to intensify. Cicadas buzz, then stop, as if silenced. I hold the phone hard against my ear, not to lose a word as his voice comes and goes. I walk up and down, to try for a better signal. "So, you have no idea?"

"No, really no idea."

"Do you think she is going crazy?"

"No, I don't think so. She sounds calm."

"Hmm. So she wants me to come to Paris, you said?"

"She wants to meet you here. In Paris. She wants you to tell Philippe that she is well, that she is going home, that she is safe. *D'accord?* And she will let you know a place to meet. She will tell me and I will call you. I have to go now. But I will see you, we must see each other, Hannah or no Hannah, yes?"

"Yes. Just one thing, Alex, when is she going to get in touch? And, am I supposed to give Philip the message now?"

"Yes, today. Not immediately, perhaps, wait an hour or so. He should go home to England and wait for her there."

"Not here? You're sure, he shouldn't wait for her here?"

"No, not there. She said in England. Don't ask me why, I don't know why, it was just what she said. *Bon.* Now I must go, but till very soon, okay? *A très bientôt.*"

He's busy, I can hear it, and sounds more than a little annoyed at being involved in all this. He likes things cut-and-dried, Alexandre does. Work has its place, and so does leisure, and so does love, and I remember what he said long ago about *"histoires de bonnes femmes"* and think that Hannah, in involving him in complex messages, has overstepped a mark he likes to stay well behind.

"Ciao, je t'embrasse." We both say it at the same time, and then the phone goes dead. I put it down on the nearest deck chair with my shirt and dive into the pool, to swim as far as I can underwater and rise shaking water from my eyes and ears, flinging back my hair. Only total immersion will do, to wash off the insanity of what I've just been told. I swim to the far end and prop myself there for a moment before swimming back, more slowly, breaststroke to the shallow end. But I can't wash off the feeling that has immediately replaced my anxiety, that we are all being used, and for what purpose? How can I tell poor Philip to go home and wait for Hannah there? How can she do this to us all? She wants me to meet her in Paris, she wants to tell me, presumably, what is going on, while she doesn't want to tell Philip. Is she involved with somebody, about to run away? Is she in some financial trouble or other? Has she simply left her marriage? All these scenarios rerun themselves through my mind. And how the hell did she get to Switzerland, without her passport being checked? Now that I know she's alive, I can be angry with her at last.

I tie a towel around myself and go back into the house, leaving my footprints' shrinking wet islands on the tiles. I want to shower and dress before I talk to Philip, who is washing his gardening hands in the sink, while Marie-Laure mops the kitchen floor. Piers has closed the computer, I'm glad to see, and has presumably gone upstairs to pack. It's all very domestic; I could be the wife, replacing Hannah, coming in from her swim, ready to dress and think about what is for lunch. Marie-Laure comes to ask me, not Philip, how many there will be at table, and do we want her to do vegetables and salad too? Is this what Hannah wants me to feel—what it is like being her? To be the wife, part of a couple, two people growing slowly old together, repeating gestures, echoing words, finishing sentences, dividing up the chores without any need to consult each other? What Alexandre has tried for several times, come to think of it, and has largely failed to achieve. His method in middle age has been—as far as I can see—to find someone apparently suitable, usually younger, marry her and then discover that she is not perfect after all. This after his first wife, Nadine the lawyer, divorced him and took their young son from him, back in the eighties. It takes work, the subjugation of the self into coupledom, however it is done, whatever premise you start from. Is this what Hannah can't do anymore?

But Hannah, why are you demanding the impossible of us—me, Philip, even Alexandre—why are you putting us through all this? What is the point, and will I ever understand it, and what must I do to follow you where you now are? Because it seems that I have to. Because even now, at this stage of our lives, I find I still can't resist your call.

When I tell Philip and his children, I'm standing at the dining table with my hand on its glass surface as if I were about to make a speech. Melissa and Piers have their suitcases packed and ready in the hall. They are both slightly tanned after the weekend, they look in their neat pale clothes like satisfied tourists; I think, I'm about to shatter that façade. They want to leave, they are relieved to be able to do so. Philip has his harassed English look, his hair strands untidy, his anxiety at their leaving, evident. We have not been able to come up with a plan, even though we have joked about Plan A and Plan B; as usual, the only plan available to us seems to be to do nothing, but of course, to keep in touch. We've all of us relied on English *sang-froid*—ironic that it can only be named in French.

"Listen, all of you. I've just had a message from an old friend. She contacted him. Hannah did. It was to say she's all right, and she's going home in a few days." Talk about blaming the messenger: they all glare at me now. What do I mean, a message, what old friend, why didn't she call us, what does this mean, a few days? I want to say, it isn't my fault. I don't know any more. I try again.

"The message was that she's okay, that's the main thing, she wanted to reassure you all. That's all I was told but that's huge, isn't it? I'm so relieved. At least she isn't in any danger."

Philip says, "This is too much, really. Claudia, why do you get a message and not us?"

"It was an old friend, from our past, in Paris. Someone we knew when we were students. I've kept in touch with him. His name is Alexandre Dutot. She asked him to call me. I suppose calling here would have seemed too hard for her, but I really don't know any more than this. Sorry, all of you, I've done what I can, told you what I was told myself." My latent anger now seems about to include them, this helpless little group, this family; this husband whose wife can't trust him, obviously, to let her do what she has to do, these immature adult children. Damn you all, I want to say, it's not my business, sort it out yourselves. And damn you, Hannah, for being so mysterious. Oh, and damn you too, Alexandre, for being the person in the middle, giving me messages to deliver. I glare back. I'm close to tears too.

"Sorry, Claude, I didn't mean to get at you." Gentle Philip, doing his best. "It's just all so peculiar. But yes, of course, what a relief. She's going home? That is, home to England?"

"Apparently, yes. But not for a few days. So, there's no rush."

Piers puts down his briefcase on the tiled floor. "Bloody hell. What a fucking stupid mess. Why does she have to do this to us? Coming all this way, and now she's going back to England? Why? What the hell is this all about?"

"I don't know," I say, for the third or fourth time. "It's as much a mystery to me as it is to you."

"Well, it had bloody well better have a solution, is all I can say."

Melissa says, "Surely the most important thing is that we know she's alive and well. You don't have any idea where she is, do you, Claudia?"

"No. Apparently she called from somewhere in Switzerland."

"Switzerland?"

"And she's traveling back to Paris. Phil, she wants me to meet her there, and for you to go home. Please let me do that. I know she'll come home to you, if I do."

Piers starts to say something, but his father interrupts him. "But why does she want *you* to go to Paris? What's this all about? Why doesn't she just come here? I don't get it, all this mystery."

"Sorry, I don't know. It's just the message I've been given. Do let me go to her, and find out what's going on and

I'll make sure she comes home after that. I'll absolutely insist until she agrees. You know," I play a card that feels false to me, but it may work. "It may be something that she can only tell to a woman friend. Somebody close. We do go back a long way."

Philip says, "I'd better tell the police in Avignon, they can stop looking,"

Piers says, "If they ever *were* looking. They can't have been checking borders very thoroughly, can they?"

I see how anxiety makes men angry; perhaps it's better than being simply worried. If I were Hannah, I think, I wouldn't want to come back at all. But maybe her trip to England will be just a visit, to tell them that she's permanently moving somewhere else. At least she isn't dead, she isn't injured, she isn't lost. I too should feel simply relieved. Yet—although I certainly don't tell them—I'm still angry, like Piers. Maybe it's nothing to do with gender, just a general sense of helplessness before the mystery of other people. None of us likes feeling helpless.

Then Philip sits down at the table, buries his face in his hands, and begins to cry. It's more of a dry groan than a sob, as if he's in pain. Melissa puts an arm around him. "Daddy, it's all right. She's all right."

"Sorry," he mumbles. Piers pats his shoulder. They don't want him falling apart too. "Nothing to be sorry about, Dad. It's only natural. You've been under a hell of a strain. Can I get you something? A drink? A cup of tea?"

Philip shakes his head, no, no, I'll be all right; but his face is gaunt. He looks up at me. "You're sure there was nothing else? No explanation?"

"No," I say, "Nothing else. Just that. She's alive. I'll go to

Paris and meet her, and we'll talk about whatever it is, and then she'll be home."

It's time for the twins to go. Piers is looking at his phone, frowning, unwilling to leave such an unsatisfactory situation.

Melissa hugs me. "I think you should go, Claudia. She trusts you. After all, it's what she wants. I'm just so relieved, I mean we didn't know anything, did we, and now we know she's alive and sounds okay. She did sound okay?"

"Alexandre, that's our friend, said she sounded okay, yes."

Piers turns to his father. "Is this all right for you, Dad? It's all very weird, if you ask me, but perhaps Claudia should be the one to go and find her."

Philip says, "I agree. Now, you two had better be on your way, or Mel will miss her plane."

"Dad, call us, please. I'll ring you as soon as I get home. Or, on the way, if you like. You've got my mobile number."

Philip's face still shows the marks of shock: relief, curiously, has done more damage than anxiety. Perhaps he didn't sleep. I feel a pang for him; he loves Hannah, he has been in agony, and in his stoic way, has kept it all in. I think now that he must have lain awake in the big bed upstairs, missing her, fearing that he would never see her again, imagining the worst. She could do that to him; she can still do that to anyone who loves her; not the first time, I wonder at her desperate self-involvement, that she can ignore other people and their feelings so entirely. But I'm the one who is now officially allowed to go and meet her, and for this I am glad.

The twins leave, with the hesitancy of people who are longing to depart but still aren't sure if they should—the kids,

Martin, you do understand Dad, and, I've got work tomorrow, look after yourself, be in touch, don't worry, take care. They aren't Hannah's in this sense: they feel guilt as they go.

The car turns, crunching grandly on the gravel that Philip has laid down, and he presses the button to open the electronic gates, and they disappear out onto the track, white dust and waving bamboo, the canal dangerously close, and set off to cross the bridge and join the main road. I see them both waving. I see Philip raise a slow hand. I feel the weight of it, the grown children, the brave pretense, yes of course I am all right, fine, fine, as he gets older without them. I am part of this, this whole scene, whether I like it or not. As we turn to go back into the house, I put my arms around Hannah's husband for a long hug, and feel him against me, his bony frame and slackened skin, the fatigue of being himself, the coping, the fear of her being gone, the exhaustion that comes with relief. He releases himself at last, sniffs, and says, "Claudia, thank you. I don't know what I'd have done without you this week. And now, this."

That evening, over our aperitifs, pastis cloudy in our glasses, a tray of nuts and olives laid out between us, he says, "There is something I didn't want to talk about in front of the twins. About Hannah."

I sip my drink, and wait. It's a time to say nothing, but be here with this man who finds it hard to speak, hard even to begin.

"It was the only time anything like this happened, that I can remember. You asked me if she'd ever just disappeared, and I said no; but there was this one time. It was when she was pregnant with the twins. She went off without telling me, when she was about two months pregnant. I was afraid she was going to try to get an abortion."

"She didn't want them?"

"She seemed very ambivalent. We'd always said we wanted children, then nothing happened. She went back to work, she was writing a thesis at the time, at the University of East Anglia, she had been planning to do some lecturing there. Then we found out we were having twins. Two babies at once, well, of course it was a shock, and I think she felt overwhelmed. She went away, as I said. Just took a train from Ipswich station and I eventually discovered she was in London. But she came back, and we never mentioned it again. The twins were born early, but they were all right, and so was she."

"Philip, you never asked?"

"I asked once. She just looked at me, as if to say, if you can't trust me, what are we doing together? It scared me, so I didn't ask again. Much later, she did tell me that she went to London, not to see a doctor at all but to spend three days going to see all the plays and films and exhibitions she could, one after another, because she thought she'd never be able to do it again for years. I was stunned. Of course, I asked her why she hadn't simply told me. She said it would have ruined it. She needed just for that time to be invisible, just a person in a crowd, without anyone knowing where she was. It was a thing with her, to be invisible somehow."

"I remember. Do you think she might be doing that sort of thing now? Just being invisible for a few days? It's only been a week since you called me in the US."

"It's possible. That's what I've been thinking. Maybe she just wanted to—get out of her life for a while."

"You haven't had it easy, have you?" I put out a hand to him, and he takes it and then obviously feels embarrassed and lets it go.

"Well, I think I'm terribly lucky to have her. But sometimes it's been quite hard."

The proud man's admission, at last. And I thought this was the perfect match, he supporting her, she finding the freedom she needed within those limits. I should have remembered: Hannah doesn't do limits.

I dare to ask him now, "She never had an affair, though?"

I hear his intake of breath. There's a long silence before he says, "Well, yes, she did. It was early on, before the children were born. I knew, without her telling me. You can feel these things."

"Do you know who it was?"

"She said that it was someone I didn't know."

"And you never asked who?"

"Claudia, a big part of staying married is not asking the wrong questions."

"But that must have left you in a lot of doubt?"

"In a relationship one can often be in a certain amount of doubt, wouldn't you say? I handled it. I still do."

I can't imagine this degree of stoicism; I say nothing.

"I thought it must have been someone at UEA, where she was spending a lot of time trying to finish her PhD. There was a crowd of young writers there, we used to have some of them over for dinner. But you see, I didn't want to spy on her. I didn't want to go any further. No, I said to her that if she broke it off, I'd never ask her about it again. She promised that she had, and so I never did. Sometimes it's better not to know. You imagine things. It hurts to have an actual person to hate."

"You weren't curious?"

"Of course. But I wanted her back, and I still do. More than ever. But then, too, I would have done anything. And I think she's kept her word.

"And then you had the twins?"

"Yes, not very long afterwards. So, you never know. She once confessed to me that she was sick of just having sex to see if she could get pregnant. It was true, it was beginning to feel like a chore for both of us. And then she came back to me, and—bingo."

"Thank you for telling me."

"Well, if you'd been around at the time, I'm sure you would have known about it all. You were always the person closest to her; she would have told you. And probably told you who he was."

"Maybe." But, I think, she was always so good at not-telling. If I had been in England, instead of in California, then maybe.

"You don't think she might possibly be with that person all these years later?"

"Well, I suppose anything is possible. But I really doubt it, Phil, that's all I can say. Anyway, I'll see her, and I'll know more then. I promise, I'll do my utmost to get her to go straight home."

"Yes. I trust you. I have to, don't I?" He sighs deeply, and rubs his eyes.

"So you'll wait for her at home in England, and not try to get in touch with her before that?"

"Oh, God. All right. Tell her I'm waiting for her. Tell her to take her own time, but to come when she can. Tell her—no, don't tell her anything. I'll stay put, keep quiet. You know, I'd been thinking she might be dead. I don't know how I could bear it if she was. I really don't think I could live without having her there. I think it's even why I didn't really want to talk to the police, because they might tell me—they might say, she's been found, she's dead, she's been killed. Or—even, I did think it, killed herself. But now. Oh, thank God."

PART III

17.

Alexandre calls me when I am on the TGV going north.
"Tell me where she is. Which hotel . . ."

"Yes, of course. And you and I, we can meet?"

"When I've seen her, yes."

Only a day later, I'm in a hotel room in Paris again, waiting
for Hannah. I lean on the windowsill, the shutters pushed
wide, and watch the swallows rise and fall between the narrow walls of the courtyard, above the garbage bins and pots of
flowering shrubs, geraniums, waxy camellias. Another hotel
room, another staging post along the journey of our lives.

In the hotel courtyard, three floors down, a ginger cat is
stalking something that disappears between big flower pots. I
watch, see the twitch of the tail as the cat waits. The backs of
these old Paris houses, always faintly mysterious, always the
same: the façades are done up, the front steps polished, and
the doors replaced with ones made of glass, but at the back,
there's always this sense of a different life going on unseen.
The cat pounces. A mouse?

My telephone's chime brings me back into the present and the room. Alexandre. That voice I used to wait for, long for, still here quietly speaking into my ear. Oh, life. Oh, time. I think, I need a drink. He tells me that Hannah is at the Hotel Fortune on rue Bonaparte, that she's scared of seeing me, thinks I'll be angry. Then, "I'll see you later? Call me."

After we've hugged, and looked at each other, she raises her eyebrows and grimaces a little, as if admitting a fault. And then she falls into alarming silence.

I wait and then I can wait no longer. Then, "What's happening, Hannah? What is going on?" I take her in: slimmer, wearing black. Her hair cut shorter, eyes that clear gray.

"I know, I've been putting you all through it, and I'm sorry. But I had to. But first, thanks for coming, Claude. Obviously, I have something I want to tell you." She's standing there, her hands clasped before her, still defensive. Against the long window, in this room, this hotel where she has summoned me: Hannah, whom I thought I might never see again.

"I went to Zurich," she begins.

"To Zurich?"

"Yes. I've just come from there. I went to book myself in, at the clinic there. I'm very ill, Claude, and I won't get any better."

The light is moving across the walls opposite, as cars pass in the street, and I long for something to happen, some interruption, a telephone ringing, someone knocking, a rendezvous one of us has to keep; but this is it, this is the rendezvous, and nothing is going to interrupt it.

"You mean, the place where you—where people end their lives?"

"Yes. I'm all signed up."

"Hannah, why?"

"And when I do—go there when it's time, I mean—I want you to come with me. Will you? Will you do that? I want both of you. You and Alexandre."

"What?" I think—Alexandre? Why Alexandre? I have to walk about the room, a luxurious room with good furniture and curtains and a bed that looks inviting, with its white cover and pillows. A four-star hotel room. There's a small refrigerator, unusual in a Paris hotel; I wonder if there's anything in it. Whisky, or even wine would help. I only ask her the simplest question as it seems to me. "Have you told him? He didn't say."

"Yes."

"And?"

"He said I must ask you first."

She sits down, her hands on the chair arms. She dips her head, shining in the low sun. She says, "I'm sorry, I didn't want to shock you, but there really wasn't any other way to do it."

I look at her. She looks fine, in her black T-shirt and narrow pants, thinner in the face perhaps, paler, the lines deeper than a year ago—a lot can happen in a year; people can change utterly, get sick, even die. Her hair is cut to shape her face, a feathery cut, no more long hair for her either, and is an ash-blonde, close to the color she must have had as a small child, before I met her. The plaits were always more honey-colored and her hair when we traveled together, streaked light with sun. She used to throw her head forward as she bent from the waist, catching her bright fall of hair in her fist to pull it all up into a ponytail. When she brushed it, it used to hang forward over her face like a zombie, and she'd giggle behind it.

"I have ALS. You know what that is? It doesn't give you much time."

Of course I know what ALS is. I can't believe it. Apparently I have to believe it.

"Give me time, I just have to take all this in for a moment." I think of people who say, if you are not with me you are against me. Like this you carve the world in two, friend or foe. Has it always been like this with us? She is asking more of me than I've ever imagined anyone would. Is it for this reason that I've avoided marriage, children, the ultimate commitments of a shared life? So that nobody can say to me, when it comes to it, I need you to be there?

"How much time do you have?"

She sits perfectly still, watching me. "Maybe a year at most."

"You're asking me to help you kill yourself, right? That's it, that's the question?" Shock has made me angry; but I don't want to be angry. I want to be on her side, now and forever. She is looking at me steadily, from where she sits in a low chair, her feet in rather ugly strappy black shoes, planted one beside the other.

"No, I'm not asking you that, I'm asking you to come with me when I go back to Zurich. It's all arranged, I just don't want to do it all alone. I've paid the deposit, and I just want you to be with me when the time comes. Please. Will you?"

"So you've been organizing the end of your life while we've all been going out of our minds wondering what had happened to you."

"I had no other choice, Claude. It's not just Phil who'd try and stop me, it's Piers and Melissa, too. None of them would be able to accept this sort of thing. They'd have kidnapped me and tried to convince me not to."

I think, Zurich. I walked through the airport a week ago and bought a watch and got on a plane and thought nothing of it. I could have walked right past her. I could have stopped her, distracted her, taken her off for coffee, made her change her mind. It could have been the turning point. She on one escalator, I on another, our amazed eyes meeting, our signals to each other, meet you up there, or down below.

"You know, sometimes it's simply safer not to tell anyone."

I can't help thinking of her escapades at school. You don't tell, or you swear your friend to secrecy. Are we back there again? "Are you sure it's not curable? Or may become curable in the future?"

Now she gives me that disappointed look, eyebrows raised, eyes wide open: the old Hannah. "You can do your own research. But I've been into it from every angle, believe me. From everything I've read, the prognosis is not nice. I will gradually become unable to move or speak or even swallow and then I will be trapped in my own body. I don't want it. I decided as soon as I got the diagnosis. I'm not going there. You of all people must understand that."

I remember my friend Joanie's mother in New York, years ago. The illness announced itself one evening in a restaurant in the Village when I happened to be there with Joanie. Her mother had trouble swallowing a piece of beef and nearly choked. The diagnosis followed, and there was only decline after that. I saw her again, only months later. She'd lost a great deal of weight and could hardly breathe without assistance. It was painful to see, and it was agonizing for Joanie. I'd resolved then never to allow myself to be in such a position, if I could help it. So how can I disagree with what Hannah has decided?

"Life on my terms, Claude, it's always been my way, remember?" Hannah bites the knuckle on her right hand then, and the gesture is the one from our schooldays, when things got hard, when she didn't want to give some bullying prefect the satisfaction of seeing her show emotion. An elderly woman, my friend Hannah, with the girl she was still inside her; a fierce frown, a bitten knuckle; as if I saw two images superimposed, one briefly blocking the other. She looks up at me, those same clear gray eyes now in their little nests of wrinkles, eyeliner pulling them into focus. We don't change. We change utterly. It's life that changes, around us. We still have to feel our way.

I say, "Yes, of course I'll be with you. If that's what you want."

"Thank you."

"But, Alexandre? Why do you want him too?"

"I thought it might be hard for you to come away from there on your own, afterwards. But there's more to it than that, actually. I want to bring our threesome together again, the way it was in Paris, remember, the way it was when we met on that train, when everything was just beginning?"

Ah, so she has it all planned; we just have to play our parts.

I take her cue. "And someone pulled the communication cord? You know, it was the only time in my life that ever happened."

"Me too. Remember, there was a fight of some sort in the next compartment?"

"And Alexandre had wine, and a sandwich."

"A ham sandwich."

"No, it was sausage. The skins got stuck in my teeth. His mother had made it."

"His mother made a sausage?" She explodes with laughter, and we're over the edge, both giggling at the absurdity.

"No, stupid, the sandwich. I remember thinking, here's a boy who loves his mother."

"And whose mother loves him. Terribly traditional."

"He still is. Have you seen him?"

"We talked on the phone, first." Then she adds, as if an afterthought, "He did come over, yes."

"And you told him? You asked him, after not seeing him for fifty years, to come on this little suicide party you've planned?"

"He's put on weight, hasn't he? But he still looks the same. I mean, we all have wrinkles and gray hair and all that, but we look the same, don't we, Claude, don't you think?"

"Well, we can all remember how we looked when we were young, and sometimes, I don't know, that young person comes to the surface. Or, we expect to see them, so we do."

"He still has those thin fingers. What people call pianist's hands."

"You remembered his fingers?"

"Well, yes. We all spent so much time examining each other then, didn't we, we looked for signs, all the time, the way we were. I can remember girls at school, exactly the way they wore their hair, how their socks fell down, the kind of shoes they had, their handwriting. And boys, we examined them even more thoroughly, didn't we? I certainly did."

She looks at me now, examining—what, the girl I was, hidden inside the aging woman? All time is present, I think. Everything that happens, happens simultaneously. There is a popular theory that suggests this, but I have never been able to take it in; perhaps nobody really can. Perhaps its truth only appears at moments like this: there and then gone. And I realize: it's Hannah and me again, it's us, it's the way we have always been. It's a relief, because it's so familiar; it's as if we're chatting on the grass at college, or outside the library at school, or late at night after she'd climbed in through some ground-floor window, or in a bar somewhere: it's the substance of our friendship, which was made long, long ago. But, Alexandre? Surely that was where it all began to get peculiar, where we stopped trusting each other, where things were not said?

She seems to catch my thought. "It was where we stopped being kids, wasn't it, when we met him. All of us. We had to be three instead of two. That was why I left him to you, because I didn't know how it could be done, otherwise. You wanted him more than I did. Wasn't that how it was?"

It was how she said it was, at the time. Giving him to me, as if he were hers to give. When I was nineteen, I was puzzled but grateful. Now, I think of it as a doubtful ploy. It was what I'd wanted, yes, and I'd enjoyed it, and him, for the whole of my life. But, what had she been playing at? Why, if she is planning her own death, does she want Alexandre there too?

She says now, "I do have to lie down, sorry. Give me a hand with my shoes? I have to wear these awful shoes, because my feet won't hold them on. It was the first thing I noticed; my left foot sort of began to flap." I kneel, and remove them. Her feet are still slim and straight. Her left foot lies in my palm.

"What did he say?"

"He said I must ask you first. But he was okay about it. I think he'll come, if you will."

Alexandre, with his sense of propriety; who wouldn't sleep with Hannah with me in the next room. Then, and now, a man of principle, whatever his life was like. A man who knows what may and may not be done in a civilized world; very French, it seems to me now, to be this clear about manners and procedure, while living in relative chaos.

She drops back on to the bed, heaves her legs up onto the white bedcover, stretches out and sighs. I go to the fridge and discover a clutch of little bottles. "Whisky? Wine? Oh, and champagne too. I think we need something, don't you?"

"Let's have the champagne," she says, and I remember, just days ago, her husband with trembling hands pouring it to drink to her safe return. "I think we need to celebrate. It's so good to see you." She props pillows behind her head and grins at me, a little forced grin, as if to remind me who we are, or were. It works.

We are back, we are together again; and if the topic of her planned death has come up between us like a whale surfacing, upheaving everything, it seems to have gone down underwater again, at least for now. The smell of whales, I remember, lingers after they have submerged; they have stinking breath. Perhaps it isn't a good analogy. I remove the foil and twist the cork in the little bottle until it pops out slowly and she stretches out a hand for her glass—there were two in the bathroom—and we inhale the breath of the champagne. It's nothing like whale breath. The prickle on our tongues makes us smile. I think, I love her; I always have, and it's not just because she's part of my life, out of my childhood, but because of the quality in her that won't give up, or fade, or accept less than everything from life. We clink glasses belatedly and I feel the fizz on my tongue and the coldness go down inside and transform the moment, the way champagne does.

"Hmm," she says, "a new widow. Veuve Rochefort? I haven't heard of this lady, have you? She sounds like a phony to me."

After a moment, in which we sip and grin at each other again and I see from her expression that she knows she has me now, I say, "But what about Phil? Where is he in all this? I know you say that he'd try and change your mind, but you're asking *us*, not him?"

It still feels unreal, as if what she has asked me is a joke, a challenge unconnected to any action—a what-if, a maybe. But I am sure, knowing her, that it is not.

I think of the man in the house in the Lubéron, aged by worry, trying to keep his life together, to will her back into it by his simple belief in all being well. Nothing serious, she was seeing a doctor, I think she's been feeling better recently. "You haven't told him anything about it, have you? About what you have?"

"What I have, let's be clear about it, it's fucking motor-neuron disease, a total entropy and collapse of me as me, ending with a tiny shrunken Hannah peering out of a completely paralyzed and useless body until she can't do it anymore and can't even breathe. No, I haven't been able to tell him. Also, as I said, sometimes it's better to act alone." She crosses her legs, wiggles her toes. "Look, my left foot is hardly managing already. I've had a couple of falls; I pretended I tripped over something, people helped me up. Nothing too serious yet. But, one day it will be."

We look at her feet. I remember them brown, dusty in sandals.

She continues, "Of course I know I'll have to, in the end—tell him, I mean. But I just wanted to set it all up first. You see?"

I see her determination to be in control, to move people about at her will, yes. But I can understand why.

"He loves me, I know that, but, you know, there are different kinds of love, and his kind wouldn't be able to hear me out. He wouldn't exactly lock me in the house, no, but he'd try to talk me out of it, he'd talk about the children and how it would damage them, and the grandchildren, and our life as a family. I really can't have that conversation now. I certainly don't want to listen to people going on about miracle cures and new-age stuff, or trying to cheer me up. My only choice is to try and go out of this as me as I am now, not as a fucking disaster that has to be nursed hand and foot and all the bits in between." She looks at me, assessing. "This is what I'm asking. I don't think it's too much. I don't think it's unreasonable. And Phil, though he loves me, can't love me in the way that leaves me free to do what I must. He can't love that Hannah. The one you and Alexandre know. Now, do you understand?"

"Of course. But couldn't you give him the opportunity to accept your decision?"

"Well, he'll have to accept it. It's done. I will tell him, in good time, and I think I'll be able to count on him. in the end. And I hope I can count on you and Alexandre, because you're my oldest friends."

"I'm with you, if that's what you really want. But I can't speak for Alexandre." I'm thinking, when she ran away from school, I lied for her for two whole days, saying I hadn't seen her, didn't know where she was, however unlikely that seemed. I lied to her distraught would-be lovers at Cambridge, including Philip, once when she went out with that boy from the sailing club, or had a brief passion for a saxophone player in a modern jazz quartet. Here I am, late in life, summoned to cover for her once again.

"Good. So that's settled, at least." She swallows the last of her champagne. "Cheer up, you look as if you've seen a ghost."

It all feels at once completely normal, and utterly strange. What do we do now? Does she want me to sign something, or swear allegiance to her plan? What now? What is the next step?

"Look," she says, again as if reading my thoughts; and stretches out her hands, the left one with the rings and watch, the right with a bracelet. Her hands are thin and white. "My left hand will hardly go up on its own now, I have to sort of heave it up there. It's like it's lying in wait for me, this thing, it delivers some new horror every day. See? My right hand will begin soon. You must have noticed, I'm sort of dragging my left foot behind me. I've managed to keep it from Phil, but I won't be able to for much longer. He thinks I've got rheumatism and that's what makes me limp. And I get the most awful cramps, especially at night. It's like being one big cramp. My muscles are giving up, you see. Eating themselves, as it were."

"And you really haven't told him anything about what you've been going through?"

"Well, he knows something is up, but I've left it kind of vague. And I'll tell him what it is as soon as I've set up with you and Alexandre, when it's a fait accompli, when there can't be any discussion. It's a death sentence, either way. I can choose a slow death with torture, you see, or a quick death without."

She pushes her glass towards me on the little table; we're sitting close to the window, a round table between us. "Is there any more of that good stuff?"

"One more of these tiny bottles."

A small detail has been waiting at the back of my mind. "How did you to Switzerland and back without your passport being checked? The police said they would check frontiers."

She grins at me. "Ah. So you thought of that too. On the train of course. Bought all my tickets in cash in England, got to the Gare du Nord, taxi to Gare de l'Est—it's a stone's throw—and on to the train to Berne. Change there and on to Zurich. Nobody looks at your passport, just the tickets. Or maybe I was just lucky."

"You still have the touch, don't you?" I see her sly smile, the one I remember from her escape plans, decades ago.

"Look, about Phil," she says. "You need to understand something. My whole married life has been about keeping Phil from being upset by things that have happened to me or us, and I can't go on doing it now. I don't have the strength. I've kept everything calm and even and working for bloody years. I wanted to give him that, when we married, the household, the children, the whole setup; the book business, too. I wanted us to be partners in everything, I had a firm idea that was what marriage was about for me. No more dashing in and out and never seeing each other and sending children to boarding school, the way my parents did."

"I always thought your parents were kind of sexy. They seemed to have a secret life."

"Yes, well, imagine being a third party in that setup? I was the gooseberry, I was well aware of that. I suppose I've swung to the other extreme."

She goes on, "I had a hard time living with my decision, for several years. It felt impossible to do it with Phil, he was so—I don't know. Different from me." She stops, and then looks at me. I catch her narrowed glance, and feel a deep apprehension.

"Claude, there's something else. Talking of Alexandre. I have to tell you, even if it's old history. Alex told me not to, but I have to. I couldn't ask you to come with me, if I didn't."

I feel cold, looking at her. What now? What more can there possibly be? "What did he tell you not to tell me?"

So, they have talked, they have plotted without me, she and Alexandre. Where was I? Waiting for her in the south, on the Paris train? Keeping her husband company, doing what I was told? Here it is, in the room with us, what I have been dreading without knowing it. Yet, also knowing it. My dream.

"I had a fling with him, oh, long ago. More than a fling. An affair, I suppose, only it was interrupted. Phil found out. There—long story short. But it did happen, and I have to come clean with you, at least, before I jump off my perch."

Change, and change again. Is there no end to it? I feel all the physical things, the thudding heart, the sweaty hands, the extreme discomfort, the breathlessness; we should not have to hear such things. I manage to say, "When? When was all this?"

"Ages ago. Before the twins were born. Phil and I were not long married, or only a few years."

We know things without knowing that we know. We

breathe them in, digest them, long before words are put to them. I've known this—just not when, or where, or how. Philip has known too.

"So it was him. Phil told me you'd had someone. But he didn't say who it was. He said he hadn't wanted to know. Jesus, Hannah. How could you? Why?"

"Because we could. Because you weren't here. Because I wasn't happy with Phil, it wasn't working, not the way we'd imagined. Because it happened. Who knows? Why do we do these things? Is there ever just one reason?"

I'm almost unable to speak. At last I say, and it comes in a rush, "Well, to tell lies to your husband and get on a train or plane or whatever it was, and go to Paris and find Alexandre and seduce him, if that's what you did, and have an affair with him, there must have been a reason, surely. Or are you trying to say it all just happened, without your meaning it to? Or were you drunk, or drugged, or in a dream? Come on, you made a decision, you did it, all of it. You have to take some responsibility." That curious expression, "come clean"—as if admitting to something absolves you of all blame.

"Claude, I'm trying to. Take responsibility. I get it, that it hurts you right now. But I didn't do it to hurt you, I promise. And I certainly didn't set out to seduce him. We kind of—fell into it together. But it was forty or more years ago. He said it would be a big deal for you, and not to tell you. Then, and again, when I saw him yesterday. But you have to believe me I am not minimizing anything. If I was going to tell you, I was going to tell you everything. Or else lie and not tell you anything. And I've done enough of that."

"Everything was forty or more years ago! Alexandre and I have been lovers ever since, did you know that? Did you even think of that? I thought you got it, how I felt about him, I thought you got it when we were in Paris that first time, when you left me that note. And all this time you've been lying to me."

"Yes," she says, "but only by not telling. And you weren't here to tell."

"It's exactly what you've been doing to Philip for all these years, and you're still doing it. Not telling, hiding things, running away. How do you expect anyone to love you? Damn it, how do you expect anyone even to know who you are?"

Silence. She looks down, so that I see the top of her head, gray in the blonde hair. I look at her hands, which are resting beside her, with their wrinkles and their rings; the hands that will soon stop working for her, signaling her whole body's refusal. For some time, neither of us speaks. She looks exhausted, there on the bed. We are aging women, about to be defeated by time. We are also back to being angry young women, jealous and afraid. The time that passes between us in this room can do nothing to help us, nothing to change the situation. I want to be able to say to her, finally, "Just go to hell."

It has been with us all along, this story, running fast like that canal that cuts through the countryside in the south, taking all the river water and rechanneling it, whisking everything along in its spate. It is my story, and Philip's too.

"I don't expect anything," she says at last. "I'm just asking. I've told you the truth, as far as I can. You know everything about me now. And I'm deeply sorry, really, I know I've hurt you. But in the light of everything now, I have no choice. All I can do is ask you to forgive me. I think I'll understand if you can't."

I hear her voice shake, and know that she means it. Maybe it's too late, maybe I really can't forgive her this time.

Maybe at last she has pushed me too far. Long ago, when we were students, she tried to go to bed with Alexandre and he refused her. What happened that second time?

I get up and stand at the window of her hotel bedroom, looking out past the iron guard rail to the street, which leads down to Saint-Sulpice at one end and Saint-Germain at the other, and the home-going traffic, and the strip of summer afternoon sky, and all the lives of the hundreds of unknown people who scurry past, or stroll, or talk on their phones, or stop to kiss: all of them caught up in their own stories, all of them feeling, struggling, planning, probably lying too. I breathe in, I breathe out. I think how cities are blown up these days; bombs on street-corners, in cafés, at concerts, on buses and trains: chaos sown in a second, destruction of lives fanning out from some dire center, some implanted wish to destroy, kill, maim, stop the peaceful trivial progress of the day and the street and the city and the people in it, just like that. I think how we all do our best with our feeble tools and our unsure intentions, how we all prevaricate and betray, in our own ways, how we let each other down and then raise each other up again, and try, and forgive, and begin again, as long as we are alive. How we insist on our stories, our versions. Hannah will soon not be alive; she will have left the party, got off the train. I turn back to her where she lies still, her head turned away, uncharacteristically quiet, awaiting my verdict. It's up to me, what I tell her. At this point in a volatile century, in which crisis can erupt out of nowhere, it does seem to matter, to be able to forgive. But, how do you go about it?

Forty years ago or more, she slept with Alexandre. And I had a dream, of standing in the street, being thrown a bunch of keys and trying one after another to find the right one.

An upper room, and Hannah perhaps up there, behind him, invisible, perhaps even naked, or wrapped in a sheet.

I ask her, at last, "Were you in love with him?"

She makes an empty upward gesture with her hands. "No. Not really."

Not really. I don't, I can't say anything.

"It just happened, as if it had been waiting to happen, and I don't even know who made the first move. He wasn't happy in his marriage, I wasn't happy in mine. We saw each other a few more times, and then Phil found out. It was almost a relief, when he did."

She goes on, and I wish she would not, "I think, to be honest, it was more curiosity on my part, and probably on his. It was something we hadn't done, when we could have. You know what it was like, in those days, people were doing it all the time."

"But you and Alexandre," I manage to say, "were not just people. You were my friends." Don't start to justify yourself, Hannah, or I will leave you now, I will walk out of this room and never come back.

At last she says, "I said before that I wanted to come clean. I'm not trying to justify what I did. All I can say is that we didn't do it to hurt you."

"You just didn't think."

"Yes, that's about it."

And yet, if someone acts without thinking, how do they know what their motives are?

"Claude, can you forgive me?" she asks me again. A small voice, her head turned away. It seems to me a childish thing to ask. You do whatever you like, do you, and then ask for forgiveness?

"I suppose I will have to. Just give me a minute, please." It seems to cost me a great physical effort. She has rearranged all the furniture of my past, and even my present with Alexandre. He has never said, never admitted it. She has relied on his tact. French men do not kiss and tell: the whole structure of society here depends upon it. But, my complete ignorance, my trust, my belief in what I know now was an illusion: what do I do with all this? How do I deal with it? Am I even telling her the truth? If I am honest, just for a moment, just with myself, I know—partly know—that it is not so much the sex as the being excluded that hurts. And this hurt goes way back, to a time before we even knew what sex was, or how it would involve us.

Do I have to forgive her, because of the times we live in? Because she is going to die? Because I always have? No. I have to because of who I am now, the person I have become in her absence, the person I choose to be. I cross the room, go to the window, look out. The street, the roofs, the sky, home-going traffic.

She met Alexandre by chance, and because of that they had to go to bed with each other? And lie to me for decades?

I turn back to her. "I want to know everything. Just tell me."

"Okay. Fine. It was when Phil was very busy, away a lot, setting up contracts with people and trying to get authors for the press. I went to Paris twice. The first time for a few days, as I said, we had this author there with a book coming out. That was when I bumped into him by chance, as I was waiting for the author, outside a bookshop. Shakespeare and Company, in fact, opposite Notre-Dame. Then another—oh, ten days or so. I think I said I was going to a summer school at UEA. Then Phil found out. He actually confronted me with it, for once in his life. And then, yes, things changed. I got pregnant with him, quite soon after that, and we had the twins. I'd promised never to see the man—Alexandre, only he didn't know that—again."

"And now you want him to come and help you die?"

I've come back to stand in front of her. She's rubbing her feet with one hand, as if she has cramps in them. "Yes."

"Why?"

"Because—well. I was the happiest I've ever been when it was just the three of us then. And maybe that's why I just went off that day in Paris, leaving you two together. Because I thought it was going to happen, the two of you together, and I didn't want to be there when it happened. Because it would be the end of my happiness even though it would be the beginning of yours. And nothing—being married, having children, having the press—has ever has made me as happy as I was in those days. And I just want that—I don't know— that sort of perfection again before I depart." She pauses. "Do you even think he'll come?"

I imagine that the centuries-old discretion practiced here by adulterers hasn't stretched yet to the question of assisted suicide. Sex is one thing, death still quite another. We are unfamiliar with its rules. And I am lost, between the two people I have been closest to all my life.

There is a long silence, a cloud briefly darkening the room, a plane going over, a shout from the street.

Then I begin again—I know I have to—to repair the silence. Perhaps the past can help us after all. Perhaps there is a safe place to be found. There, if not here. Then, if not now. I tell her, "When I was waiting, in my hotel, I thought about those times, those summer holidays when we sat on the seawall, in Suffolk, when your parents were at the yacht club, remember?"

She nods. Is it a relief to her too, to go back to this old story?

I say, to lighten things, "Do you remember the song we used to sing?"

"What song?"

"It was like a marching song. It was nonsense. 'Two—blue pigeons'"

"Yes!" She sings the first notes, and then it comes to me in a rush.

'One was black and white—pom!'

And then we sing together, loudly, laughing, the song that probably nobody else in this world remembers: 'Sandy he belongs to the mill, the mill belongs to Sandy still, Sandy he belongs to the mill. And the mill belongs to Sandy!'

"It was complete nonsense. 'Two blue pigeons!'" She sings out the four notes again. We both have tears in our eyes. We skip in memory all the way up through town, girls together, all the way to the Moot Hall and back. Young, carefree. Perhaps we are saved.

'One was black and white—pom!' We fall across the bed, laughing. I lie beside her; we both look up to the ceiling, where a little light winks—a smoke detector? If there's an edge of hysteria, it passes, and we turn our head sideways to look at each other.

"Your mother taught us that, after she'd had her G and T at the yacht club."

"Did she? I'd forgotten. She must have had several if she was singing."

Her mother, the hardworking doctor; yes, she did have a lighter side, with her gin and tonic, and her love of the cinema. I remember the back of her head, her streaked light hair, in the car, and how she turned and sang us the words. I was fascinated by Hannah's mother. She exuded, what was it, well—sex, of course, as I've just told Hannah, while my mother for all her production of babies, did not. Hannah's mother worked, and had sex with Hannah's father, and helped people not to have babies.

"We sang songs in the back of the car, all the time. It was fun."

Hannah says, "I feel exhausted. Do you mind if I just lie here for a bit and we don't talk anymore? Or anything?"

I'm thinking, I could go on like this: like nailing something back into place that has begun, disastrously, to come apart. Too much is going on here; it's as if our lives are in fast-forward, rushing towards the end that Hannah has decreed..

"And the maroons went off that night, remember, and we went down to the beach, the lifeboat went out and they saved people."

"It was exciting, wasn't it, going out in the middle of the night?"

"And there was one young man who was already dead, and we saw them carry him past us."

"I don't remember seeing anybody dead." Hannah says.

"It was a foreign ship that went down, and the sailors who came ashore didn't speak English. They were Norwegian. Your dad stayed, to help out. Surely you remember?"

That body on a stretcher, an arm dangling, a hand. You don't forget the first dead body you see. She lies back with her arm across her eyes, and says nothing. Death is already in the room with us, all too present. I should not have evoked the drowned sailor; I don't insist. Her silence tells me eloquently: no, not this, not now.

I lay a hand on her shoulder. "Okay, I'm going. Back soon."

She opens her eyes, half sits up. "He's down there, or should be. I told him to wait in the café, till you came."

I told him to wait. How we still do as she wants, no matter what.

"You mean, Alexandre? Which café?"

"The Flore, of course." As if there were no other possible café. "He'll be upstairs, waiting for you."

So, one more time, I do as she directs, as she pushes me back towards Alexandre. He's all yours. Except that he wasn't, hasn't been, will not ever be now.

18.

I leave her stretched out on the bed, her shoes off, arms at her sides, the little light winking above her; the outside light changing the colors in the room, as clouds come and go towards evening. I go down one flight of stairs and through a glass door, out into the small courtyard and then the street. I'll come back, I've promised. I walk along rue Bonaparte towards Saint-Germain-des-Prés. I feel dizzy with all she has just told me—loaded upon me, it feels like—the request about going to Zurich "when the time comes," the announcement of "a fling with Alexandre." She has always had the power—have I given her the power?—to turn my life inside out. But there's also the new meaning behind all this: her decision to die. I've often thought about this—dying—you don't reach the age I am without it crossing your mind from time to time; but it's always been in a far-off-enough future, in which I will be really old. Hannah and I are not yet really old. Yet a disease has fastened on her, made its terrifying threat, she will change, suffer, and die in its grip, and she has decided on her escape from it, her way out. She has said no. No, not like that.

Calmly or not calmly, she has decided; have there been lonely nighttimes when she has sobbed and groaned about it and gone back and forth in her mind? I'm stunned by her decision and her ability to go there to set it up alone. But she has taught me: you can say no to pain, as you can say yes to pleasure. Whatever we think, or say, she has moved us roughly on to the next stage of life.

Yet we can still sing "Two Blue Pigeons" and laugh until we cry. And I will lose her. And in losing her, I will lose part of myself.

I cross the boulevard with a hundred others, Japanese tourists following a woman wearing a black hat and knee socks and carrying a flag on a stick, and walk into the café, past the waiter who stands in the doorway and lets me pass to go up the stairs. The bells of the church of Saint-Germain are ringing; is it time for mass? Is there a wedding, or a funeral? It's as if we are all fleeing beneath the din of the bells. I go upstairs and find Alexandre sitting by himself at one of the tables in the upper room of the Café de Flore. Because it is summer, and warm, the downstairs tables and those on the sidewalk are all full; but up here it is empty, and fairly cool. He has a glass and a bottle of Perrier in front of him on the little square table; he's sitting on the banquettes that line the room, facing outward. He gets up to kiss me on both cheeks. I let him: we could be acquaintances, or old friends; there is nothing about our meeting to suggest that he is my lover. It's as if Hannah has changed things between us already.

"Bonjour, Claudie. So. You've seen her?"

I sit down beside him on the bench. Up here, everything is so untouched—or has been restored to its former glory? Light filters in through the thicket of flowers growing outside the windows. Everything is all of a piece, art deco down to the glasses. "Yes, I've just come from her hotel. She felt tired, she's having a rest."

"So, you know? She told you what she wants?" He sounds almost angry; certainly agitated. I haven't seen him like this in years.

"Yes. She told me you'd said she must ask me first."

"How was she?"

"Oh—calm, decisive. Not in bad shape, physically, yet."

I'm hoping the waiter will come soon to ask me what I want to drink. The champagne I drank with Hannah stings still at the back of my throat and I have a slight headache and am very thirsty.

"You know it's illegal?" Of course, he's a lawyer; I almost forgot. Of course, this aspect of it would come first with him. We sit beside each other like plotters, not lovers; as if neither of us wants to turn our back to the room. A Chinese woman in what looks like a designer silk suit comes upstairs to use the toilet, glances at us on her way; otherwise the upstairs room is empty. The mirrors show you who is coming up the stairs, before they can be seen in reality. He must have seen me come up, my mirror image before me; maybe braced himself for what we'd have to say.

"She's not planning to do it here. She's doing it in Switzerland. She's already been there to sign up."

"Claudie, why must you always do what she wants?" Alexandre keeps his voice low—in case the Chinese woman hears, on her way out? He sips his Perrier. The wood paneling of the room makes it feel like a club, but the orchids and palm leaves at the windows let in today's hot late afternoon light as if we were in a greenhouse.

"Why do I? She's my friend. More to the point, why do *you* do what she wants, Alex?" I see that he doesn't know what I mean. "She told me about you and her, and what happened. You never told me. You both lied to me. How do you think that feels?"

He makes a restless dismissing gesture with one hand. This infuriates me. "You will not diminish this like you have so many things."

Now he's really rattled. "It was forty years ago," he says, looking down at the table. "It was a mistake."

"A mistake! A mistake happens once. More than once is not a mistake. You lied to me, that's what hurts most. And finding it out all these years later makes me feel like an idiot."

"She asked me not to tell you, Claudie. She said it would hurt you too much."

"No, you asked her not to tell me. Admit it."

At just that moment the waiter ascends the stairs, white-jacketed, mirrored too as he comes. "Another Perrier, please," I say to him.

Alexandre has his head propped in his hands and isn't looking at me. I want a sign from him, just one. That he understands me, at least. The waiter has seen everything, and these days sees and hears it in a dozen different languages every day. On the wall, a group of badly dressed Parisian intellectuals looks down from the only photograph and I wonder who they all were. Did we really come up here, when we were young? It would have been expensive, even then. Didn't we drink at a smaller, unknown café down one of the side streets off boulevard Saint-Germain? I couldn't, now, remember. I wait for him to speak, agitated, even slightly ill with tension.

Alexandre looks around him as if still afraid to be heard;

but we are alone. "You know how we were then, how easy it was, it was a whole different era. We're not the same people anymore. You can be upset about it now, of course, Claudie, really. But you must see, it was so long ago. Also, you know that there have been other women. We have always said that it doesn't make any difference to us, no?"

"Others, maybe, and actually that was hard enough. But not Hannah. Not her."

I remember his theory, the one he explained to me when we were young and his infidelities still hurt: that he was completely present with me, body and soul, here and now, and that this, what we had, was eternal. I wonder now if he has said exactly the same thing to other women. To Hannah, even.

As for us not being the same people—I want to say, then who are we? And why are we together?

The waiter comes up the stairs again with a round tray, and more bottles of Perrier; we both seem to hold our breath.

He looks up at me. "Claudie. It was something that happened, without either of us expecting it. I probably shouldn't have done it. I'm sorry, that you had to find out now."

"Well." I swallow my fizzy water.

He says quietly, "Don't let's fight, Claudie. I'm sorry, I said I'm sorry. I'm sorry I did it, I'm sorry I lied. I really never wanted to hurt you. But would it had been better if you had known? This passion for telling everything is very American, it seems to me."

"What are you trying to say?"

"Would it have made you happier, would it have made things better or different if you'd known about it back then? We might not have had all the times together, the love, the attention for each other that we have had."

I look at him. He has a point, of course. I would have been angrier, more upset, when I was younger. I have to accept that it could have been much worse, and done more damage, and yes, it could have put an end to what became a long liaison that has brought both of us a great deal of pleasure. I also think, we have been having our first fight in years, if that is what it is. But what is a relationship, really, if it consists entirely of pleasurable sex and never an argument, never a scene like this one where we sit stubbornly opposed to each other, not giving way? I realize that Hannah has put us here; she has orchestrated this, we can blame her—or, be grateful. The world is caught up in so much misunderstanding and antagonism, my only chance is to be different from that, to accept what is, and not fight it. I think, for some reason, of the old woman sitting on the rocks on the shore in Greece, everything lost to her, except her life. The woman whose photograph I saw.

We should be talking about Hannah, her decision: not about ourselves. It's best for all of us that I don't stay angry with her. I should be able to let go of this. But what we should feel is not always what we do feel, and therein lies the whole confusion of life.

I look at him. "Hannah wanted to tell me the truth because she's going to die."

"Of course. And for her it makes sense, perhaps. But can I tell you something? You can believe it or not. Me, I can hardly even remember how it was, what it was, how she was. It was probably nice. It was also not important, compared to everything we have had, you and I. But I also want to say that we all go to our deaths with secrets, with things not said. It's how life is."

At last, after a long silence, I say to Alexandre, here in the Café de Flore, "All right. If we don't say any more about it, where does this leave us?"

"Well. She has left us in this position, asking us to go with her."

He is right. Once again, and in another context entirely, Hannah has preempted us. I wonder what must it feel like to know that an enemy is marching inside you, wreaking its damage day by day? To have gone alone, first of all to face a diagnosis, then to make the arrangements for your own death? To prepare yourself to give up the world? To ask friends for help, and not be sure that they will come through for you? I look at my lover of forty or more years, and think, yes, this is a test of us together, of what we have made.

"I think that we have to go. I think we have to help her." As I say this, he reaches out and for a couple of seconds squeezes my hand.

We are who we are now. He is a successful French lawyer and I am a college professor from the United States. We are nearly old enough to retire. We have obligations, ties to other parts of life, we are social beings. And yet, here we sit in the café of our youth—for we did come here, and what's more, I remember the pattern in the carpet—the same carpet, or its duplicate—in a café where we met once when he lived in the rue du Dragon, in a maid's room under the eaves of pigeons and rusty gutters and squares of the Paris sky above rooftops.

Alexandre spreads his hands upon the table and looks at them. I imagine he does this in court, before he begins to speak for the defense. While he looks at his hands— Hannah is right, he does have long thin fingers; why was I not suspicious when she mentioned them?

Then he says, "You talked with her about her husband?"

"Yes. She says he would try to stop her. She wants to present it as a fait accompli."

"But in fact, could he stop her? If he did, perhaps it would be for the best. Maybe this illness can be endured for a long time. We don't know the quality of other people's lives."

"Alex, you obviously don't know about ALS. It's horrible. The suffering it brings. I've known people who've had it. No matter what I want, what she wants makes complete sense to me. Especially because it just gets worse and worse. And every case is a death sentence. You don't get better from it."

"True." He looks sideways at me, slides back in his seat. "You know, it is complicated."

I say, "No, it's actually simple. It's yes, or no."

"No, it's complicated for us. To be with her there. Because we are not relatives. Will they accept us? Will we be accused of trying to kill her, of persuading her against her will? There is all this to consider."

"Well," I say, "you're the lawyer." For a lawyer, I'm thinking, his arguments are fairly illogical. He must be as confused by this as I am. "They can't accuse us of anything, surely?"

He frowns. "I'm not sure. I have to look at all sides. You must see this. Yes, we must help her, but is this the best way? Is there not another way?"

"What other way is there? This is assisted. It's dignified. It's what she wants. And what she wants makes sense to me."

Is it at this moment that I see what has changed? We are no longer in a bedroom, focusing simply and willingly upon each other. That is what we know how to do. This is different. With everything he says, I see him slipping away. He is right, of course, in the real world where we sit. Yet where it matters, in the country of the heart, he is not.

"*Allons*, let's go."

"But where?"

"I have to go back to my office, at least for an hour or so. Will you go back to see her?"

"Yes." I want to say, what about later?

"And we can have dinner?"

"If you're free."

"Of course. I'll book. There's a place at the end of boulevard Saint-Germain, Chez René, number 10, I think. You can find it?"

"Of course. Anyway, call me if you need to, otherwise— what, seven-thirty? Eight?"

"Eight, rather."

"And Hannah?"

"Ask her, if she wants to come. But we can't talk about all this over dinner. We must talk about something else."

He leaves twenty-euro notes for the expensive bottled water at the Café de Flore, and goes down those stairs, mirrored, his jacket over his shoulder, his elegant work-self on its way to the next meeting. Again, he's had the last word. But what was it, exactly?

As soon as I leave the café to cross the wide street and walk up rue Bonaparte back to Hannah's hotel, I know that we can't do this: we can't all three sit in a restaurant and, as Alexandre has stipulated, talk about other things. Hannah's request, Hannah's confession, Hannah's death fill all the space available, whether we like it or not. I'll call him, tell him no: what you are asking is impossible, even in the context of French manners and behavior. Hannah and I are not French, we can't do this, we aren't even going to pretend. In her room, she's still lying on the bed and I realize I haven't been away long in real time. I've knocked, she's called out, it's open.

I tell her, "He has to think about it, he says, and he wanted us all to have dinner together in some restaurant and talk about something else."

She sits up, her hair on end, her legs in their creased black pants, ankles pale and swollen. "Oh well," she says, "if he can't, he can't. I'm over asking people to do more than they feel capable of. Let's just accept the fallibility, all round, of the male gender. He probably feels squeamish, they all do."

"Well, I'll call him, shall I? Tell him we can't make it? Dinner, I mean."

"But, Claude, don't you want to? I don't mind, really. I can probably have something sent up."

I say, truthfully, "I'd rather be with you. I could go out and bring us in some dinner, if you'd like."

"Oh, I don't eat a lot these days. But I tell you what, I'd love some good bread, some butter, some ham—you know, like the old sandwiches, *jambon-beurre?* And probably some more champagne. I might as well enjoy it while I can."

"It shall be done." Relieved to have something simple to do, I set out again to walk what seems like miles to find a bread shop on the rue du Cherche-Midi where they have *pain Poilâne,* and then to a grocery on rue d'Assas where there is both ham and butter; and of course, there are innumerable wine shops in the *quartier* that sell champagne in real-sized bottles. At the corner of rue d'Assas and rue de Rennes, I call Alexandre and leave a message. He must be still in his meeting. "Alex, she doesn't want to come out. I'm buying a picnic for us to eat in the room." Then I carry back my booty and hide my grocery bags as I go up in the elevator to Hannah's room. She's up, and sitting at the table, her hair brushed, lipstick renewed.

"Claude, if you could but imagine, how wonderful it feels when someone just does exactly what I want, without thinking up something completely different that would do me far more good. You are an angel. Did you have to walk miles?"

"Yes, there isn't much actual food around here, these days. But look, we have a real Widow this time, and she's chilled."

"What would I do without you?" It's rhetorical, but I think—you have never really had to.

"Did you call Alex?"

"I left a message. I said we weren't going. He was in a meeting with a client."

"Who would have thought that scruffy kid would have become a lawyer? Wasn't he going to do something arty, when we met him?"

"Yes, but he realized doing something arty would never make him any money. He likes money, Alexandre. Or, the things money can buy. And let's not forget he has expensive divorces."

"Are you still in love with him?"

I pull the gold foil off the top of the bottle and begin to twist the cork gently so that it will be eased out, not forced, and the champagne will flow as it is supposed to. I hesitate to tell her, but I do. It matters to try to be truthful with each other now, whatever Alexandre says about the relativity of truth. "I don't think so. But we are close. We are very good friends, but I can't feel the way I used to, no. I just realized it today."

"Today! Only today? Because of what I told you? Oh, Claude."

"No, not really. You've just told me what I've always half known, in a way. You know, he and I have been lovers for years, on and off. Of course I knew he had other women, I just didn't know one of them was you."

She dips her head away from me.

I say, "It's more that he's gone too far away. At least, I think so."

"Far away?"

"Into his life, his pursuits, being a lawyer, his compli-cated divorces—all that."

Considering this, she sits up, her glass held out. I think, the champagne is a good idea: we are celebrating, not yet mourning. We are together in these simple acts: opening a bottle, cutting good bread.

"Was it to do with what I've asked you both?"

"Bring your glass closer. There. Ah, lovely. No, it wasn't just that: it was seeing each other out of the bedroom. Meta-phorically speaking. If you can stay in the bedroom for more than forty years, that's something, I know. But now, we're out of it. I can't explain more. And, your plan, yes, I suppose so. But it needed to happen."

Once, somebody said to me, you have to prefer reality, whatever it gives you, and I recognize now that this is and will always be true. Reality is this. It is these four walls, and Hannah and me together, and this evening's swallows falling down in the gap between the buildings, dusk coming in at last, and Alexandre sitting in a restaurant without us. It is the age we are, and the world we live in.

Then I think—my glass halfway to my mouth, the little

bubbles sparking at the rim—she wanted to separate us; she wanted this, perhaps even without knowing it. All these years later, she wanted all my allegiance for herself. Now, all I can do is be with her, and accept what comes. Her death preempts everything. This is her end game, it has to be.

My cell phone rings. I'm halfway through a mouthful of ham and bread but I grope for it and listen. It's Alexandre. "Sorry you couldn't make dinner," he says. "But of course, I understand. Tell her—that I will do all I can to support her."

Still so ambiguous. "You'll come with us, then?"

"When the time comes, yes. I'll try. If that is still what she wants."

I make a one-thumb-up sign to Hannah and nod to her. It's easy to forget that it's her death we're talking about: it feels more as if he's simply joining us on some risky adventure.

"Thank you," I say. "We'll talk later."

Once I am off the phone, Hannah and I smile at each other. Alexandre will always need to believe that he has arrived at his decisions alone.

She says, "Well, it only took him an hour."

"And eating dinner alone."

She chuckles. Right now we are two, against his one. It's always like this with three; and can shift in a second. All this feels familiar, if dangerous.

"Claude, would you stay here with me for a while?" she asks me, "That is, if you haven't anything better to do? I'm going back to England tomorrow, I've a ticket on Eurostar, so this is the last time we'll be together, until—whenever it is."

"Of course," I say, and stretch out beside her on the vast white-quilted bed this hotel has provided. "Do you know when it will be, by any chance?"

"I think some time next year. It rather depends how this horrible thing progresses. I also need to know when you'll be free."

"I'm nearly retired." I tell her. "Two more semesters. Next year can be all yours."

"Good. That's settled, then." She stretches her legs, wiggles her toes as if to test that she still can. Then, "Are you involved in making any more films? I never even asked you what you're doing, I'm sorry. Illness tends to make one so self-absorbed."

I tell her it seems as if I've already retired from filmmaking, though they have sent me off each year to conferences, the Society for Cinema Studies; I even gave a paper once. And they do even show my short films from time to time. "I suppose I have a small reputation in that world, at least."

"You sound disappointed."

"Well, nothing is quite what we imagined it would be, is it? But I do miss being involved in it, with other people, being in that sort of hum of activity, making something together."

"You wanted it so much, I remember."

"Yes, but I had no idea what it really was or what it demanded. Not until I jumped in with both feet. You know, success isn't what we thought—it's more evasive, it's less spectacular. It's not solitary. It's more like a sort of love affair. I feel it when I catch myself watching, say, the Wallace Stevens film, or *Susana*. I think *Susana* is my favorite."

"Hmm. You shouldn't stop, Claude. You've still got loads of time."

That she says this to me now matters more than it might have in different—normal—circumstances. "Any more in that bottle? There's no reason not to get rat-arsed now, is there?"

I pour the last of the champagne. "To you," she insists.

I say, "To us."

Outside, the sky darkens after the late sunset. Swallows swoop once again between buildings. Noise comes up from the street: there's a siren wailing far off on the boulevard. Life goes on, Paris goes on, in spite of terrorist attacks and soldiers strolling the streets with machine guns, in spite of the turmoil that we hear about daily: with all its flaws and disappointments and the messes we make, it's still a lovely world. And all the contradictions we have been through are true, and yet there is something—something—that may be as brief as four notes of a silly song, that links us and always will. Her glance of complicity as she raises her glass to me. Her raised eyebrow, as I answer only, "Perhaps."

Before I leave, she says, "Claude, you know that feeling we had at the end of the summer holidays, that term was going to start and we were going to be sent back and there was absolutely nothing we could do to change that? Well, I feel like that now. I want the holidays, but not the going back. I can choose now. I'm not at anyone else's command."

Running away, someone has said, or written, is a prelude to suicide. True or false? Hannah was always an escaper. I wanted to run away, but never enough. I thought of outcomes. I knew I'd be sent back.

"School," she says, "it was bad, wasn't it?"

"Hmm. Maybe it wasn't as bad as all that," I say. "We seem to have turned out all right."

"Have we? How do you tell? But Claude, no, it was that bad. It was cruel."

I put the empty champagne bottle beside the wastebasket, I lay a hand on her outstretched leg. "Yes, you are right. It was."

"I'm going back home tomorrow," she says. "I'll wait for Phil there. I'll tell him. It's not going to be easy, but I will. Then, can I call you? Where will you be?"

I give her my cell phone number, to avoid having to say where I will be: my ticket to the US has not yet been changed. Will I stay on in Paris? I don't yet know.

"Tell me, what was the best moment of your life, the one you'll always remember?"

"I think—the best time of my adult life was when I went all the way to Sundance, to the film festival, you know it's out near Salt Lake City, with mountains all around it? I took my film *Susana* there, and Robert Redford asked all the directors to his house. That was amazing. But the best of all was seeing it screened there. Sitting in the dark with all those other film people—everyone there is obsessed with film—and seeing my film with them."

"So, it was worth it?"

"It?"

"Your going to America. Your pursuit of your dream."

"Yes. There were very hard times, but I was doing what I wanted, what I had to do. And you?"

"I don't have an actual scene, or moment. I never wanted to make anything that much. Maybe I've missed out on something important. But you know, those early days at the house in France, when we were building it. When the twins were little. Doing it together, Phil and me. That was a good time. It was what we needed, to do that together. Or when we brought our first book out. I've had a lot of good days, and very few hard ones, well, until now. Though nothing ever really lived up to those times we traveled together, the three of us—you know? It may sound pathetic, but there was something—some promise, something waiting just ahead of me—that I never really had."

I hug her for a long moment then, feeling her body frail and small in my arms. I stay with her till midnight, hug her goodnight, and then walk through still-warm streets to my hotel near Odéon, just down from the restaurant called Les Editeurs, where they are stacking chairs before closing. I need to be alone for at least the next few hours, so I don't call Alexandre—or anyone. The habit of telling people where one is gets tiring: I like to let myself into a hotel room and think, nobody knows where I am. Perhaps this is my own form of escape.

I think as I walk along the emptied street, that she has been envious of me—perhaps always—and that I have had something that she has not. It is not, was not, Alexandre, it was my passion for something, for film, the way it has allowed me to be single-minded, the way it has filled my life. But Alexandre stood in its place, that time, there for the taking. She wanted what I had: he was the nearest substitute.

In my room, I kick off my shoes, take off my clothes, lie face down on the bed in the welcoming cool of air conditioning. The curtains are drawn. A wrapped chocolate lies on my pillow. I get between the smooth cool sheets of this twenty-first-century hotel room that I will pay for with an American credit card, and sleep.

19.

In *"L'Avventura"*—the film I showed my students earlier this summer, the one I first saw with Hannah at the Arts Cinema in Cambridge—we first see Claudia as she sets off from her father's house to meet Anna and her lover, Sandro, to go to the island. She goes to the house where Anna and Sandro are making love. She has to wait for them. She wanders around the house. Claudia is blonde, she is Monica Vitti; Anna is brunette. Sandro is one of those handsome but essentially ordinary-looking slicked-down Italians. He has none of the pathos and wit of Mastroianni. Claudia has to wait some time, while Anna and Sandro are together in another room. Then they all set off to meet their other friends and get in the boat to go to the island, where Anna will disappear. On the island, Sandro gets more and more irritated by Anna, and complains to Claudia. Anna has become more demanding, even irrational, he says. They are obviously on the point of breaking up. Then suddenly, Anna is not there. She has disappeared. You turn a corner and the person walking just ahead of you is gone. They search the island, daylong and into the evening, in their pale Italian summer clothes, their espadrilles, their mid-twentieth-century haircuts. The boat waits. Nobody eats anything or even drinks any water, although the boat-owner's wife sits on the boat drinking coffee. The others roam across the island calling Anna's name; they interrogate an old peasant who lives there; they grow disenchanted, even bored, and gradually they begin to give up. Sandro is with Claudia; in searching—or pretending to search—for Anna, they have become close. You can pretend to be doing something while actually doing something quite else. They are in collusion; yes, they are relying now on not finding her. You, the audience, see him watching her, Claudia, closely. You see that they will have an affair. That they want to be together and alone. Without her.

This is the film that we all saw nearly fifty years ago. Anna and Claudia at one point borrow each other's clothes; are they trying to become each other? I asked my students about this. But girls are always trading clothes, they said. They exchange shirts. At one point they put on similar wigs. This is before the island. And I remember that in the Arts Cinema in Cambridge, where Hannah and I saw the film, people began to leave, flipping up their seats as they went with an angry bang, streams of cigarette smoke following them out of the cinema. We stayed, still mystified but unwilling to leave simply because nothing was happening, because there was no plot, because the searchers even seemed to be giving up the search and returning to the ordinary aspects of their lives; because we weren't used to the new cinema, in which mysteries were not solved, endings were left in the air, and you had to argue furiously with your friends afterwards about what was really going on. We stayed because we wanted to understand.

It was the era: the very edge of a welcome newness, a

mark of being hip, or with-it, or cool; yet it was what still annoyed us, because we didn't get it, really, we felt left out. Was there really a period between 1960 and about 1980 in which people came to accept that mysteries could exist without solutions? That life went on, carrying you with it, all endings out of sight? We who grew up at that time breathed in this idea; it entered us and never let us go.

I think of my class in Virginia, and how it creaked and shuffled around me that last afternoon like a ship beginning to break up. I heard the incipient wreckage begin, the dismissal, the scattering into the world; I would not have them for more than minutes now. Students are like nuts about to split open in the sun; you never know where and how far the seeds inside may shoot. Into another era, perhaps, in which nothing will be recognizable to them as they age; in which what matters, once again, is not the outcome but the procedure. It may come back to them, then. They may remember an old movie, black-and-white, on an old-fashioned screen in the afternoon, and a teacher who told them that life has no neat endings. That the mystery cannot be solved; more, that people do not even want to solve it.

In the late morning after a long sleep, I put on lipstick and go to meet Alexandre. We'll have lunch, on this last day in Paris before I leave. After that, who knows? I can no longer imagine us in a hotel bed together, after the conversation in the Café de Flore. Something has shifted. I'm about to find out.

We meet in a small bistro on a corner of boulevard Raspail, near where he works. This lets me know that lunch will probably be a short interlude between work hours; is what I feel relief? It's too crowded, but then everywhere is too crowded between noon and two around here. We push through, one after the other, to find a table. As always in Parisian restaurants, other people are so close that we can hear their conversations and they, ours, although we all pretend that this isn't so. There is a general unfolding of napkins and placing them on knees, a hovering of waiters, an opening of menus; all this after discreet two-cheek kisses that take place as the second arrival at a small round table greets the first, who half stands to allow this. Water jugs appear, and baskets of bread, and wine lists, and we are so caught up in all this that we only manage an amused glance at each other, eyebrows raised, as we settle at our table, I hooking my jacket across the back of a chair, he following me in doing the same—it's warm in here, but at the outside tables we wouldn't be able to hear each other for the traffic, and the car fumes these days are intense. Lunch in Paris. Lunch with my lover. How many of these couples are lovers, I wonder. Many of them are men, colleagues I think rather than lovers, but it's sometimes hard to tell.

Alexandre, settled, puts his elbows on the table, leans towards me. "*Bon*." It lets me know that we have arrived. We smile into each other's eyes, as we often do, he a little more questioning than usual, I giving back my acceptance. "So—how did you leave our friend?"

"All right, I think. I stayed till nearly midnight, then went back to my hotel, I just needed to sleep." His slight nod tells me that he has understood, isn't—or is trying not to be—hurt. "I'm sorry I didn't let you know sooner. It was one of those times, when, you know, you just have to be completely available."

"I understand." In here, he looks so much like other men of his age, it's almost hard to remember that he is the one I have been making love to all these years, that our lives are this much entwined. People of our age become invisible; but not, surely, to each other.

"Alex."

"Yes?"

"She says it's to be next year. That we'll all go, and you and I will come back."

"All right."

"You're really all right with it?"

"Listen, Claudie. I said I will do it if she still wants it, at the time. She may change her mind."

"Knowing Hannah, I very much doubt it."

"But there is always room for doubt."

The lawyer again, I think. I dare to place my hand on his, which is on the table. I just lay it there lightly, not so much a caress as a contact. Then the waiter appears, and asks us if we have decided, and I withdraw my hand and Alexandre asks, what is the *pièce du boucher* today, and the waiter says, *filet de boeuf*, and we both choose that, for simplicity, and the *terrine* first and a bottle—you can drink, yes?—a bottle of Côtes du Rhône. There, that's done. My hand is back in my lap. But he's seen: I want the connection, I'm claiming him, I'm not letting him be one more anonymous suited Frenchman in a restaurant full of them. We matter to each other, still.

"Yes," I say, "there is room for doubt, things can change, but we need to be very sure that we will be available." I'm saying, don't let me down; and he gets it, he reaches out and takes my other hand, the one playing with my wineglass, and holds it in his own warm, firm grip. We have the habit of touch; it still feels easy. Yet I know that I can't let it all go this easily, what he did with Hannah all those years ago, and the lie of omission that has kept it fresh and painful in a way that surprises me. It's as if their collusion has kept it fresh; even if they never saw each other, never talked of it, again. Does death really eliminate everything else, make it unimportant? Alexandre believes that the body—and in this case, the hand briefly, warmly gripping mine—can stand in for words, taking their place with a lack of accuracy that I sometimes find irritating, false, and then ultimately, compelling. Sex, touch, to remove the need for words; now, I find this too easy an assumption. He has used it, probably too often. I look at our joined hands, their nails, the hair on the back of his, there on the white tablecloth; then I withdraw mine.

He makes an almost exasperated face, blowing out his cheeks. "Let's eat our lunch in peace first, and then, I would love a long afternoon with you, it is after all your last day, and who knows where we will be when we meet again, at an airport in Switzerland, in some discreet suburb, in a clinic where everything smells of disinfectant, and death."

So, this is not just a quick lunch in between a morning and an afternoon of work. He's taking the afternoon off. But do I want him to? Where do we go from here? The wine comes, he tastes it, offers it to me. The plates of meat arrive, with their garnish of roasted vegetables. Everything begins to feel more normal, as it always seems to when you begin eating and drinking in France; as if Hannah is nowhere in the vicinity, and the clock may even be turned back, to a time in which we have not yet had cause to doubt.

The afternoon develops a little strangely. We walk after lunch along the boulevard in the direction of the Bon Marché department store, where there is a little park with green benches. Here we sit for a few minutes under the plane trees and I think, with a newly sharpened awareness, he has something more to tell me. In the past, we would have both smoked cigarettes; it would have given meaning to sitting here, it was possibly why people did it, to invest these small spaces in life with meaning. Today, we just sit and watch pigeons land, and a woman at a nearby bench reach into her bag to feed them. Men in white shirts go past, their ties loosened and jackets hooked over their shoulders in exactly the same way as Alexandre's. Some are smoking. There's a well-dressed young mother with a child with a doll's pram, preventing her daughter from picking flowers.

Alexandre says, "You still have your hotel room?"

"Yes, till tomorrow."

"You aren't seeing Anna again?" He always has difficulty with that H.

"No. She's going home and so am I."

"Can we go to your hotel?"

"If you like. Do you want to?"

In answer, he pulls me up off the bench, and his expression is hard to read: a decision made, one way or another. There was a question— is it now that we end this, or do we continue?—and he has answered it for himself; and because I haven't yet answered it, because I am slower than he is in nearly everything, I simply follow him once again, where he has decided to go.

As we approach my hotel, he takes my hand, "Let's try to be simple, Claudie. So much has happened, and will happen. But you and me, you know? It's simple, really. It's what I love."

All I can say, later, is that something is missing, and

something else has taken its place. Our attention is not on each other, nor on the intensely focused place in which we have always met.

We go up in the elevator to my floor, I push the card into the slot, the door opens, the bed has been made in my absence, my suitcase is already half packed, a scatter of bottles and lotions still stands on the glass shelf in the bathroom, where he goes in to pee as soon as we are inside. I am already half here, half not. Alexander begins undressing without more ado, shedding his ironed shirt, his pressed trousers, his black socks; he faces me in his underpants, a stocky man with gray hair on his chest and a slightly swelling stomach, tanned from a trip to Nice in May. "Please, Claudie. Take off your clothes. Or do you want me to?"

I shake my head and begin to undress. My heart is doing something strange in my chest, I am close to tears, I want him simply to take me in his arms and blot out Hannah and her plan, the anxiety of it, the intrusion: to take me back to where we were, before I knew what I know now. He sees this. He is sensitive. He pulls me close and begins to undress me to my underwear, and then he helps me out of my last remnants of what feels today like protection, and we lie down together once again. I want to forget, to go back, to find our way together, to be there in the place of total closeness that there are really no words for. But we don't. We can't. He knows it, as I do. He tries for the magic of touch, and fails. We are two people lying on a bed in the afternoon, the drawn curtains and closed shutters protecting us from too much light; and his skin is still his skin, he smells of himself, he touches me with all the subtlety he's learned over the years with women including myself; but we are marooned, cast up on a dry shore, separated. Tears slide down the sides of my face and fill my ears as I lie on my back.

"Claudie? Claudia?"

"It's no good. Don't let's go on trying."

"I know, I'm a useless man—but you?"

"Don't insult yourself, Alex."

"All right. You are right, we have been talking too much, too much involved in all this business with Hannah."

I think how she said it, "A fling with Alexandre," and how "affaire" in French is for business rather than infidelity, and I try to smile, but the tears keep on flowing: for us, for him and me on this last bed we will share, I think; and for the passage of time.

He props himself on one elbow, turns towards me, strokes a lock of hair back from my forehead, kisses me where the tears stain my cheeks. He can be very persuasive, and I have—oh, so many times—been lulled like this into silence and acquiescence. We're always, literally and figuratively, speaking his language. But the body doesn't lie.

"Claudie? What is the matter?"

I think: you know what is the matter. It's not just Hannah and you in some bed together forty years ago; no, it's that you have brought us into the real present, you and she, you have pricked the bubble, you have brought this—this—to an end.

I say, "We can't go on like this."

"I don't agree. I think what we have, Claudie, is eternal."

And if I don't say to him that I'm sick of everything being explained away like this, by invoking the eternal, the essential, the transformative power of sex, that it's an easy way out, a cheat—it's because I so want it to be true. Simple, he said. It has never been simple, except in the way of bodies that know what they want, and that now have let us down, or begun to tell a truth we don't want to hear.

He kisses me goodbye at the street corner with a warm pressure on each cheek, no more, and turns to go. I watch him walk away from me in his lawyer's uniform, his white head bobbing as he strides into the crowds going down towards Odéon, where he'll take the Métro back to work. If his heart is beating a little too fast or irregularly, if he's late for a client, if after all the early afternoon love-makings and snatched rendezvous of his life, he's feeling a little more strain than usual, if his blood pressure is high, I can't see it or know it, any more than I can see the inside of his head, where his busy brain will be on to the next thing, the next problem, the next chapter of his complicated life. I have never felt more alone.

So, what to do now? Being the age I am and not nineteen, or twenty-nine, or even thirty-nine, I don't burst into tears on my street corner; I don't go into the nearest church and light a candle; I don't reach for the nearest drink. I examine my options. Age does at least do this for one: no more histrionics now, nor leaping into impulsive activity as a way out of self-pity. At least, this is what I tell myself on this afternoon in Paris when Alexandre has gone back to work and I am alone again and know that we may never again be lovers; we will only meet again to help Hannah die, for that is our role now.

You can't mix sex and death: they are two opposites. One cancels out the other, I think, always will. You have to choose which one will get your attention. You have to accept one ending—not the happy one, maybe, that will not be possible, but the one that fits.

20.

Antonioni's women who walk alone, swaying on heels, along an empty street. Fellini's dancing crowds, the linked hands, the processions. Truffaut's close-ups: a child's face. Godard's car on a road that is all perspective. Bergman's silent couples. I have staked my life on images, these images, and many more, since Hopalong Cassidy was William Boyd galloping through a canyon. The peculiar excitement of film: that you can see in, you can see through.

Alexandre is right, I have been running the movie through my head. I see her leave, on an early train to London. A note on the kitchen table for him where a stack of old bills is skewered and he will see it as soon as he comes through that door for lunch. (There was nothing unusual about this, really; she often went to London for the day, or overnight; sometimes to stay with her friend Penny in Fulham, sometimes to see a writer who might have work for the Press, sometimes to shop; or to do all three. He wouldn't worry. This time, it was for a long weekend in Paris, to meet a young writer who had sent them a manuscript about his family home in Brittany;

but it was also time to be on her own, time to get out of the village, time—she wouldn't admit this to him—to be invisible, out of reach.)

It's 1979. She's packed a small bag, and taken her passport. She already has tickets. It's a cold spring, light glassy across the fields as she takes a taxi to the station (not to bother him, she explained, not to take up his time by asking him to drive her). The trees are bare, still black, but if you look closely, there are buds. Unde the big oak at the corner of their garden, primroses; and the snowdrops already plentiful, and crocuses poking up their heads.

(She had become, in the years of their marriage, the years of their living in the country, a gardener, a tiller of the earth. A planter of bulbs that hid in the dark earth till it was time to put out a green shoot. She had also become a secret-holder, if not quite a liar. How this had come about, she wasn't sure; it had begun as a necessary withholding: he loved her too much, said so too often, held her too close with the strings of both affection and need. This trip was to be an experiment, performed in secret. It was also a quite legitimate business trip, for the Green Ivy Press. She needed something to be just hers; she needed a space, or a time, or a mixture of the two; a little slice of life, a sliver, a shred.)

She pays the taxi and walks into the station to wait for the Cambridge train. You can see her walking a little more buoyantly, an excitement in her step, her body. You watch her move, from behind. (This journey was all hers; she trusted that she'd see nobody she knew at the local station and nobody on the platform in Cambridge, nobody on the London train. Anonymity was what she longed for now, even if it wasn't strictly necessary; she had her alibi.) She wears black trousers and a long warm jacket, and she has a hat pulled down over her ears, and gloves. The slow train moves through flat land-scape, inland, away from the east coast, across the black slabs of fen, past the cut waterways and sedge, towards the yellow brick of town, the towers of Ely Cathedral dimly seen, like a lighthouse across the marshy distance, then Cambridge, its ugly outskirts, its yellow brick, its rather dingy station. (Here she changes trains, to get the faster train to London.)

She's at Heathrow, late morning, in time for her Paris flight. It's in the last century, 1979, when she is in her early thirties. You can tell from the clothes, the scenery. (People talked about a tunnel beneath the Channel, a shortcut to France, but this seemed unlikely, if not crazy. The only short cut was flight: a brief swoop up, another brief swoop down, with hardly time for the tray tables to be set up and a drink placed on them, in between. The English Channel a wrin-kled stretch, gray-blue, curling at the edges against a gray-green stretch of land that was northern France. England left behind. Girt by a silver sea, which never was exactly silver, was it? This happy land—how Shakespeare had glorified it for them, once and for all, and how happy one always was to lift up above it, and leave.)

She looks out of her porthole window, down. Close-up, and then out. The land turns to cloud, then is mistily visi-ble, then rushes up. A thud of wheels, a tremor like earth-quake, a sudden braking, and that is it. Now there was only the journey into the center of the city; she'd get a taxi, treat-ing herself, wanting to look out of the window and take it all in as they arrived, wanting the river and the bridges, the crowded streets, even the traffic of midday rush hour, rather than the dark underground clatter of the metro. (Of course, when they'd come here when they were young, she and her friend Claudia, they had never had money; they had arrived on the packed train at Saint-Lazare and taken the grungy smoky Métro of the time to wherever they were going, even skipping past barriers without tickets, chancing it all the way, running when they saw an official or, worse, a cop. She had money now. It was one of the good things about the settled life, the business, Phil's and her hard work, the daily assiduousness of it all.)

From the back seat of a cab, she watches as Paris comes to meet her, the boulevards branching like opening arms, street names, cafés she might once have been to, and at last the bridges across the river, the crossing to the Left Bank, Notre-Dame, the streets smaller and narrower, the little park, the tree-shadow, the cobbles, the dark-green water fountains and benches; life going on here as it always had, although she has been away so long.

The bookshop: Shakespeare and Company, set back a little from the street. She pays the cab and walks over cobbles. Notre-Dame begins its long tolling bell: eleven o'clock. She waits. The young writer is late. She looks at her watch, waits outside because the shop is crammed with young Americans. Then she sees him. Alexandre? Unbelievable, it's really you! Yes, it's really me. But what are you doing here? She gestures towards the shop doorway, where a young man hesitantly comes forward. Can you wait? This is too extraordinary. Can we have lunch? Yes, of course. I'll wait. Take your time. I'll have a coffee. Hannah, I can't believe you are here. What a coincidence. Yes, what a coincidence. We must celebrate it, don't you think?

He is waiting for her at the café next to the bookstore; sitting outside in spite of the cold, he is wearing a dark overcoat and jeans and a knotted scarf; traffic blurs the space between them as she comes towards him, there are the crowds of young

Americans, she is saying goodbye, shaking a young man's hand, he doesn't move to greet her until she's finished and is stepping towards him, carrying her bag; then he gets up almost lazily and comes towards her. (All this so far has been rapid, almost without words. You know from the images what is going on, what has to happen next.)

She sees, we see her notice, he is not much changed. Same dark fall of hair, a new moustache in the current fashion, his face pale after the winter, and his clothes, winter clothes; it was always summer back then.

"Anna." The way he always leaves the H out of her name; it's hard for him to say it. (It is the first word you hear spoken. She has been traveling towards this.)

She shivers, approaching him. (You see it is not from cold. A cold spring. Breeding lilacs out of the cold land. She couldn't help it, the words always came, even if she tried to ignore them; out of the books that had brought her somehow to this place, the books that had saved her when she was young. Shakespeare, Eliot, Hardy, Lawrence, they moved her still, moved inside her, made her peripheries. But you don't see this; it is in her, it is how she is.)

"Bonjour, Alex." He kisses her quite formally, on both cheeks. (But you see him linger just a second.) The warmth of his cheek in the cold.

"So, you came to meet a writer? You are a publisher now?"

"Yes, I just met him. We made a date for tomorrow, to talk for longer." (It was true. It was her official reason, if asked. She had something about her, subtle, like a spy.)

"Shall we go? Do you want to drink something? Or, just have lunch?"

He leaves a few coins beside his empty coffee cup. She shakes her head. "Lunch would be good. I left early." He stands up to leave with her. His hand at the small of her back as if he already owned her, as if he already knew. (And all that time behind them, flowing, inscrutable like the river; in which what could have happened had not happened, or at least, not to her. But this, of course, you do not see.)

You look the same, you've hardly changed, how long is it, what an extraordinary thing, I can't believe it, all these years, I like the moustache . . .

"You're married now?"

"Yes. And you?"

"Yes. I married another lawyer, she was in my year at the Sorbonne. It's complicated." (She doesn't ask him more, as they turn the corner of the street. But you see her expression.)

"And, do you have children?" he asks her.

"No. We've tried. Nothing happened. It's got rather boring, trying. Do you?"

"We have a little boy. That makes it harder. But he is lovely. His name is Dominique."

(She thought that was a girl's name. Perhaps it could be a boy's too. You see her think this.)

They have crossed two bridges. They are arriving at the Île Saint-Louis now. A musician playing, a scatter of people listening. The far-down water, its glitter on a cold day: the trees bare still, leaning. Perhaps a barge passing, serious river traffic, the emphasis that this is a working city.

"He's two. But already he notices, I'm sure, that his mother and I—but, I don't want to talk about all that. Here we are, it's a place I quite often eat at, but it's changed hands since you were last here, you and Claudia. How is Claudia?"

(She doesn't say, "Surely you know? Surely you are in touch with her?")

"Oh, fine, I think. She has a new job, she's working for a film director, in California."

"So, she is making films?"

"Not her own, yet. But she will. She did a postgraduate degree in film, in Los Angeles."

"And you, Anna?"

"I'm fine. Well, I'm okay. And the business is doing well these days." She says nothing about her own marriage, and he doesn't ask

"Hmm." Then, "Here we are. This will do, I hope? It's not pretentious, but neither is it expensive, and the *plat du jour* is usually good."

They go in. They sit down. The waiter comes. The menu. The carafe of water. The wine. (You have seen this all before, in how many other films?) They look at each other across a little table. They raise glasses to the extraordinary chance of their meeting.

I'm there with them, close as the waiter, as I lean in, to listen. Every filmmaker is a kind of voyeur, after all.

In a good film you wouldn't have to say what they said, you could just watch the hands rise to take menus, the whole pantomime begin and end, the words exchanged across the table indistinct and vague; a decision could be made, wordless, incontrovertible, and they would get up again maybe even without eating, leaving the wineglasses half full and the table in disarray and the waiter surprised and irritated, lifting his hands to see them go, with a "*ça, alors*" in his stance; and the door to the street opening again to let them out, and away. You would add in the sound afterwards: a chink of glass, a chair scraped against a bare floor, a door opening and closing.

Then you could see them from behind, watch them walk

down the street together, arm firmly in arm, to their next destination, the hotel he may already have in mind; or you could be disturbed, uprooted in your assumptions, and see them part out there on the pavement, with the traffic passing, agitated words spoken that you cannot hear, and everything to suggest the impermanence, the transience, of life. You could end it there. Cut. FIN.

I could make this film, as I have made it in my mind, and give it the ending I choose. I could reclaim the story, take charge of it as the Anouk Aimée character does in *A Man and a Woman,* coming back twenty years later as a filmmaker, in charge of the action, to the same beach with the same man where she films their story. But I already know, I can't. My directing days are past, and anyway, this is not my story, not anymore. It's too late. Hannah's departure to Zurich, her impending death, have taken up all the room there is; to forget this would be to turn from reality into an idle dream.

I walk away, my vision blurred by tears, heading for the Pont Neuf and the statue of Henri IV on his horse, just to walk, just to work this sadness through my system. At Vert Galant, Hannah and I used to sit with our baguettes and Vache Qui Rit cheese in its round box and our bottle of rough red vin ordinaire, and watch the willow trail its branches in the water, and the boats and barges pass. I see us there as I pass, talking about our futures, our successes, but I don't, can't go down. The cobbles are the same, the green benches, the river flow. Only the trees have grown. A couple, boy and girl, sit where we once sat, their picnic set aside, kissing. Everywhere you go in Paris, people are kissing. It's a city famous for it; it invites it, even. I remember sitting in a café on Place Dauphine with Alexandre, who told me then that somebody, some writer, was it Aragon, had named it *"le sexe de Paris"* and I remember laughing, and his hand on my knee, and a whole afternoon before us in some bed we'd rent, and life in all its wonderful complexity ours to enjoy.

What will happen if I just sit still—all afternoon, if need be, and into the coming night—and let go of it all? If I forget plans and tickets and rendezvous and work and become simply a woman on a bench, letting the whole insubstantial pageant pass me by? I think of Hannah and her Shakespearean quotations, she who first quoted him to me on the banks of the Cam; I think of my images of her, the ones I have assembled over a lifetime: the latest being the woman drinking champagne with her shoes off, on the bed in a Paris hotel. We keep these images of each other; how many of them are invented, misremembered, wrongly juxtaposed? It seems not to matter, when you are telling the story. Yet in between the shared memories we have of each other, the other person is always off living her own life, out of sight.

I sit on my bench, let time pass, let clouds gather and suggest rain and move away again, reflected in the water, and the light change on the buildings opposite, and the dark river run. In fact, I don't let any of these things happen, because they happen anyway, with me or without me; but I notice them. I'm still a part of this moving, shifting world; I'm here in the heart (or sex) of Paris, and I'm alive while millions of my exact contemporaries are not. I am not the woman sitting empty-handed on the beach in Greece, where she has been washed up; even if at times she seems to have become a part of me. I am not Hannah, who will soon be leaving it all behind.

PART IV

21.

She was clear about it, what she wanted; we all saw and felt it, her inexorable clarity. Philip, astonishing us all, came on board without protest, because as he said, he loved her enough to let her go. I—well, I was still in thrall to the old Hannah, the adventurer who would do as she wanted whether or not I was with her—and whom I had decided to be with to the end. I looked up her illness on the Internet—of course I did, this is what you have to do now with your own symptoms or another's. Google has the monopoly these days on all our hopes and fears. What did I want to find? Details, medical terminology, a philosophical reason to go with her, in case the emotional one was not enough? I found it, and presumably the others had too. As have Phil's and Hannah's children. You can't dispute, or forget what you find in the medical facts that are now available to us all.

I read as many of the details as I can bear.

I read about Stephen Hawking. I read about MRI tests to rule out other diseases. I read about drugs. I read about stem cell research, genetic research, chemical research. I read about Jean-Martin Charcot, who discovered the disease in 1869. I read about Lou Gehrig. I read what the Mayo Clinic said—there is no cure (again) and eventually the disease is fatal. Then I think that I have read enough.

I fly to England as soon as I can, during the October break. I land at Heathrow and cross London to take the train from King's Cross. The Cambridge, then the Ipswich train. At the station, a trained hawk swoops across the platforms above our heads to land above the board announcing train departures and then to fly back to its handler, who wears a falconry glove and settles it for a minute back on his wrist before letting it loose again. The passengers thronging below it look up to watch; I think, this is the new England, someone has thought of using a hawk to control pigeons. The great bird sails above our heads, scouring the grimy air: its cruel beak, its claws, its dangling accouterments, and I watch its progress, its exact homing.

All the way up through East Anglia I look out on country-side that's already turning brown and gold with autumn—no, not fall, it's different here. I feel the pull of nostalgia, that you can feel only for the country you were born in. I have been gone so long. The land lies low under the sky. Dusk comes early. Everything happens more slowly than in North America. The lights in houses twinkle, as if even electricity is used differently. A bloom settles on roofs, on fields, like the bloom on a plum. You feel the sea at the edge of things, coming nearer.

He is there to meet me again—Philip in his greeting mode, shy, heartfelt, with a one-armed hug pulling me to his side, his muttered, "Wonderful to see you, so glad you've come." Once again, I am made welcome, because needed. Once again, I am the oldest friend. We drive east towards their house that has always felt to me like a last outpost, beyond the village even, with its open aspect to the wide low salty flood fields and the long shingle of beaches, within the sound of the sea. Or do we imagine the sound of the sea, is it the grind of stones, the endless battering of them against each other, as if matter is being ground down day and night? He drives, and I ask him, once again, how is she, how are you, how are things going?

"It's not easy. But she's determined."

"Have you told the children?"

"She didn't want to. But yes, of course. I told her it was essential."

I hear a new firmness to his tone; he has had to assume responsibility, even contradict her. I look at his profile as he drives, and see the bone structure, the nose, the lifted chin, the proud—or is it shortsighted?—stare ahead down the road we are on. Trees on both sides of us, then the land opens and empties as we drive towards the coast. A pheasant scoots across the road with its whirring croak, vanishes into low undergrowth.

"I can't wait to see her."

"I'm afraid you'll see a difference. She's weaker. Physically, I mean. We have a nurse coming in."

"So, it's to be soon, you think?"

"Not sure. She hasn't fixed the date yet. She wants to be here for her birthday, in April. Maybe after that."

"I'm sorry I can only stay for such a short time. Still have to work—but after next spring I'll be free.

"It'll make a difference, Claude, that's the point. She is so looking forward to seeing you."

The white road going east narrows and we come into the village, past low houses with the lights coming on under the blotted silhouettes of big trees, sycamore and ash. His house is the last one. I remember the walnut tree at the gate. As he turns the car into the drive, I think: I am connected to these people as I am to no one else. They are my family. And yes, there she is in the lighted kitchen, sitting at the table, her face bright with pleasure at seeing me, and as I bend to hug her, we are both in tears.

"Oh, Claude. Coming all this way to find me."

"It's only a hop across the pond."

"Still. You're working."

"Only a few weeks more, after this. I've a light load, until April. Half the work and half the pay. Then, I'm free!"

"I can't tell you—oh, it's good to see you."

Her voice is deeper, then whispery at times, and her words come more slowly, as if she's searching for them. I see her left arm limp at her side. A stick, propped against the table edge. Her blonde hair is short and closer to white.

"Go on, Phil, take her to her room. You must be flaked out, Claude, aren't you? Then come down and we'll have a drink and talk, until whoever's energy gives out first."

I follow Phil, who carries my small bag upstairs, the creaking stairs I remember, the turn on the landing, the carpeted corridor, yes, I remember, the bathroom, and at the end of the passage, the guest bedroom. It's a cottage, their house, built in flint and brick with low ceilings, uneven floors. I'm home, I think. This is as close to home as I'll ever get, after my years of exile. Yet I had to leave to discover it, as I had to leave her.

When I come downstairs, I notice the photographs on the landing and windowsills: the twins as children, laughing. The wedding. The two of them, their best man—Who was he? Someone from Cambridge?—and myself in my Biba dress and hat, bought hastily in London for the occasion as in

California at that time I had no real clothes. A lineup, facing the future with such insouciance, raising our glasses to it all.

She sips from a cup, using a straw. "Maybe this makes it more alcoholic, who knows?"

She has her food pureed. "Kind of boring, but babies seem to like it." I think of her pleasure in the ham sandwiches we made, only a few months ago.

Phil helps her to bed, in what used to be the TV room, where she has her favorite painting, a seascape, above her bed, and her books around her.

We hug, long and heartfelt. She says, "I'm hoping for next spring, see. Thought I'd see in one more birthday. Will you come?"

"Of course, if I can get away." I remember, of course I do, her April birthday, as she remembers mine, in September. She will be sixty-nine.

Alone in my room that evening, I look out towards the east, towards what seems like the permanent pale glow over the sea, to where the land ends, to where we saw it when we were children, just along this same coast where the drowned villages are deep underwater and people used to say they heard the bells of churches long sunk beneath the sea. Then I draw the curtains, undress and fall on the bed, and stretch my limbs out to its corners. I curl and uncurl my toes, feel all my extremities, am aware of the warmth between my legs, in my stomach. I can feel pleasure in my whole body, just in its existence—in spite of the fatigue of travel, maybe because of it. It's mine, all mine. A vast quiet darkness gathers at the back of my eyes as they close.

* * *

In the morning, breakfast is laid out for me at the kitchen table and Phil is already busy in his office, with his secretary who comes in the mornings. The press is expanding, just when he had thought of retiring, he has told me. He's taking on some essays and fiction, as well as the environmental writing that's popular now. There's a young Scottish writer, he says, who walks about Scotland and has written a marvelous book, doing very well.

He comes in, perches at the table beside me, a half-drunk cup of coffee in one hand. "Sleep well?"

"I hardly moved."

"I'm glad to have a minute. Stephanie will answer the phone. Hannah's still asleep after all the excitement of your arrival. The nurse will be here at ten." Like this he describes his household, how he has organized it around this changing, transforming being that is Hannah.

I say, "I did want to ask you. How it's been. You seem to be managing magnificently, Phil, but it must have been hard."

He pushes the toast rack towards me. "Boiled egg? I've put the coffee on." Then, "Well, it's not been easy, I can tell you. She doesn't want me to tell anyone, so I've had to tell a few lies, gloss things over, you know, hint that it might be Parkinson's, but we aren't sure. No firm diagnosis yet. Luckily, out here we don't see that many people. The kids come, but they're busy, and it's a trek to get here. She wants to stay at home until it's the moment to go."

"But you. When did she tell you?"

"When we both got home, in the summer. What a different time. I can't believe it's only been months. I was furious and very upset, and at first I couldn't accept it. Even the way she'd treated us all by disappearing seemed almost trivial beside her making that decision alone. I felt excluded, yes, and as if she didn't trust me or even particularly care how I felt. It seemed as if our marriage counted for nothing. Then I did begin to understand, that it is the sort of thing you have to decide alone. Yes, she was right, I would have tried to dissuade her. Part of me still wants to. Part of me still wants to save her. But I can't."

The coffeepot starts to hiss and he gets up to fetch it. The room is quiet, otherwise, and everything feels very normal.

"Claude, you know, it's against everything I believe in, as far as I believe, but it's also her life. She isn't me. And I've been hers, as you know, from the very beginning, when we first met in Cambridge. I've had to accept that all I can do is support her as best I can."

I see his hand tremble above my coffee cup. "I think that's admirable."

"Admirable or not, I haven't any other choice."

"And, the kids? I mean, they aren't kids, of course, but how did they take it?"

"Disbelief, shock, anger. You can imagine. Piers was the worst, oddly enough. I think Melissa took her mother's side almost at once, she just cried a lot. But Piers—he wanted me to prevent her, he kept looking up more possible cures on the Internet, and going on about Stephen Hawking. I shut him up by just telling him it is her life, and he must grow up and accept it. He went away in a huff, but he got it. Since then—well, they've both been good, they call often to talk, but they aren't here. Actually, it's a relief that they aren't here."

"Really? You don't feel too alone?"

"I'm with her." He smiles. "How could I feel alone? The kids came later. We two were there from the beginning. Just us. It's how I like it."

"It's gone faster than we'd thought, hasn't it?"

"Yes. Time seems to be rushing, suddenly. It's why I have to treasure every minute."

I sip my coffee and accept the egg he hands me, damp patches drying on it fast, and set it in my eggcup. Everything has to seem as normal as possible, he has decided. He's right, I think; this framework both soothes and protects us, and allows us the space we need in which to assimilate the rapid changes taking place.

Yet I have to ask him. "Phil, you know she asked Alexandre Dutot to come with us?"

"Yes, of course."

"And you're okay with that?"

He faces me: I've punctured the normality, the calm. But he looks serene—only a slight tic, a vein at his temple. "Yes, I'm okay with it. It's what she wants. We're just doing what she wants now." Then he adds, not looking at me, "He's been in her life too. As of course have you. I've always known she was not entirely mine."

"Oh, Phil."

"Well, none of us belongs entirely to anyone, isn't that so?"

"You probably know too—he and I have been lovers for many years."

"Claude, I don't have to be protected anymore. Do you understand? You and he—whatever you do, it's your affair. Hannah—she's all I've got, and I soon won't have her. Nothing else matters any more. You see? I've got to the end of all that. Really. You don't have to look after me. Now, eat your breakfast."

Then his secretary, Stephanie, looks round the door to ask about an order, and he goes back to work. Life goes on, this is what he is showing me; his house is in order; he is not the panicked man of last summer, when he did not know where she was, but calm and even purposeful now that she is with him till the end.

I finish my breakfast and slip into Hannah's room, to be there when she wakes, before the nurse comes.

"Hannah? Han?"

"Oh, darling, it's you. How lovely. I thought I was dreaming. But you're really here."

"Yes, I'm really here."

"Now tell me." She reaches out a warm arm to pull me closer. "Have you heard from Alexandre? Is he still onboard?"

"We emailed a few times. Yes, I think so." I don't tell her that the emails have been short, even curt, and that I have not had one from him for at least a month.

"How are you, the two of you? You and Alexandre?"

"I don't know. I don't know that we are a two anymore."

"Not because of what I told you?"

"No. Because of—oh, the passage of time. Things change, they have to."

"Do they? I suppose so. It's sad, though. You've loved him for so long."

"Well, it seems that we're all on to a new stage."

She says, "Well, that's certainly true for me. Phil has been marvelous, all round. You can't imagine. What a brick."

I smile at her old-fashioned slang. "He's certainly that. Han, he's just told me he's okay about Alexandre coming."

"I told him the truth about everything. I had to. All the lies and inventions. He simply said, it's the past, it's over, we have to pay attention to now. Water under the bridge. Isn't it funny how that image has stuck around? I mean, water always looks as if it's not going anywhere, when it goes under bridges, it always looks the same."

"That was it?"

"Yes. He didn't want to know who it was. He was quite clear about that. Then when we talked recently, he said, nothing like that matters anymore. What we did when we were younger. He's remarkable, in his way, I really see that now."

"He's a good man."

She says, almost casually, "By the way. The twins. They are not Alexandre's, in case you wondered. But he somehow made it easier for me to go back to Phil that time. It's strange, isn't it, how things work out? He made me feel better, and I went home and got pregnant."

She has decided on her version. Phil has decided what matters for him. So has Alexandre. It's only me who is still thinking about that long-ago time when she slept with my lover. When she knew what he smelled like, when they were naked together for a first time. When she—but I can decide too, perhaps, that that one event, that small series of events that was Hannah and Alexandre, their nakedness, their closeness excluding me, holds no danger now.

"Isn't it strange, so much seems to depend on whether we think we're still the same person we were? We are still us, don't you think?" We look at each other. "The eyes don't change, anyway."

"No. But what they see does."

"I see you, Claude, I'd know you anywhere."

"And you. Coming here, I can see it. Yet you've changed so much."

"Not just for the worse?"

"You are more you. More complete."

"Shame, just as I'm about to fall apart." Then she says, shifting a little in the bed, holding out a hand to me, so that I take it, "But look, we have to talk about everything now, because next time maybe I won't be able to. Apparently this disease comes in two forms, one called bulbar, affecting speech, the other affecting limbs first. I seem to have got the limbs one. But in the end—well, it all goes pear-shaped. So we must make the most of the time."

"That's what Phil said. He seems so calm and serene compared with last summer."

"I told him about my plan," she says, "As soon as I got home from Paris. He was shocked, at first. Then he cried like a kid, and when he was done, he said, I want to be with you in whatever you're doing more than I want to make you stay. And then I cried like a kid too, and there we were. I'd really underestimated him, Claude. I thought he'd try to hold on to me, or make me feel bad about the children or something, that it would be too complicated, you know. But I was wrong. Oh, I've had to learn so much in the last little while. You wouldn't believe it."

I'm close to her on the bed, holding her hand that feels very thin, small bones knit frailly under skin. I feel its slight pressure on mine, as she squeezes back. After a moment I get up to pull back the curtains so that we can both see beyond the big walnut tree at the gate, the pure line of the land where it meets the sky. Just beyond that line, where the sun has risen and the sky is eggshell blue, the North Sea pounds and pounds at the shingle, cracking open stones, taking centuries to do it, grinding everything at last into fine sand.

She pulls me back. "I've something else I want to say."

"Oh?" I can't help the immediate feeling of alarm.

"No, nothing drastic. Silly. It's just, you must make your next film."

"What? But I've stopped."

"No, you mustn't. Retire; make another film. You know what it is, Claude."

"What do you mean?"

"Think about it," she says, "us, of course. When we were young."

"Really?"

"Don't say you haven't thought about it."

"Okay. I'll think about it. But it's hard to get funding, especially when you haven't done anything for years."

"Forget funding. I've left you some."

"Hannah, you mustn't. I don't want your money. What about Phil? The kids?"

"This was in a trust, from my grandmother. I had to use some of it for Zurich, but I've never touched the rest, I didn't have to. It should be enough to make at least a small film. What do you have to do, get a crew, find a studio? Well, do it. Don't you dare say no."

I sit on her bed and look straight at her: those gray eyes fiercely looking back into mine. "Thank you. It will be dedicated to you." Then tears fill my own eyes, and spill, and she pokes me, "You sentimental old thing, you," and we begin to laugh, because she wills it so.

22.

It's a cold early summer, hardly emerged from the chill of Northern European spring. Hannah and Phil have flown from England, I from the US. We find each other, as arranged, in a coffee shop in the arrivals lounge where they serve Illy coffee and tiny madeleines, as if Proust might drop by on his way to somewhere. I sip my good coffee and look at my two companions, who are sitting with me at a round table in this quiet, glossy version of an Italian coffee shop. It seems amazing that we have arrived and met. I glance at the people at the next table, the man in the wheelchair, with a woman who is helping him to sip from a straw, and the way his Adam's apple moves up and down, and a younger man, perhaps a son, who leans across towards the other two to speak in a low voice, almost a whisper. I don't catch the language, but wonder, are they going to the same place, for the same reason? Is every wheelchair traveler in this airport immediately suspected of being about to end his or her journey in death? You can't tell. And I think, nobody could tell about us, either. Hannah is not in a wheelchair as we sit here, although she used one to cross the miles of Heathrow to the waiting plane and was met with another at this end. She has slid on to the red-cushioned banquette, in order to be on a level with us. She has a stick, sometimes two. Her stick is an expensive-looking hardwood with a rubber tip, almost an accessory. ("Well, I'm not waiting till I'm too decrepit to get there on my own two feet.")

"Good coffee," she says, lifting her lidded cup with a shaking right hand, to drink it. ("I have to be able to drink the stuff myself, no good spilling it all down my front.") She's wearing a trouser suit of pale linen, a black sweater and a necklace of small gold links. Pink lipstick and some eyeliner and a pale foundation. She has bought some Chanel 19 at the Duty Free—"I want to go out smelling good"—and a small bottle of Laphroaig, her favorite whisky. Phil is wearing a dark jacket over pale trousers, a blue shirt, and a flowery tie, as if, packing, he decided that flowery was right after all for the occasion; who wants to look at navy blue, or gray with a thin stripe and be reminded of offices or, worse, funerals? His hair, what's left of it, is brushed back and so far has not started to fly around his head in strands and wisps, and his expression is of a man forbidden to think a single dark thought, and having a hard time with it. And, where is Alexandre?

We sit there, and wait for the Air France flight from Paris. Surely he remembers where we are to meet? Half an hour passes, then three-quarters. Phil says, "Claudia, perhaps you should go and ask?"

We've watched well-dressed French people stalking along with their little wheeled suitcases, until the crowd dwindles, and no more seem to be coming past from the Paris flight. I go to investigate. I haven't told them about my last email to him, which went unanswered. I try him on my cell phone; leave a message. I think: surely, he can't have let us down? What was our last communication, I try to remember; scroll through my old emails, till I find his name. Ambiguous, as usual. If he can get away, he says. If. I think, oh, damn you, now of all times, don't do this to us.

The doors are closing in front of me, the announcements on the board changing: Dusseldorf. He was not on the flight from Paris. There seems to be nobody to ask. I say to him in my mind, You must come. Please. Don't let us down now. I think—he's not coming. He's decided as a lawyer, not a friend. He's simply not up to it. We are not the people we were, the three students on the train, the way we have always remembered; that story is gone, has been deleted, he doesn't remember, doesn't care. He and I are finished; he is telling me this. I watch the doors close and the flight attendant walk away, through a blur of tears.

I go back to where Phil and Hannah are, and they look small and somehow cowed, he bending over her. "No luck?"

"Seems not." I think, Alex, I will never forgive you. You have ended something that was not yours to end: my belief in you.

"So, should we go on waiting?"

"I think we should go. He's got the address, if he comes late."

I look at Hannah. She gives a little shrug. Ah, well.

And then I see him, coming from a quite different direction, his wheeled bag at his heels like all the others, his free hand waving. He's walking fast, towards us. Back to us, I think, back to where he knows he should be. He is in designer jeans and a green linen jacket, as if he were on vacation, or as if this is all he has when he isn't wearing a lawyer's suit. His white hair is flattened, cut shorter than I've seen it. It suits him, makes him look younger; also, he seems to have lost weight. We have not had time alone together since that last afternoon in Paris when he walked away from me without a backward look.

I watch him now, coming closer, at each step more real. I think—there is this total opposition between absence and presence. Absence leaves you alone in an emptied world: presence fills the world up again, so that you can move on. So that you can live.

He says, seeing me, "What's the matter?" He reads me accurately, always.

"I thought you weren't coming. I watched everyone come off the Paris flight."

"Ah, I came on a different one—Swissair, it just got in. The Air France flight was full, they asked me if I could get on a slightly later one. But it was only minutes later. Claudie, why, you look strange?" He kisses me on both cheeks. I stand, tears in my eyes, taking him in. It was so nearly true that he did not come; but here he is. We have been reprieved, brought back from the brink.

Philip gets up. He and Philip shake hands. "Bonjour." It is a meeting of men: matter-of-fact, smiling, the way they have been taught.

"Bonjour." From Phil's face, I can't guess what he is feeling. I remember him in England: *nothing else matters now*. Alexandre, with his impeccable sense of the appropriate, is simply friendly and polite. He's unaware, Alexandre is, that we nearly gave up on him—or I did. Everything changes in a moment. Life, even now, rushes us on. Alexandre bends to kiss Hannah, one on each cheek. She gives him a little nod.

"Claude, come with me? I need to find the loo." Hannah and I leave the two men together. I go to help her into the disabled toilet in the Damen and wait for her.

"So, he came."

"Yes." What else can I say? The threesome she wanted, and the man she married: all here, for her.

She reaches to wash her hands at the basin. "The thing about Alexandre was, that you never could rely on him. I suppose that was what made him interesting. But look, here he is, reliable after all."

I don't want to comment. There were all those meetings, across time and space, when as if by a miracle he and I came together; like birds to a cliff-top, a cliff-top homing, exact. "How has everything been, since last year?"

"Good. No, of course not good, pretty terrible in most ways. But, good between me and Phil. He's kept the whole show on the road, the business, the house, my nursing arrangements, everything. He's calmed the kids down. He's lied to our friends and neighbors, as I didn't want the whole of England knowing, obviously. But anyway, here we are, and he's going to come home with you two afterwards. Claude, if you can be with him a bit, I'd really like that. Now, can you pass me some of that hand lotion, we might as well make the most of all the freebies, don't you think?"

I squirt lotion into her hands. We both smell of gardenias now. A woman comes in wearing huge dark glasses and carrying a tiny Gucci purse and Hannah and I glance at each other in the mirror and smile and raise our eyebrows.

"I feel like a conspirator," she murmurs.

"I always do, with you."

"You see," she says, "I didn't need to protect Phil, after all. I wanted it all to be very discreet, and it has been. It's brought us together, him and me, in a way I'd never imagined. A sort of daft honeymoon. Now, can you pass me my stick?"

I say, "I'm so glad. For you and Phil, I mean. But what do you think they'll be talking about out there?"

"Him and Alexandre? God knows. What do men talk about when we aren't there? The World Cup? Outer space? I've never been able to guess." Her gravelly voice, speaking slowly, even sounds quite sexy.

"You sound like Lauren Bacall. I'm sure someone must have told you that before."

"No one who isn't as old as us even knows who Lauren Bacall is anymore."

"You know, I thought Alexandre wasn't coming. I thought he'd panicked and dropped out."

"And you minded, that much?"

"I minded for you. I didn't want him to let you down."

"Ha. Claude, you should have seen your face when he showed up."

"I was feeling furious with him, on your account, and then there he was."

"So, you see? Everything has turned out all right, and they're even talking to each other like the civilized fellows they are. Thank God. Perhaps there's less testosterone around than there used to be. Now, let's go and join them. Do I look all right?"

We go back to meet them, our dates as I now think amusedly to myself, and they even get up slightly from their seats to welcome us back. Hannah waves them down again.

"No need for the regal treatment, boys. We're fine. So, when we've all finished our coffee, shall we be on our way?"

Alexandre takes my hand briefly and squeezes it in his own warm one as we leave the café, walking slowly behind Hannah in her wheelchair. I glance up at him, and he lets me know with a flicker of his eyes that he's there, for me as well as for her. I take a deep breath, adjust my stride to his. Phil is pushing Hannah along, and we come behind them, like bodyguards.

We leave the airport terminal, trailing our small bags that hint, I suppose, at the short time we are planning to stay here, and a taxi rolls up, and we all get in, and Phil gives the driver the address of the hotel, in a small town that is about an hour's drive away. The driver, a big blond man with hair short as wheat stubble, nods, no problem. He must have done this before. I watch the back of his neck, where sunburn ends in green polo shirt. As we give the address, I shake inwardly, as if guilty of some crime about to be discovered. It goes back, this feeling, to being with Hannah at school, about to break another law. I pull myself out of it by leaning forward to mutter in her ear, "What would Miss McKinley say?"

"Poor old dear's pushing up daisies by now," she says back over her shoulder in her new slow voice—she's in front with the driver, the rest of us are in the back with Alexandre sitting in the middle, his knees in their clean denim pressed together. "Or thistles and nettles, more likely. Actually, I hope she rots in hell."

"Hannah!" says Phil.

"Well, she wasn't nice to us. Claudia will tell you."

Alexandre asks the driver, in French, how far it is. Not so

far now, says the driver in English, only about fifteen minutes. Maybe a little more. We watch Swiss suburbs become countryside, and suburbs again. Phil looks out of the window, silent. He may be thinking that he shouldn't have corrected her. But it's what you do with the living, you react, you say what's in your mind. Alexandre starts asking him what he thinks Portugal's chances are against Germany in the Cup, and the two of them chat quietly in French, Phil's accent as clunky as ever, Alexandre knowing what his job is, to draw him out.

"Your French is quite good," he says, squashed up against Phil in the back of this speeding but silent car.

"Depends what I'm talking about," Phil says. "I can do football, and cars, and sometimes politics. Oh, and restaurants, of course." He sounds relieved.

"What do you think, is Britain going to leave Europe?"

Phil says, "I think it's a crazy idea. This bloody referendum, nobody can talk about anything else. But I don't think it will happen. I don't think anyone takes those clowns seriously."

Alexandre says, "Yes, it would be quite a mistake. Not good for any of us."

They have switched to English. The driver is listening to the radio in German. We are slowing into a small town now. I poke Alexandre with my elbow to tell him, good job, keep going, the referendum will keep his mind off what we are doing. I see how men use their familiar topics for covering up feelings, how they feed each other lines, spark off controversies, just to stop themselves from focusing on what is going on underneath. Today this seems to be an excellent idea. We women are always digging for what's underneath—feelings, truth, experience—and sometimes in life, as now, I don't want to do it, not at all. If we can see Hannah off while sticking to the World Cup, the British referendum on Europe, the coming US election—it will be Hillary, surely—or even if her anger at Miss McKinley can go on fueling her, so much the better.

"So, how was it?" I ask her as I help her settle into the room she will share with Philip for their last night together. He is downstairs in the bar with Alexandre, being plied with drink, I imagine, or more questions about British politics. "When you came here before and fixed it all up? You never told me."

"I went to see the doctor—no, not in a hospital, not even a clinic, it was a largish house, nearby, very comfy, sort of lived-in. With lots of bookshelves and books on them in leather bindings, in French and German. They were mostly on psychology and medicine, some on history, some poetry. I found Goethe, remember, we had to read him at school? I was just looking for that poem about the oranges in Italy, when he came in."

"Lemons, they were lemons. *Zitronen*."

"Oh, well, lemons. They didn't grow in Germany, either. Anyway, he offered me tea, said, I hope I never see you again."

"What?"

"I think he meant he hoped my diagnosis was wrong. I was shocked, because I thought for a minute he was refusing to do the deed. But no, he patted my shoulder, and said, I always hope that, because there is always, in this life, another chance, something we have not yet thought of. Then I went back to my hotel and had a stiff drink and watched Swiss TV."

"The doctor said that, about there always being another chance?"

"I think he wants to know that his patients will only use

him as a last resort. Anyway, I'd already paid my money, so I said, thanks, and goodbye. I probably won't see him again, because he can't be the only one, can he? I imagine they must have a team. Tomorrow it might well be someone else."

Tomorrow. She says it so lightly. I want to ask her, Hannah, are you sure? But I can't. Just as I could not at her wedding: are you sure this is what you want to do? We have sworn, all of us, not to do this, however hard it gets. If Philip can decide not to do it, so can I. I hang up her dressing gown and lay her nightdress on the bed and ask her, "What would you like to do tonight?"

"Oh, find a good restaurant, I think. I noticed an Italian place down the street, we could try that. And a good bottle or two. Don't they have some decent wines here? Let's ask the guys if they are up for it, when you've finished fussing with my clothes. Claude, I'm not going to need any of that, you might as well leave it in the suitcase, that skirt. I'll wear the old silk outfit tonight, it's nearly in rags but Phil likes me in it, a bit of cleavage may cheer him up."

I want to hug her, and cry, but have promised not to: no scenes, Claude, promise? There will be a moment for it; but it will be when it is right for her. She's leading the way. The rest of us are stumbling through the jungles of our feelings, stepping over roots and snakes.

I say, "That's a lovely suit, where did you get it?" The dark blue silk falls over her thin shoulders, her smaller breasts; there isn't much cleavage anymore, but a pair of fine clavicles, an elegant if stringy neck.

"Armani. It's ancient. Phil said to me once, after the twins were born, just buy something you love, no matter what the price, and I did. Even though I couldn't really get into it, at the time. I knew it would last a lifetime and I'd always feel good in it, and look, here I am, and it has. Could you do up this necklace, I can't manage the hooks?"

I reach the lapis lazuli around her throat and lift the strands of her hair to fasten the hook and eye.

"Thanks. But look, you must stop behaving like my lady's maid, you must go and change too. Oh, are you and Alexandre in the same room? I never thought."

"No, we aren't. We have two separate rooms."

"Not even adjoining?"

"Not even adjoining." I know she's teasing me, but it still hurts that she asks this. About Alexandre and me, I simply don't know anymore. We have this job to do, that she has given us, and beyond it I can see nothing. It's become a cul-de-sac, a dead end.

"Claude, just to be serious for a moment, I'm sorry, I didn't mean it like that. But you must go on living. I said this to Phil. He must live, he must enjoy himself, he must if he can find someone else. And the same goes for you, and Alexandre. You've loved each other a long time. Remember on the train? And when we met him with that Italian chick in the Uffizi—I saw your face, then. You looked just the same in the airport today."

"No, I can't see what can possibly happen between us now. He's still officially married, I live in another country. You just can't organize our lives for us after you've—gone. We're here now. We're all four here this evening. Beyond that, we simply can't go. Sorry."

"Okay," she says, "but don't forget what I said, will you. You could do me at least that favor."

"I won't forget."

"And another thing. You're retired now, right?"

"Yes, I've said all my goodbyes. They gave me a new camera, I didn't dare say I mostly use my phone these days, but it's a complicated beauty."

"The film. Our film. You won't forget that."

"No, I promise. Of course." I can see, written at the very end before the credits, between its two dates, her name.

When I see Philip standing alone in the lobby, I take my chance.

"Phil."

He turns. I'm not going to tell him what Hannah has said, any of it, at least not now. He looks so alone; I slip my hand through his arm, feel the hard bone under the sleeve. An aged man. What was it Yeats said? "Unless soul clap its hands and sing." Everything speaks to me of our mortality; not just Hannah's. Hannah is out in front of us, laughing, grimacing, even making jokes. She knows the day of her death; is this what has freed her? She is clapping her hands and singing, till the end.

"Claude."

It's one of those moments in between, in the wings of life, its corridors, when you can't tell if the time passing is a minute or half an hour. I say almost shy with him, "How are you?"

"Well, I'm simply following her lead. I always have, really. It even simplifies things. Afterwards, I'll have to— well, make the best of it. So, here I am. I'm hers. I always have been, you know that."

"I admire you for it," I tell him, and I squeeze his bony arm, and for a moment, there in the hotel lobby, we stand together, awkward, heartfelt.

He says, "At least, for these last months, I've had her

with me, and nothing was in the way between us. It was out in the open. We've been closer than we've ever been. That has made such a difference. It's been, in its own way, quite amazing." Then, "Don't admire me, Claude," he mumbles into my hair. "It's too remote. Please? Just be my friend?"

Before dinner, the doctor comes to see Hannah. He apologizes for not having come earlier, he got held up. He comes into the room where all of us are assembled, and now it's not possible to talk about the World Cup or Britain or Armani suits or dinner or any of the frail props of the living. He's younger than all of us, not surprisingly, but it still surprises us; you expect doctors, like judges, always to be older, however old you may be. He has all his hair, it's dark, and he's a handsome man who could be our child. He brings forms to sign, and Hannah signs them, over and over, her hand only a little shaky, her signature slightly better than her usual scrawl, as if she's decided it must be legible. The young doctor asks her three times during this half-hour if she really wants to die tomorrow, and she says yes. The third time I want to ask him, why do you doubt her, do you think she would be here, if there were any doubt? But I don't, and then I see that it is part of the protocol, he has to be sure beyond a shadow, a sliver of doubt. Doubt is not allowed.

He stands to shake hands with each of us in turn. "Have a good evening." Then he leaves. We look at each other. Alexandre puts a hand on Phil's shoulder, man to man, and once again I am grateful that Alexandre is here, and knows so surely, it seems instinctively, what to do.

Hannah says, "Some people take a lot of convincing, don't they? Now, for God's sake, let's go and get some dinner."

* * *

Watching her suck up her spaghetti—"no, I'm absolutely not going to have baby food on my last night on earth"—her white napkin tucked around her neck over the Armani silk, I feel relieved and grateful after all that she can do this exactly the way she wants, even if the *vongole* are too chewy and are left in a little line on the rim of her plate. I sip my strong red wine and am grateful too for the way it goes to my extremities, and, presumably, hers.

"Remember how we lived off spaghetti when we were in Italy that time? Remember how we used to swig wine from the bottle? Remember how thin we got, running away from Italian men? Remember that time we hid in the railway station to have baths, and that guy was still waiting when we came out? Remember that young Frenchman we met on the train? Alexandre, I think his name was. Remember how you fancied him?" It's as if she spins a tighter net of memory, with which to draw us in. The past lives in its details. You remember the detail, and you recapture the scene. I drink my wine and feel what she is doing to us, for us, even on this last night of her life.

The dinner comes to its end, with small glasses of *limoncello* offered by the maître d', and then we have to collect up our purses and jackets and move on. On, into what awaits us. Phil pays, and we all let him, as if this has been arranged. We get a taxi for the short distance back to our hotel. There, Philip and Hannah say goodnight and are about to go up in the elevator to spend their last night together. I don't want to think this. I want, we all want it to be casual, a normal thing, goodnight, goodnight, see you in the morning. I can't imagine what this is like now for Phil, who is taking her arm a little stiffly to lead her across the foyer; but I have more of an idea now. He's already walking with the upright careful gait of someone at a wedding. I see her stumble at his side. I go to hug them both, one at a time. Alexandre kisses Hannah, one on each cheek, then Phil. Phil says, "Thank you."

Hannah looks tired. She says, "Beam me up, Scotty," and steps forward to the elevator. I see them step inside, and the door closes, and the little light shows where they are, the second floor, the third.

Alexandre takes my hand again, with his brief caress, holding and letting go. "Shall we go to the bar?"

I don't want to drink any more, but where else can we go? I agree, and follow him into the padded red recess of a small bar, where one barman is polishing glasses. We sit on bar stools.

"No, let's sit in the corner, over here, it's more comfortable." He orders cognac and it comes in big glasses, and all I do is breathe it in, as if its fumes are enough.

"This is so strange, isn't it?" We've been speaking English all evening, but move into French, the language of our intimacy. I'm glad of it, it makes him feel closer, more real. Alexandre speaking his accented English in an Italian restaurant in a small Swiss-German town where my friend has come to die: well, it was all adding to the unreality, the sense of detachment. I want him alone with me, in French, in the half-dark, if only for a short time.

"Yes, it's strange."

"How are you, Claudie? You have known her longer than anyone."

"I'm all right," I say finally. "I feel strange, but it feels right too. It's Phil I'm worried about, it's worst for him. And he's been so marvelous. By the way, you were so good with him this evening, I noticed, *entre hommes*, you know what I mean?"

"All I did was what I'd like someone to do for me, in his position. But I'll never be in his position. Nor will he, ever again. That's why it is all so bizarre, it's as if we are people in a play, acting our parts, hoping to get through to its end without forgetting our lines, or letting each other down."

"I'm so glad you are here."

"So am I." His hand finds mine across the little table, as it did in the restaurant the last time we met. There's a warm silence. Time seems to have stopped. The man behind the bar stands still, and for a moment nothing moves, there is not even a clock in this Swiss bar to remind us. There is no point in planning anything. We have let memory play and reconfigure us this evening, and now it's all done, we are who we are, we have arrived.

23.

The place we are going to in the morning is immediately across the street; we saw it as we reached the hotel, but I didn't know what it was then: an ordinary house, quite innocent, divided into apartments, with an outside staircase and separate front doors, and a garden at the side. We cross the street, looking both ways, Phil wheeling Hannah in her chair. This morning she is wearing the Armani suit again, and I don't know if she never undressed, or if she is wearing it because of Phil and their past, or if it's like a talisman to her now, the perfectly tailored outfit she bought when she was still young. She has a faint pink lipstick, and eyeliner, and I can pick up the waft of her Chanel No. 19. The summer morning sunlight hits the end of the street and the sun pours light down the sides of buildings, shade sharp at its moving edge. It's like a tide coming in. I can smell new bread from a bakery somewhere. A blackbird is singing. Alexander asks us, can you hear it, I think it's in the garden, listen. *Le merle*. I

remember how he notices birds, as I do. This morning everything is a sign. I don't say this, because of the pact between us
all, because of being there for Hannah, who doesn't do signs
and portents. She won't want any of us to think she's turned
into a Swiss blackbird, or a butterfly, or a black cat we see
crossing our path. She's going out on her own terms, bleak
though they may be; she's a realist to the core, her scientist
parents' child, who only hid her face to pretend to pray in our
school services so that she could glance sideways and smirk
at me. But I know her, she's not cold or cynical or unfeeling,
she's the person she has been over all these years, she's Hannah. We're sitting on the seawall sharing our fish and chips.
We're singing, as we skip all the way home. Her parents are
at the Yacht Club, drinking gin and tonic. She doesn't complain; she never complains, but she does run away, she makes
her bid for freedom. She has run here.

As we go inside the place I think: we will come out of
here without her. We will be people we do not recognize.

Then Alexandre looks sharply at me and I feel him catch
my arm and hold me up.

"Claudie, are you all right?"

"I just felt a little dizzy. I'm all right." The moment
passes, and he doesn't let go of me.

A big solid woman with a knot of blonde hair greets us.
She's like a matron, built like a brick shithouse as Hannah
might say, the right size for this venture. Hannah has to sign
more papers. The rest of us wait on, not speaking. Then I see
Phil's face move and begin to break up, it's like watching a
wall begin to crumble, from the bottom up. He's at the point
where he can't take any more; he's arrived there after days
and weeks and even months of self-restraint, and he's going

to collapse and howl. The blonde woman sees this just as I see it and she steps forward on a long stride and imprisons him in her embrace. She holds him with her bare fat arms, muscle flexing under the little blonde hairs. She's done this before, she knows what happens. She holds him so that he droops against her, and I can't see his face, and Hannah won't see it because she's still signing papers, she has her back to us in the wheelchair that met us at the door, she's simply doing what she has to do next.

The blonde woman holds Phil against her as if he were an infant. She says, "Sir, you cannot do this now. You cannot." She gives him a little shake. Phil straightens, as she lets him go. It's enough. Her strength has held him up, held him in, and now he can do it. Hannah signs the last page. She looks exhausted. I wonder how their night was and think, I will never know, and I don't need to. The blonde nurse says, "Good. Now, would you like to be in bed, or just sitting, or, would you like to be outside?"

Hannah says, "I can be outside? I'd like to be outside." Everyone is speaking English, or I think they are. The nurse has a strong accent, she is Swiss-German; she must have learned to do this in many different languages. We follow the nurse. She isn't wearing a uniform, but she's obviously a nurse: those scrubbed hands. Hannah says, I don't need the chair, let me at least walk out there, okay? She seizes her stick, and Phil's hand, and they set off together. I once saw them walk down an aisle, young and striding towards an open church door. We follow, Alexandre and I, he still holding my arm. We are their attendants. I can do this, I tell myself. There is a garden, fenced in and bamboo growing, and a lilac tree that has just finished flowering, and I think that the blackbird we heard might be in the lilac, and there are seats, like chaises longues, and a little table, as if someone were about to serve us drinks, or lunch. None of us ate much breakfast, earlier, just sipped our good coffee. My stomach rumbles, and I hope nobody hears; but really, what matters anymore, stomachs rumbling, tears, even howls, even fainting; in just a short while it will not matter what sounds our bodies emit, or how we control them. We sit out on the patio in sun and shade behind a carved Indonesian screen with figures on it. It's hot already, but there's a breeze. The young doctor we met yesterday comes out carrying a small box and greets us in English, and we all say good morning, and Hannah smiles her ironic smile when he asks her for a last time, are you sure?

"Yes, I'm sure." He opens the box, gives her the cup. The first drink is a sedative, to settle her stomach, so that there is no chance of her throwing up. She takes it, asks for a sip of plain water, licks her lips. After a few minutes she takes the second drink. She has to lift it herself, even as the doctor's hand cups hers to support it. I see a shadow pass across her face: this is it, no turning back. I am stunned by her courage, her clarity. It's not hemlock, it's not Socrates dying in agony, it's nothing that has happened before anywhere, it's my friend Hannah, lifting a plastic container in her good hand, as she looks at us—a small toast, even?—and sucks it all up through a straw. I see her pursed lips, her effort. The blonde nurse films her as she does this. For the police, she says. To be safe. I dare not look at Philip, but take his hand. Hannah closes her eyes. The sun on her eyelids—does she see red, and patterns? We all sit still, and the blackbird starts up again in the lilac. I see tears on Phil's cheeks. Alexandre and I are motionless and

silent and once again time stills and stops around us, as it did
for him and me in the bar last night.

It takes about fifteen minutes, as we were told it would.
The world stands still around us, silent except for the blackbird. Hannah is here, and then she is not here. She looks
unconscious after five or six minutes, her head lolls as if she
has fallen asleep in the sun. I think, but do not say, goodbye.
We all sit there without moving, and if tears fall, they are
unnoticed, and nothing has to be done or said. I feel the garden begin to move around me: a swirl and rustle of leaves,
the spring light altering patterns on the grass, the bird in the
tree, the air that shifts and goes on shifting invisibly as the
wind currents pass across the earth and flutter matter into
life, here in this garden, in a village outside Zurich, in Switzerland. It's like being at the center of the world. It is the
center of the world. Perhaps it will always be. We are still, as
Hannah is still; and then there's a creaking and shifting into
slight movement, knees, stiff backs, faces lifted, hands grasp-
ing chairs, a breathing out, a wiping of cheeks, a common
agreement that we will begin to move on.

Then—now, suddenly—it is the time after. We can't
stay at the center of the world. Life is centrifugal, sends us
staggering out to its edges; it always will. How do we do this?
How can we manage the next thing? By acting as if it's normal. As if she's asleep in the sun, as if we are coming back for
her soon. As if. Life, real life has passed us by; death has come
quietly, it has taken Hannah, she has drunk it down. She is
not breathing now. The young doctor has felt for her pulse,
in the moments after, nodded at us: she's gone. I don't know
how to let this in. None of us knows. We get up and stand
there for a moment, a little huddle of three, not knowing,

until he says, that's it, you understand, you can go now; and picks up his phone to call the police and speak to them in German. He's dismissed us: we aren't needed, we've done our job, and he has done his. We have to move, to leave here, to go outside into the rest of life, and never return.

Philip stutters a little as he asks, "What happens next?" As if there has to be a next, as if he has to ask, because otherwise there is a blank, a sheer drop.

"As I say, that is it. She has gone, sir. We will see to all the rest. You can go home."

All the rest: what you normally have to do after a death, prepare a body, order a coffin, arrange for cremation or burial, tell people, put a notice in the paper, choose hymns, order in food, receive ashes, whatever people do; all the rest. They will cremate Hannah and send her ashes to him at home. Philip looks stunned, pale, exhausted. Alexandre takes him by the arm, "Come. We'll go back to the hotel."

Holding on to each other like the road-sign picture of old people crossing a street, we cross the street, walk back to our hotel. On the threshold, where it says *Willkommen* on the doormat, Philip stalls like a horse that won't go into its stable. "We can't go in there. I can't go in that room. We have to leave."

I see his panic, his refusal. He can't live life without her. He can't do what's asked of him. Yet he knows, oh, yes, he knows what he absolutely won't do—and that is, go back into that room. At least he knows that.

Alexandre sits him down in the bar, with a brandy in front of him. Alexandre, with his hand kindly on Philip's back, his murmur in English, sit here, you don't have to do anything, we will do it, Claudia and I. Then he and I go up in the elevator to our floor, and collect our things from our rooms first and then, using Phil's key, go into his room, the one he shared with Hannah on her last night, and start packing everything into suitcases, his and hers, just as if she were going too. He doesn't speak as we do all this, and neither do I. I'm hardly able to see through my tears, as I pick up her bottle of Chanel, her nightdress, her toiletries, her dressing gown, the underwear she wore yesterday, the clothes she traveled in. It feels like the last possible thing I can do; but Alexandre is here, he is putting Philip's things into the other suitcase, folding his sweater, his pajamas, his socks, as if he's spent his life as a gentleman's valet. If we weren't both in pain, it would even have been funny. I see him brush a tear away, this man I have seen cry only once, after his mother died; I'm touched, move towards him, we drop the clothes we are holding on to the bed and are in each other's arms just for a moment, holding each other hard. In all the years I have known and loved Alexandre, I have never seen this side of him: this practical kindness, this ability to help another person. He is perfect, I want to tell him, he is exactly right. I will tell him one day: I will say, on that day, you were perfect, the essential friend. You were kind, and practical. You were exactly who was needed. And yes, I am always moved by kindness between men. It seems so rare, and they are rarely brought up to show it; when they do show it, it disarms me, and this, one day, is what I want to say to Alexandre.

He strokes my hair; I cry on his shoulder, noisy sobs at last. He hands me a handkerchief. "Claudie. You did well."

"So did you." I blow my nose, scrub my face, hand him back the handkerchief. Who carries real handkerchiefs around with him these days?

"No, keep it, you may need it."

"We have to get out of here. Don't we?"

"We have time," he says, "but I don't want to leave that poor man sitting alone for too long. We should go down. You know, I never thought I could do this, take somebody to their death. I never thought I would have to. When she asked me, first, I thought, no, never. Then you asked me, and I thought, I can't refuse. I didn't imagine it would be like this. So simple, really. I can't believe it. Perhaps none of us will be able to believe it, it will seem like a dream."

"Perhaps."

"I thought, this has nothing to do with me, it's not my business, *ce n'est pas mon débat,* you understand what I mean. But today, I feel I could not have missed it, it has shown me something—I don't know exactly what."

I smile, though I'm still sniffing back tears. Alexandre's first thoughts about everything have always been about the interesting effect it has on him. He's already examining himself for signs of change. But he's shown me his kindness, his practicality, his sympathy for a man he didn't even know until yesterday. I've already seen a new Alexandre, or one I haven't fully known until now. He's all these things, practical, self-absorbed, kind, obtuse, sensitive; he is, I know, a person I love.

"Yes. It will take time. Where will you go next? Home?"

"Back to Paris. I have a case on Monday, as usual. I've a flight at four-thirty. And you?"

"I'm going back with Philip, at least for a few days. I don't want to think of him going into their house alone."

We close the suitcases, glance around the room, check that we have left nothing behind: no clue of what has happened here. The maids will come and clean, change the sheets and towels, all signs of anyone's passage here will be removed. A good hotel is always a clean blank page. Alexandre and I know hotels, and they were not always this way.

He touches my shoulder, squeezes just slightly, and lets me go. We drag the bags behind us, call the elevator, wait for it side by side. We are once again a couple that is not a couple, leaving a hotel room, and we smile together through our tears, at the irony that I know has struck us both.

Epilogue

At the end of the film *L'Avventura,* Sandro and Claudia sit alone together on a bench looking out over the city. We see them from behind. We can't see their faces. But just before the film ends and the white letters come up, we see her lift a hand and touch his head, in a gentle stroking motion that has some regret in it, as if to reassure him, or herself, or perhaps even someone out of sight, that she cares for him. It's almost like an animal licking another animal, because that is what they do. A gesture of tenderness; of reparation. What humans do, Antonioni shows us, is care for each other with this slight yet instinctive animal warmth. A lick, a touch, a caress. When all is said and done, whatever has gone before, whatever is remembered, forgotten, forgiven. Then the letters come up and that is the end.

Acknowledgments

I would like to thank all who supported the writing and publication of this novel, especially my agent, Kimberley Cameron; Lori Milken of Delphinium Books; and my editor there, Joseph Olshan. Thank you all for your enthusiastic commitment to this book, and Joe, for sterling editing advice.

To Ellen McLaughlin and Andrew Greig, who first read the book in its infancy, many thanks for your thoughtful suggestions. To Marie-Claire Blais, thanks again for your early reading and constant encouragement.

Thanks for encouragement, writing lunches, your stories, and general support to Simone, Jessica, and Brooks in Key West, and to George in Prague.

Claudia's film career in California owes much to both Linda Dittmar and Barbara Hammer, and to The Conversations—Walter Murch and the Art of Editing Film, by Michael Ondaatje (Knopf 2002). I am also grateful to Alicia Malone for her timely book The Female Gaze (Mango, 2018).

Appreciative thanks to all the film-makers mentioned in this book, especially to Agnès Varda for L'Une Chante, l'Autre Pas.

To my husband, Allen Meece, thanks again for being there throughout.

About the Author

Poet and novelist Rosalind Brackenbury is the author of *Becoming George Sand, Paris Still Life, The Third Swimmer,* and *The Lost Love Letters of Henri Fournier.* A former writer-in-residence at the College of William and Mary in Williamsburg, Virginia, she has also served as poet laureate of Key West, teaching poetry workshops. She has attended the yearly Key West Literary Seminar as both panelist and moderator. Born in London, Rosalind lived in Scotland and France before moving to the United States. Her 2016 novel, *The Third Swimmer,* was a 2016 INDIES Silver Winner in Adult General Fiction. She now lives in Key West, Florida, with her American husband. Her latest poetry collection, *Invisible Horses,* was published by Hanging Loose Press in May 2019.